BEFORE THE DAWN

Rupert Copping

SKYLIGHT
PRESS

First published in Great Britain in 2013 by Skylight Press,
210 Brooklyn Road, Cheltenham, Glos GL51 8EA

Typeset by Rebsie Fairholm
Publisher: Daniel Staniforth
Cover painting by Rupert Copping

www.skylightpress.co.uk

Printed and bound in Great Britain by Lightning Source, Milton Keynes.
Typeset in Minion Pro.

British Library Cataloguing in Publication Data:
A catalogue record for this book is available from the British Library.

ISBN 978-1-908011-29-9

To Jemima

the claw will be soft
leave me hope.

— *Miguel Hernandez*

List of characters in order of appearance:

Punimillo *(pu-knee-me-yo):* a chief elder.
Cuspi *(koos-pi):* an apprentice elder.
Rumicuri *(ru-mi-cu-ri):* the sovereign.
Cascarina *(kas-ka-ree-na):* the sovereign's mistress.
Mountain Trotter: guide and intermediary.
Calchas *(kal-chas):* guerrilla, lover of the sovereign's wife.
Illapacta *(eeya-pak-ta):* an elder who has fallen from grace.
Macaruca *(ma-ka-ru-ka):* an elder.
Chotavalo: an elder.
Illani *(ee-ya-knee):* the sovereign's wife, the queen.
Guaneque *(gua-ne-ke):* Cascarina's sister-in-law.
Amataba: a medicine woman.
Rupuche: a medicine woman.
Agustina: the sovereign's aunt by marriage.
Federico: Agustina's son.
Victoriano: the sovereign's uncle, living in exile.
Capayambe *(ka-pa-yambe):* Guaneque's husband.
Tusuma: an Indian.
Jamana: an Indian.
The Major: an army officer.
Lieutenant Echiveira: an army officer.
Captain Maldonado: an army officer.

PROLOGUE

FROM a hole in the roof of the cavern a shaft of light shone down on where a boy sat cross-legged. Beyond the shaft of light the cavern was in darkness, but this did not disturb Cuspi, for he had never seen the orb of the sun, he did not know that beyond the cavern there was a world of vast skies, of mountains and forests and people.

Cuspi had been removed to the sacred cave as an infant. He was now fourteen years old and during none of these years had he been allowed to venture beyond the four caverns contained within the sacred cave. As far as he knew the caverns – and all their contents, the things that gave him sustenance – were 'worlds' the Holy Source had dreamed for him, and beyond them there was only the Holy Source.

Ever since he could remember, the three elders who looked after him had promised that one day he would know all the answers to all the questions. When this happened his confusion would vanish, they said, and the true nature of the Holy Source would be revealed to him. Cuspi had been bitterly disappointed in the past. On several occasions he had felt so close to the revelation that he had collapsed in despair when ultimately it had eluded him. His guileless, nut-brown eyes had filled with tears. He'd lost his appetite and been so assailed by hopelessness that all he had wanted to do was sleep. The elders, however, hadn't given him a moment's respite. They had been assiduous in their efforts to soothe, encourage, and if necessary, to bully him into perseverance.

And so it was that Cuspi, dressed in a plain woollen smock, was seated on a straw mat, in the shaft of light, intent on solving the riddle the elders had given him, when the wooden door of the cavern opened with a clatter and Punimillo, the chief elder, stepped out of the darkness. Cuspi wasn't surprised to see him. The elders were in the habit of appearing at odd hours, but as Punimillo stepped closer Cuspi noticed that he had a purple robe folded over his arm and was carrying a gourd. Cuspi was puzzled. The more so because at that moment, without knowing why, he thought the chief elder looked different from his usual self.

Punimillo was a corpulent, square-set man with dark skin set off by striking white hair and white eyebrows. Though of advanced age he spoke in a booming voice and when entering the cavern he had the custom of greeting Cuspi by loudly calling his name. But this time he approached in silence, with heavy tread, and when he sat down it was almost as if he had shrunk overnight, such was the absence of his usual vigour.

Cuspi didn't know what to make of it. He was worried by the chief elder's manner, but at the same time excited by the purple robe. The elders themselves always wore purple robes. He wondered why Punimillo had brought a spare one. Was it for him? He dared to imagine that something unusual was about to happen. Almost, he wanted to believe it was the revelation that for so long had been promised him. But what was wrong with the chief elder? Why did he look so strange? Why wasn't he happy?

While Cuspi fretted, Punimillo, for his part, was making a grim attempt to mask the sorrow that inside him had opened up like an abyss. Gazing at his charge, seeing the apprehensive expectation on his vulnerable face, it was as much as he could manage to stop his own visage from crumbling.

How he loved this child. When an infant he had rocked him in his arms and cleaned his bottom. He had fed him and watched him grow and had schooled him in the stern path to elderhood. The child was precious to him, more precious than his own flesh; but what was his own flesh now? What was life? The vision was dead. It had shown itself to be a poisoned illusion. Only destruction and madness – a world that was forever dying, this was all that remained.

His spirit broken, Punimillo made an effort to simulate vigour and cheerful confidence.

'Cuspi', he said with artificial loudness. 'Go and wash and then come back here'.

Cuspi jumped up and stepping past a bed of bamboo and fleeces he came to a large earthenware container. After divesting himself of the woollen smock, he stood naked and used a bowl to scoop water from the container. He became queasy, his heart thumped, and his hand shook as he washed himself, for he was ever more certain that something very unusual was about to happen. When he'd finished washing he dried his unnaturally pale, pubescent body with a cloth and returned naked to the shaft of light.

Punimillo indicated the purple robe. 'Put it on.'

Cuspi obeyed. He put on the robe, noticing that it fitted well, his eyes large with wonder as he stared down at himself.

'Sit down,' Punimillo commanded, and when Cuspi was seated: 'Have you discovered yet the answer to the riddle?'

'No, *tata*,' Cuspi admitted, fearful.

'But you want to know all the answers to all the questions?'

'Yes, *tata*!'

'Very well. So it shall be. In a moment you'll know the true nature of the Holy Source.'

Cuspi quivered. A stunned gasp escaped his lips. His eyes glowed.

Punimillo tried to smile in response. His throat was choking him. He lifted the gourd and passed it to the boy.

'Are you ready?'

'Yes.'

'You aren't afraid?'

'No… A little.'

'We're proud of you. I want you to know this, we're very proud of you. My brother elders are waiting beyond the door of the world. In a moment we will go to them, but first take a drink from the gourd, Cuspi, it'll give you strength, for it's a great thing that's about to happen.'

Cuspi did not hesitate. He'd been brought up to trust the elders and to obey all their commands. So he lifted the vessel to his lips. The liquid had a strong sweetish bitter flavour. After drinking, he lowered the gourd, wiped his lips with the back of his hand, and, suffused with happiness, he thought: I'm ready. Soon everything will be clear and I'll know all the answers to all the questions.

It was the last lucid thought he had. A fierce burning flared deep in his entrails. His chest became constricted. He couldn't breathe. He opened his mouth, gasping, staring at the chief elder in bewildered incomprehension. His vision blurred, he keeled over, hitting the floor with a thud, his body convulsing as blackness invaded his consciousness.

Punimillo sat quite still. Only the horror in his eyes, and the tremors in his face, betrayed his turbulence as he watched Cuspi thrashing beside him. When Cuspi was still at last, his body grotesquely contorted, Punimillo reached over and closed his frozen, staring eyes. Now he knows the true nature of the Holy Source, he thought.

Standing up, placing his arms under the body, he lifted it with difficulty and lowered it onto the bed. Next, he manoeuvred the body into a curled, foetal position – the position in which all Arayana Indians were buried – but then, on a quixotic, almost maternal impulse, he extricated a blanket from the bed and placed it gently over the corpse.

The gourd was lying on the mat and some of the brown liquid had spilled out, but not all. Punimillo sat down, his legs crossed, clutching the gourd in both hands. Images filled his mind, of fire and smoke, of dwellings reduced to rubble, of corpses – hundreds of mutilated corpses; the air heavy with their stench and the vultures that fed on them so bloated they couldn't fly… So be it, he thought. This is all there is. This is the true nature of the Holy Source. And then he raised the gourd to his own lips.

PART ONE

T HE voice was loud, urgent. When he opened his eyes – in a warm bed, Cascarina stirring beside him – he heard it more distinctly.

Rumicuri got up quickly and in dark twilight walked across the cold stone slab floor. Cinders from the night before were alight in an open fire, still giving heat, casting a red glow on his naked legs and rump as he stepped towards a flimsy wooden door. In the faint light of dawn a man wearing a woollen smock stood before him, agitated, breathing fitfully.

'Loma-Cayapa is at the bridge. But he's not alone! Others are with him. People from his village!'

Rumicuri – his name meant Stone Face – stood without moving. He wasn't conscious of his nudity. The hard, chiselled features of his face showed no emotion. Only his eyes changed; expanding, opening wide.

'They're all from his village? You're sure of this?'

'Yes. That was his message.'

'How many?'

'Ten or twelve. Men and women.'

'Anything else?'

The messenger shook his head.

'I'll be down,' Rumicuri said. 'They're to wait. That's all...'

The messenger left, footsteps rustling as he hurried across a patch of dry earth, then vanished into dark vegetation.

Rumicuri did not go inside at once. He stood in the doorway, inhaling the cold air, staring at the faintly blue and green stars scattered like tiny jewels against the dawning, violet sky. It was a familiar sight, and he stared around him as if to reassure himself that the world was still there, unchanged, that everything was in its proper place.

When he returned inside Cascarina was already up. She was standing naked by the fire. Her skin glowed like dull copper. Rumicuri loved her body. There were times when her nakedness surprised him, for in her broad hips, in her thrusting breasts, he perceived not so much a yielding softness as a formidable weaponry. Women were warriors. With their provocative voluptuousness they commanded and conquered. But now he didn't see this. When he beheld her nakedness, and the alarm in her eyes, he was aware only of her frailty, her defencelessness...

'What is it?' she said. 'Is there trouble?'

He was silent. From a line strung between two posts he removed a short robe-like garment and pulled it over his head. 'My sandals,' he said, sitting down on a low stool by the fire. She brought him a pair of grass sandals. He put them on but didn't rise to his feet. For a moment his disquiet was such that it drained him of strength. All the message told him was that something out of the ordinary had occurred. It was pointless to speculate. Yet he couldn't help fearing it was the start of a sequence; predestined, reaching him like the first tremors before an earthquake.

Like all his people, Rumicuri was superstitious. He believed in omens, signs, the invisible world of the spirits, but he wasn't always fatalistic. As the ruler of the Arayana it was his duty to govern with resolve. If crops failed and stores were depleted he did not resign himself to letting the community starve; he organised hunting parties and sent people into the forest to gather wild fruit. In order to rule he, above all others, had to find ways of overcoming difficulties. So why such unease? Why the clammy foreboding that from this moment on nothing would be the same?

Rumicuri made an effort to compose himself. He straightened his shoulders and looked at Cascarina hoping no emotion showed on his face. 'Don't worry,' he said. "No one can cross the gorge.'

'Do you want to eat? I'll get some food.'

He stood up. 'There's no time. I'll eat later.'

Outside, above the trees, a rose-coloured light was spreading into the sky. How many more dawns? He thought. We're so few. We endure like a wounded jaguar in its lair. The purinis, they seethe like marching ants...

He hurried down a narrow path, barely visible in the dim light. He hurried between trees, past silent mud huts and shadowy fields. With deep fear he hurried to stop an event that hadn't yet happened, but which had been seeded in the distant past, in the time of his ancestors, when the first purinis had come from across the great waters. And mounted on horses, wearing their creaking clothes of metal had spat fire and destruction upon the Arayana.

Rumicuri had been brought up to respect old people – even if they were not of his caste – but now he had difficulty containing an alarmed anger towards the old man who stood before him. And no matter if he looked exhausted and fearful.

Cayapa, who was known as Mountain Trotter, stood in grubby shirt and trousers, clutching a straw hat in both hands, strands of grey hair flattened across his balding pate as he tried to explain that he had no choice. The whole village had been taken over. Soldiers with firearms (Mountain Trotter used Arayana words but Rumicuri understood the concept of armed soldiers, for he had some knowledge of the outside world) were threatening to kill the relatives of anyone who tried to leave. The villagers were frightened. They didn't want to stay in the village with the soldiers there. A few families who lived beyond the village had managed to escape. 'And so what could I do, highness? Where else could we go?'

'Why didn't you leave them behind?' Rumicuri whispered fiercely. 'You know our laws. Haven't you always come on your own?'

Mountain Trotter pleaded that he had no choice. Had he stayed behind another moment the soldiers would have located him. He had left at once, intending to come in secret so as to warn Rumicuri of all that was happening. But others had seen him and had started following. What could he do? He was an old man, his legs weren't so strong any more, he couldn't outpace them. What could he do? Would it be better had he stayed behind and not come to warn him?

Standing in his red woollen robe, Rumicuri stared impassively at the dozen or so people huddled some yards behind Mountain Trotter, anxiously awaiting his decision. They looked tired and dirty. One woman was trying to hush an infant in her arms. There was a lean young man with cropped hair and wearing a green jacket made of a shiny fabric such as Rumicuri could not remember ever seeing. The man was tainted; a danger, he feared, noticing moreover that the young man was staring at him with an expression that was not merely challenging, but defiant, even insolent.

In olden times, centuries ago, such insolence could have merited instant punishment. A ruler had only to give a sign for an offender to be executed on the spot, without question. But that was in olden times, when Rumicuri's ancestors had lived in great palaces and had worn ornaments of gold and sacred feathers and had ruled over a vast kingdom that not even the Incas, their powerful enemies, had been able to subdue. Now, of that kingdom, only this small enclave remained. For more than seven generations the Arayana had lived here, following the traditions of their forefathers in secrecy, undetected by the advance of civilization. So Rumicuri was angry with Mountain Trotter for bringing to him people he didn't personally know and who might not be trusted with absolute certainty.

On the other hand, these people were of his blood, the same race. All that time ago, before the Arayana had moved to their present location, the kingdom had split into two groups. One group had elected to remain behind, no longer to run from the advance of the outside world. Mountain Trotter and the refugees were descended from this group. They lived in tenuous contact with the outside world, but they still considered themselves Arayana. Among themselves they spoke a corrupted but still very similar language, they retained some of the old traditions, and secretly, stubbornly they clung to the notion of being Rumicuri's subjects, even if they had never set eyes on him and knew of the high kingdom's existence only by report, through chosen intermediaries such as Mountain Trotter.

Staring at the refugees, Rumicuri tried to assess them, anxious lest any of them might have managed to remember, from this one outing alone, the route through the jungle...

'It will have to go before the council,' he addressed Mountain Trotter, finally, "But... well, there's nothing for it; bring your people across.'

At once Mountain Trotter dropped to his knees, his hands and forehead touching the ground. Once up again, he gestured to the others. They came forward in ones and twos, following Mountain Trotter's example. Only the young man resisted. He stepped forward but instead of making the obeisance, his lean, pock-scarred face regarded Rumicuri with stubborn, contemptuous defiance. Rumicuri wasn't accustomed to such disrespect. For a moment it confused him. His nerves frayed, in a flash of temper, he half pushed, half struck the young man on the shoulder. The young man stepped back; he seemed surprised, he started to flush, but before he could recover, as though of one mind, the whole group of men and even a couple of women jumped on him, pushing and beating him, forcing him to kneel.

'You know our laws,' Rumicuri reminded Mountain Trotter. 'That's a purini garment he's wearing. He can't enter like that.'

Mountain Trotter and his companions made the young man remove the green jacket. After it was discarded, tossed aside in thick undergrowth, Rumicuri turned and began walking to where shafts of early sunlight illuminated a narrow basketwork suspension bridge.

The kingdom's terrain began, properly speaking, beyond the gorge that was spanned by the bridge. Even more than the many miles of hostile, virgin jungle, it was this gorge that made the kingdom unassailable, since it was up to hundred feet wide and it extended in a circular trajectory around the base of what eventually, after a long climb, became a high mountain. A mountain, however, that whereas only a few years ago had an abundance of snow, now barely had a smattering of it. During the wet season snow fell upon the high kingdom in scant bursts. It hadn't snowed properly for three years.

Immediately beyond the gorge (a gorge so deep and overgrown you couldn't see its bottom) stood a circular mud hut with a straw roof. This hut was manned day and night. Had the refugees not been accompanied by Rumicuri they would not have got across. Aside from Mountain Trotter's sporadic visits, and the still less frequent ones from one other person, this was the first time in nearly a hundred years that the kingdom had admitted outsiders.

There were no other dwellings beyond the guard hut. There was instead a path through a terrain of mountain forest; steep, lush, and muddy, for this far down there was no shortage of water. Here, somehow, the jungle managed to produce its own rain.

For some four miles the group travelled in this steep, mountainous world of shadows, of hanging lianas, of tree trunks overgrown with moss and climbers, of sudden flashes of colour – a flower, a bird – and of a canopy overhead so dense that daylight filtered through it like stars. Around midday they emerged into a sparser terrain where the dwindling forest had been cleared to allow cultivations of maize, yucca, potatoes…

Small groups of people, for the most part dressed in plain smock-like garments, were working the fields, irrigating and planting and weeding, but upon seeing Rumicuri with a group of strangers they stopped work, standing motionless and speechless. Then, recovering, they hurried towards the path.

There was very little talk. The arrival of strangers into their kingdom was an event so extraordinary that they could think of nothing to say. In shocked silence, therefore, and always at a respectful distance, they began following the sovereign and the group of strangers through more fields and tracts of forest, until they came to the first dwellings.

The Arayana community wasn't all one unit. It consisted of separate clusters of mud and straw huts without windows, with roofs of palm leaf or grass. The huts were separated from each other by spaces of earth or grass, and each cluster was separated from the next by tracts of forest.

As the procession passed by the huts more and more people joined in, so that by the time they reached the main part of the community the crowd had swelled into many hundreds of men, women and children. All were wearing similar garments, although the smocks of the women were more brightly coloured and also they wore striped head-scarves, bead necklaces and bracelets. As for the main village itself, it was located on the uppermost border of the forest, which meant that while it was surrounded by lush vegetation, a short distance further up the vegetation began to thin abruptly. Thereafter only bushes grew – no trees – and further up, not even bushes; a yellow green pampas grass interspersed with thistle-like plants, and finally nothing at all: the barren sand, the craggy black rock of an all but snowless mountain that rose into a limpid, azure sky.

Besides the dwellings of the community's ruling class (such as Rumicuri, the elders, and various others) the main village contained two long, relatively large edifices. One of these was the granary, the other the gathering house. After placing the refugees in the gathering house Rumicuri sent word to the elders, all three of whom were at a secluded location, engaged in a sacred ritual. Then Rumicuri addressed the silent, anxious crowd that had assembled outside, explaining little, asking them to be patient, saying he would have more to tell them after the meeting with the elders. Finally, having addressed the crowd, while waiting for the council to convene, he went to summon Illapacta.

Illapacta was a shrivelled, arthritic old man. When Rumicuri arrived he was sitting on a log outside his hut, warming his bones. As usual he was wearing a scruffy woollen robe, his long white hair was wildly unkempt, and on the ground, close at hand, stood a gourd of mishqui.

'Ah… It's the sovereign himself,' remarked Illapacta, showing his rotten teeth, addressing Rumicuri in an off-hand manner no one else would dare.

Rumicuri was silent.

Illapacta lifted the gourd, took a good swig, put the gourd on the ground, wiped a trickle from his chin, and then was still, staring at his visitor with a sort of bleary intentness.

Rumicuri went down on his haunches, leaning his short, compact body against the wall of the hut.

'There is trouble.'

And when there was no reply: 'Mountain Trotter is here. His village has been taken over, he says, by soldiers with firearms. But that isn't all. He came here with other lowlanders: nine people from the village.'

If Illapacta had been tipsy before Rumicuri arrived, now, in a moment, the dullness vanished. He was stunned.

'*Here?*' he asked. 'Are you telling me he brought them *here?*'

'He says they wanted to follow him,' Rumicuri replied. 'He wanted to warn us, he says, but he couldn't stop the others from following.'

'So where are these people now?'

'In the gathering house. I've sent word to the elders.'

Illapacta passed into a frowning silence. At last, he said. 'Who are these soldiers Mountain Trotter speaks of? What do these soldiers want? Has he told you?'

'I don't know. No… You've got to come.'

Illapacta gave a nod.

Rumicuri didn't press him. There were some who said Illapacta had lost his wits. When not in pity, they said it in scorn because he was an elder and they couldn't forgive a man of his high office for falling from grace. But Rumicuri knew the old man hadn't lost his wits. Whatever it was that had caused his undoing, for Rumicuri he was the same man he had loved as a child, and who, long ago, had accompanied him on their one and only journey to the outside world.

Apart from them there was no one else in the kingdom who had first hand knowledge of the outside world. They were the only ones and it was for this reason he was anxious the old man should be present when the council convened.

'There's no need to wait for me,' said Illapacta. 'I'll be along.'

Rumicuri stood up. He had things to do. He must change his clothes; a meeting of the council was a serious matter... Serious! When had his life not been serious? He could hardly remember a time since becoming the sovereign when he'd had no cares...

He tried not to let them weigh him down. To the people he presented a calm and determined disposition. They had no knowledge of the fear prowling his entrails. They didn't know there were times when he doubted his strength to withstand adversity...

It wasn't by choice he had become the sovereign; he was born to it, fated, and he tried to be worthy of the task. But always people were coming to him – because a crop had failed or because a rogue puma was after the llama or because neighbours were feuding...

Just yesterday he'd been obliged to mediate between two women. One of them had reprimanded the son of the other. The purported offence was trivial. The boy had apparently tied a piece of twine across the doorway, causing the woman to trip and drop a pitcher of water. But there was past acrimony between the women and neither was prepared to give ground. So both had stood before him, hurling insults, shrieking at each other. The mother shouted that the other woman had no right to scold her son. The other woman shouted back that her son was spoilt and undisciplined. The boy himself, meanwhile, stood between both women looking from one to the other with wide-eyed innocence, although Rumicuri had suspected he was secretly enjoying being the centre of attention.

Had it not been himself but his father who was mediating – depending on his mood – he would have either dismissed the women with a shout of his own, or more mischievously, he would have sided with the boy, whether or not he was guilty or deserving of punishment. In either case his father would have promptly rid himself of the women because he had little patience for the day to day chores of governing the kingdom. But Rumicuri wasn't like his father. As a child, growing up, he had seen how the community had suffered under his father's capricious rule. And determined to do better, he attended conscientiously to all the problems, large or small, that were brought to him.

In the end he had managed to pacify both women and to extract a solemn promise from the boy that he would desist from causing mischief. But it had taken half the morning, and soon afterwards something else had come up to do with irrigation for the fields in the high ground, which were affected by drought.

It never stopped. The problems he had to contend with came one after the other, without end. For himself, for the people, survival was at the best of times precarious. The task of governing wearied him, but he had no choice, it was his duty to protect the people, and so he did as best he could, holding on like a tree at the river's edge…If only snow would fall on the mountain, he thought. It would make the people happy. And the river would rise and he would be able to swim in the pools and dive from the rocks. There were few things he enjoyed more than a lazy, carefree day by the river…

But there was no time now for idle thought. Abruptly Rumicuri stood up and started walking towards the village. Illapacta raised his head and watched him leave. He watched with one eye half closed, squinting because his vision was blurred. It was his green eye. He'd always had trouble with the green eye…

Illapacta had one eye that was brown and the other green and it was on account of his unusual eyes that he'd been selected for elderhood.

Where had the green eye come from? The elders of those times, when Illapacta was born, had been at a loss to explain it. After consultation they decided it must be a sign from the Holy Source that the infant was destined for elderhood. And once this was decided he was removed to a sacred cave in the foothills of the mountain.

The sacred cave – forbidden to all except the elders and those they chose – was a huge natural cavern containing many interconnected chambers. Four of these chambers, each selected for a specific reason, had their entrances artificially restricted, as well as other necessary adjustments, and it was in the innermost of the four chambers that the infant was placed. There Illapacta spent the first six years of his life, in almost total darkness, and was allowed to see no one other than his mother and the three elders in whose absolute charge he was to remain for fourteen years. Because he was so young, in later life Illapacta had very little memory of the first chamber, but he could remember the second one.

When he awoke each morning this chamber – the only world he

knew – was invariably at its darkest (so dark that he could see nothing at all) and there would be a chill in the air. Reluctant to get out of bed, he would burrow under the thick blankets, whose provenance was beyond his powers of comprehension, so unfathomable that he could not even begin to guess. He knew only that they were part of his world, and therefore he accepted their existence in wonder but without bewilderment, just as another small child, living a more normal existence, accepts a tree, the sky, the sun…

While it was still utterly dark, and he lay under the blankets, a creaking sound would come and his mother (although he didn't know her by that name) would be there, sitting down beside him and enfolding him in her warm, sweet smelling flesh. He couldn't see his mother, it was always too dark when she was present, but he knew, intimately, the feel of her, the scent of her.

His mother was not allowed to speak to him. Sometimes she made sounds, ripples of laughter, sighs, and once, touching her cheeks he felt them wet with tears. But she never spoke, not even after he learnt to speak, so that his entire knowledge of her was limited to touch and smell. Nevertheless, without being able to explain it to himself, without ever having the words for these things, he sensed the intimate bond that united them, he sensed the love that flowed from her, and though invisible she was as much a part of him as the invisible air. During those early years, emotionally, for his inner sustenance, Illapacta was more dependent on the mother he could neither see nor hear speak than he was on the elders, who were the ones to talk to him and feed him and teach him. When lonely or sad or frightened, it was not for the elders he yearned, it was for the tender solace of his mother's arms.

After spending some time with him (always too brief) his mother would depart as she had arrived – mysteriously, from darkness into darkness. Then, later, the same creaking sound would announce the arrival of one or other of the elders. The elder would bring him an earthenware bowl of warm food, which he ate greedily, savouring the taste, but as with the blankets he hadn't the least notion of its origin. After breakfast the elder would wash his hands and face and other parts of his body with cold water (another unfathomable) and by the time all this was done it would no longer be quite so dark, for the first small, but flashing, brilliant rays of light would begin to pierce the dark through a hole in the roof of the cavern.

He cherished the sight of that first light. He marvelled at the way it appeared high above him and soon spread into the blackness, making the darkness retreat until little by little he was able to discern the outline of his own body, as well as that of the elder. When the light was at its peak, falling through the hole in a single golden shaft, he could feel the exposed skin on his hands and face tingle, and he could see as far as ten or twelve yards around him. But he couldn't see as far as the walls of the chamber. The walls of the chamber, the walls of his world, were always black; hard, cold, and black.

It was during the first two years in the second chamber that the elders taught him to speak and count. They pointed to the roof high above and called it 'sky'. The hole where the light came through they called Father Sun. They told him his name was Illapacta, and one day when he asked why he was called Illapacta, the elder who was teaching him did something extraordinary.

Squatting on the ground in the shaft of light that came from above, the elder reached under the folds of his purple robe and as he drew his hand out there came from it a blinding flash. Illapacta jumped back. The small, white haired, frail looking elder gave one of his cackling laughs. He told the child to come close and not be afraid. When he'd been obeyed, the old man slowly opened his hand to reveal, or so it seemed to Illapacta, the very Father Sun resting in his palm!

'Take it. Pick it up,' the elder commanded.

Illapacta gingerly seized the object. He thought it would be warm and slippery but to his surprise he found it was hard and cold.

'Now hold it between your fingers, stretch your arm; look! look!'

He obeyed. He looked at the object, expecting to see it flash again, but what he saw caused him such consternation that he nearly dropped it. A face! A face was staring at him from within the shiny surface.

'What is it you see? A face?'

Illapacta couldn't speak. He nodded, his eyes fixed on the face staring back at him. It was a strange face, not like any of the elders; a face that was smooth and unwrinkled, a face like none he'd ever seen. How could this be? Where did this face come from?

'That face is you,' the elder said. "That's your face you can see. That is how you are.'

Such was the first time he saw his reflection. He was confounded. How could he see his own face? But presently the elder showed him it was true: he held up a stone and Illapacta saw the stone reflected in the object. Then the elder carefully manoeuvred the object so the next thing Illapacta saw in it was the elder's own face. After that he no longer doubted the elder. Holding the object at arm's length, he grinned into it and saw his reflection grinning back at him. He laughed, and then began to examine himself intently. He lifted his fingers, trying to touch the places he could see, but to his confusion he saw instead his own fingers. In a while the elder directed his attention to his eyes. Reaching under his robe again the elder brought out a tiny but glowing green stone. The stone didn't flash like the object; it glinted with a warm, luminous light. The elder explained that the stone was called an emerald, and because it was green, like one of his eyes, they had named him Illapacta: Eye of Emerald.

Illapacta was delighted. He had seen his own face and now he also knew how he had been named. His curiosity inflamed, he began to ply the elder with questions. He wanted to know where the stone and the shiny object had come from. He asked about the clothes he wore and the food he ate. He wanted to know how big the whole world was and if the elders lived in a place that was like his own. Many of these questions weren't new, he had asked them before. But if he hoped they would be answered this time he was again disappointed, for the elder refused to answer them. As with all the others who'd been sequestered, Illapacta was told that he must wait, that he must be patient, and if he did exactly as he was told and learnt all that the elders had to teach him, then one day he would know all the answers to all the questions. To everything? Illapacta asked. Would he know the answers to everything? To everything that was important, the elder assured him. He would know all the answers.

After the green stone and shiny object had disappeared back inside the elder's robe, he began to teach Illapacta the names of the shadows. In the chamber, at that time of day, there wasn't one darkness, or two, or three... there were many shades of darkness: At one extreme a darkness on the edge of light, at the other extreme a darkness deep as the heart of night, in between these two extremes a whole range of shades waiting to be identified, named, remembered...

So many years ago... All that, the sequestration, the rigorous apprenticeship had all occurred so long ago there were times when

Illapacta remembered it like a distant dream. Only the ultimate moment, when he had seen the world being born, remained completely undimmed, blazing inside him, even now that his bones ached and white hairs sprouted like bushes from his ears and nostrils.

But in truth Illapacta no longer cared for the birth of the world. It blazed inside his time-ravaged body against his own desire. The mystic experience of seeing the world being born had become for him a source of violent affliction, of profound anxiety. A curse. For this reason he chewed coca, drank more mishqui than was good for him, and turned a deaf ear to the things people said about him. As an old man – more, as an elder who had fallen into disrepute, he didn't think that he had much left to lose.

With a sigh, Illapacta struggled up from the log. On his painful, arthritic legs he started hobbling towards the main village. As he followed the path the twigs crunching under his feet sounded to him like the rattling of bones. A moment later he brushed against a bush, snapping one of the branches, and where the branch snapped the old man saw not sap but crimson blood.

Within the gathering house, in a shadowy light, the three elders sat in a row on a low bench close to a wall. They wore white, long sleeved tunics under purple robes hemmed with dark red borders. At an angle to the elders' bench, in the centre of a rough stone slab floor, Rumicuri sat alone on something that was half stool half chair and was intricately carved out of a single block of wood. His official attire consisted of a white tunic, like the elders, but the robe he wore over it was black instead of purple. As for Illapacta, in his position of disgraced luminary, he wore nothing more than a scruffy brown robe and was seated on a bench opposite the elders, which was normally reserved for the community's lesser dignitaries.

Gathered on yet more benches, facing the council, Mountain Trotter and the group of refugees tried to answer the questions put to them by the elders, until presently it became apparent that there was one person among them who seemed to know more than the others. And this was the young man who, on arrival, had stared at Rumicuri defiantly, and for that matter continued to behave, if not with outright insolence, at least with obvious disrespect. Showing none of the obsequiousness of the others, rather with barely concealed arrogance, the young man, whose name was Calchas, told the council that purini soldiers had taken over the village because they were looking for the Radiant War. And what was the Radiant War? the elders queried. Calchas then reached under his rough cotton shirt and from the colourful waistband of his trousers he removed a slim red book. As he did so he wished he also had a digital camera to show them. Photographs, moving images of the Radiant War on a digital camera, now that really would've been something! But the one he'd had, given to him by Chairman Mateo, had been lost some time ago; so now, holding just the red book, he stepped up to the elders and in the sudden, total silence he dropped the book in the lap of Punimillo, the chief elder.

No one spoke as Calchas returned to his place on the bench. What he had done was without precedent. It was the law that nothing, no artefact from the outside world should be allowed into the Arayana kingdom. The refugees all knew this, which is why they had arrived with no more than their clothes. Not so Calchas. Quite apart from the provocation he'd already shown Rumicuri, now, as if his manner wasn't rude enough, he had the temerity to smuggle a foreign object into the kingdom and furthermore to flaunt it, to drop it unceremoniously into the chief elder's lap! Such impudence was unheard of. Under different circumstances it would have called for severe retribution. However, at this moment the elders had no room for such thoughts because Calchas had not yet explained himself, and also because this was the first time in their lives they'd seen an object from the outside world so close at hand. They were amazed and mystified by it.

As the book had been dropped in Punimillo's lap, it was he who first examined it. Corpulent and square set, his dark face stared down at the book frowning so intently his white eyebrows were joined together. Finally, making up his mind, he reached for it with both hands; lifting it from his lap, fumbling with the cover, and once the book had fallen open, his stubby fingers seeming to stick to the pages as he clumsily inspected them with an expression of utter bafflement.

After Punimillo had finished, he passed it to Macaruca, the elder on his left – a tall thin man of seventy, gaunt, with cavernous cheeks, who, in contrast to the chief elder, stared at the book with snooty disdain. Yet when his long fingers riffled the pages, they did so gingerly, with nervous distrust, as though afraid the book, more than a mere object, might contain unaccountable malevolent magic.

The last elder to examine the book was Chotavalo, a comparatively young man of forty-five. Like Rumicuri, he had black hair, and black eyes, but his features were softer, more rounded than the sovereign's. Chotavalo took longest in examining the book. He went through it slowly and methodically, pausing to stare intently at each page, as though by so doing alone he might be able to glean its significance.

At last, after the elders had finished examining the book, without being the wiser, they beckoned Calchas and returned the book to him indicating he should pass it to Rumicuri. But unlike the elders, Rumicuri, who all the while had sat in his place impassively, had no wish to examine the book, for he already knew that such objects existed: he had seen them once before, as a boy, when he'd made the journey to the outside world. So when Calchas stepped towards him, he made no move to accept the book. Instead he stared at Calchas with cold anger. Be careful, his look warned. One affront too many and I will crush you like an insect. Calchas, for his part, hadn't forgotten the slap he had received. To flaunt a forbidden object, more to belittle the sovereign by deliberately showing the book to the elders first, was his way of getting even. When he returned to his seat he wasn't displeased with himself for riling the sovereign.

Besides Rumicuri, one other person who had seen a book was Illapacta. However, such was Illapacta's undignified appearance that Calchas had not thought of showing it to him, nor, for that matter, did Illapacta care to examine it.

The book having been examined, the council now awaited an explanation. With an air of self-importance, since all eyes were intent on him, Calchas began by explaining (in a dialect that was not so different that it couldn't be understood) that the book was like the symbols on their own artefacts. The book contained many, many symbols, and if you knew what these symbols signified you could understand the thoughts of the person who had put them in the artefact.

After a number of questions from the elders (for it wasn't a concept they could easily grasp) Calchas went on to inform them that the book contained the teachings of a great leader. This leader wanted to change the outside world because it didn't belong to the downtrodden, the dispossessed. As the elders must have heard, the outside world contained people of all different colours, races, and castes. They were all purinis, but not all purinis were equal. The rich and powerful among them stole land, corrupted women, enslaved men. And when had it not been this way? Ever since the first white men, all that time ago, had come to this land with their firearms and treacherous gods and lust for gold, it had been this way. The rich grew fat and powerful on the hunger, the suffering, the toil of the dispossessed.

But no more! A whirlwind was coming that would sweep the land clean. Invincible flames would leap up and from the roar of battle with its sacrifice and its unquenchable fire would come redemption, a luminous glow, and there would be a new dawn, a new world.

Calchas had been sitting when he started speaking, but now, moved by his own eloquence, he rose to his feet, his lean, hungry, pock-scarred face regarding the council with challenging, defiant pride.

The great leader of the Radiant War – Mateo was his purini name – had assembled a powerful army and had declared total war. Mateo's war was a just war, a war full of radiance, a war of deliverance. It was a war the rich and powerful couldn't hope to win for the armed struggle gleamed in the minds of the Radiant Warriors; it beat in their hearts and leapt irresistibly from their will.

That was how it was. They had justice on their side and the moment of complete victory was drawing closer all the time. And when victory finally came the oppressors would be stripped of their arms, their riches, their power. All those who resisted would be as sticks to a fire. There would be no mercy. Whereas for the victors it would be the beginning of an everlasting dawn; a world in which the land belonged equally to all: for the dispossessed first and foremost, but if the oppressors repented, if they obeyed the laws, there would be peace and plenty for them as well. Yes, even for them. This is what Mateo had announced in the symbols the elders had seen. Only the oppressors did not want to give up their power. They did not want the dispossessed to be strong and free. That was why the purini government had sent their warriors, which they called 'soldiers' in their language, to the village. The soldiers had learnt that the Radiant War was gathering many followers in the region. The soldiers had come to search for the Radiant War. But how would they find it? The warriors of the Radiant War were hiding at secret locations in the jungle, two, three days march from the village. The jungle was very dense where the warriors were hidden. The soldiers wouldn't be able to find them. But the warriors of the Radiant War knew how to find the soldiers. Those soldiers who at this moment were getting drunk in the village, and raping Arayana women, and beating Arayana men, every one of those soldiers would soon be meat for worms. It could happen this very morning, or another day soon, but this much was certain: One night the Radiant War would come for its revenge. One night not one of those soldiers would be alive...

Calchas had finished speaking and now he stood in expectation, waiting for the council's response. But there was no response. Nothing happened. Moments passed and Rumicuri and the elders stared back at him in enigmatic silence. Calchas didn't know what to make of it. Rumicuri's silence he could accept; they didn't like each other, he didn't expect the sovereign to greet his words with favour. But the elders? Hadn't they paid attention? Did they not understand what he'd told them? The Radiant War had singled him out. Chairman Mateo had personally instructed him to 'sow seeds of fire', and he had prepared his words carefully, he thought he'd made a good speech, so why did they sit there, without response, staring at him in silence. He was baffled and not a little disappointed. Not a single question. He could not understand why they didn't ask him a single question.

Cascarina, her name meant Blue Morning, had to laugh when the boy tripped and fell. She couldn't help herself because first the boy had been stung by a wasp. Cascarina – a woman of twenty-four: heavy hips, almond eyes, an easy laugh, hair as black and lustrous as a raven's wing – was on her way to the women's house, where she intended to do some weaving, when, coming across a group of children at play, she saw one small boy jumping up and down, crying out that he'd been stung. A moment later the boys scattered as more angry, droning wasps appeared. The boy who'd been stung started running, but then he tripped and fell down on his face. As Cascarina went over to him she couldn't stop herself from laughing at the double misfortune. But when she saw his look of wretchedness she helped him to his feet and spoke to him gently.

Later, walking slowly up the path to the main village, she forgot the laughter that had briefly lifted her mood. A troubled melancholy was burdening her: Early that morning, before the dawn, Rumicuri had gone.

He had risen from her side and dressed himself in the clothes she had made for him. Awake under thick blankets, she had watched him dress in the red glow of the fire, putting on the trousers and shirt and poncho of an Indian from the outside world. The one thing he could not do, though, was to plait his own hair, so he'd asked her to do this. She complied with reluctance, for it was only in the outside world that Indians plaited their hair; it distressed her to see her lover, the ruler of her people, forced to submit to an alien custom and thereby to demean his dignity.

As Cascarina knelt behind Rumicuri, her skilful fingers plaiting his long hair into a single pigtail, she couldn't help being deeply afraid for him – of the perils he would encounter, and of how exposed and unprotected he would be in the remote, and for her incomprehensible, world of the purinis.

Dwellings with walls you could see through... Animals made of metal that could carry people in their bellies and travel at unbelievable speed... Miniature suns that lit up at night... Boxes that spoke and some with moving, coloured, changing images inside them... She had heard of many strange and frightening things existing in the outside world, and while she was thinking of them, still plaiting Rumicuri's hair, a shadow appeared: The flickering shadow of beating wings which emitted a soft fluttering sound. It was a large moth, only a moth, but Cascarina nonetheless gave a start. In agitation, dropping her lover's hair, she jumped up, and, as the moth fluttered erratically above the fire, she stalked it, clapping her hands, trying to catch it, succeeding on her fourth attempt.

No sooner had she caught the moth, while it was wounded but still alive, she urged Rumicuri to open his mouth, then she placed the moth inside his mouth and quickly clamped his lips, now urging him to swallow it.

Cascarina was pale and her heart beat in agitation when she went back to plaiting Rumicuri's hair. She shuddered to think what might have happened had she not seen the moth or had she not been able to catch it, for it was her people's belief that at particular times – in illness or sleep, in moments of weakness or danger – a person's soul was liable to desert the body, and in deserting the body it often took the shape of wings, be they the wings of an insect or a bird. So who was to say the moth wasn't Rumicuri's soul taking flight from his body?

Cascarina could not imagine that Rumicuri would falter before the task he had set himself. If she understood anything about his character it was that he had a will of stone. He was not a man to be deterred, she couldn't imagine that he would ever allow his body to succumb to fear. But that was his body. It wasn't his soul. A person's soul, she knew, was different. A soul had half a life of its own. It was said that a soul never grew up; always it remained as it was on the day a person was born. A soul was childlike. It was mischievous, unruly, easily frightened, and worst of all, forever wanting to leave the body and return to its home in the spirit world. And when this happened, when a soul forsook the body and couldn't be made to return, a person soon weakened. That person lost his mind. Or became ill. Or died.

Rumicuri had been fortunate on this occasion. To Cascarina it was alarmingly obvious that his soul did not want to accompany his body on the perilous journey. So his soul had tried to desert him, it had tried to leave his body by taking the shape of a moth, but she had spotted its shadow, she had heard the slight, fluttering sound a soul will always make when it's in the air, and she had caught it and returned it to his body. He'd been fortunate on this occasion, but what if it should happen again when she wasn't there to look after him? What if it should happen when he was in the terrible world of the purinis?

As she entered the main village, walking between brown mud huts towards the women's house, Cascarina heard the sound of female voices. They were coming from around the corner of one of the huts, and because they were voices she recognised, and moreover heard Rumicuri's name being mentioned, she paused to listen.

'Nobody tells us nothing, that's the truth,' one voice was complaining. 'First they say there is a war going on but we're safe and shouldn't fear; then just now we hear the sovereign has gone to the purinis.'

'*Aee, aee*, he's gone to consult his uncle, the one who lives in the world of the purinis.'

'But why has he gone? Why, if we have nothing to fear?'

'*Aee, aee*, I tremble to think what's coming to pass. I tremble. First it doesn't rain. Everything is dying. *Aee, aee*, the river is dying, the grass on the mountain is dying –'

'Hush now, in the forest it rains and there is water for our crops.'

29

'*Aee, aee.* Do you see a cloud above? And why is there no snow on the mountain? And everything has been tried. Everything. Even the dead. Even the bones of the dead have been dug up. But it doesn't rain, and now the lowlanders have come, fleeing their village, saying there is a war in the world of the purinis, and then this morning we hear the sovereign has gone to consult his uncle –'

'Hush, woman, hush. Soon a new elder will be here. Soon. And when the new elder sees the world being born it'll rain, you'll see. And the sovereign will return saying we're safe...'

Cascarina lost interest. As she walked on, past the corner of the hut, glancing sideways she saw the women who were talking. They were three elderly women, all of whom she knew, and they were standing in the harsh light of the sun, their heads protected by striped black and white scarves. On the ground numerous, many-coloured guinea pigs were scurrying and squealing in between their legs, sniffing out the grains of corn that one of the women had tossed for them. The women dropped into silence as Cascarina walked past, but she could feel their eyes on her back and she knew they would start talking again as soon as she was out of sight.

Further into the village, Cascarina passed a shepherd taking a flock of llama to the scarce pasture on the foothills of the mountain. Dust rose from the thick-fleeced, sad-eyed llamas, as the shepherd, wearing a pointed woollen hat, followed behind them with long, loose-limbed strides, and made clicking sounds to urge them forward. After the flock had passed, a woman appeared through the settling dust, her small figure doubled over under the weight of a huge bundle of firewood. Further on, yet more women ferried gourds of water, or sat outside their huts grinding corn in stone mortars or hand spinning yarn from wicker baskets piled high with rough flax or wool. Some of these women ignored Cascarina, others smiled and greeted her, and perhaps on another day she might have stopped to chat with those who greeted her. As it was she barely acknowledged their greetings. She walked on, towards the women's house, distracted, thinking of one of the old women whom she had overheard talking, the one who kept saying, *aee, aee,* and who at this very moment, Cascarina was certain, would already be blackening her in her thoughts, if not openly maligning her, for this woman was a close relative of Illani.

Cascarina didn't like to think she was the sort of person who harboured ill will, but the truth was that whenever she caught sight of Illani, or even thought of her, she became upset. Illani, her name meaning sweet, was anything but sweet. She was cruel, twisted with hatred, because she'd tried to steal Rumicuri from her, and in the end, for all that she had managed to seduce Rumicuri, to marry him, to bear him a child, she hadn't been able to keep him. She hadn't been able to steal his heart from her.

Illani had bandy legs, thin lips, a sharp crooked nose. She wasn't beautiful, certainly not to Cascarina's eyes, but she had very white teeth, black hair so long it reached below her waist, and a body that contained something feline in its sinuous, predatory motion.

Illani was a woman who could arouse lust in men, and envy in women because of the effect she had on men. But she herself, while doing nothing to discourage the admiration or envy, gave the appearance of being haughtily indifferent to it. Of course, in reality she wasn't indifferent; no woman ever is, Cascarina knew. Even a plain woman is susceptible to vanity. It was only that Illani gave this disdainful appearance because it increased her sense of power. She liked people to admire and envy her. And she enjoyed being able to despise them. Illani was drawn to power. That was why she had chased after Rumicuri. And that was why, in her youth, she had ingratiated herself with Amataba and had become her apprentice. Cascarina had no doubt it was sorcery that Illani had used to seduce Rumicuri. All her life Illani had had a passion for sorcery. And it was Illani who, when they were children, had dared Cascarina to help her steal Amataba's gajuru – the bone stick that in the hands of Amataba was said to contain so much power it could make the skeletons of the dead rise from their graves.

That day, standing in the doorway of Amataba's hut, acting as lookout, Cascarina had never been so scared. She felt Amataba's presence everywhere; an invisible but fearsome presence, as though the air were full of watching eyes, as though Amataba could see them from afar and knew exactly what they were up to and at any moment would materialize before them in a whirlwind of fury. Before any such could happen, however, Illani came hurrying out, clutching the gajuru, and at once they raced into a nearby cluster of trees. When they stopped, Illani was gasping, her brown eyes shone with mischievous excitement, and the white knobbly-smooth gajuru stick was trembling in her hands. But then, while they both stood staring triumphantly at the gajuru, Illani gave a shriek. The gajuru was burning her hand! She couldn't open her fingers!

Cascarina froze. She wanted to help her friend but at the same time she was too frightened to dare touch Illani's hand. Illani, meanwhile, started sobbing, shaking, and in real panic now they ran from the trees, racing back to the hut, not caring any more if they were seen. At the threshold Cascarina stopped, not daring to go further, but peering into the shadowy interior she saw that Illani, astonishingly, was now able to open her hand and drop the gajuru in the place where she'd found it.

When Illani emerged, she was clutching her hand, which, Cascarina noticed, did not look sore or inflamed. Her face though was drained white, and there were tears in her eyes. But soon, once they were safely away from the hut, Illani stared down at her hand in wonder, her thin lips smiling through her tears in a curious, secret way.

The smile made Cascarina suspicious. She wondered if Illani had pretended more had happened than actually had.

'When I'm older,' Illani told Cascarina, 'I'm going to be a medicine woman. I'm going to ask Amataba to teach me!'

And that's what she'd done. She'd become Amataba's apprentice. And she was still Amataba's apprentice when, years later, when they were young women, the gossip started, the rumours…

For days, weeks, Cascarina refused to believe what she heard. Anybody could start a rumour. It could be Illani herself had started it. For a long time she'd known that Illani had her eye on Rumicuri. It could be that Illani had been making advances, and, rejected, out of revenge, she herself had spread the rumour. Cascarina wouldn't put this beyond her. That woman had no scruples. She could believe anything of Illani.

But Rumicuri? How could she think badly of him? They went back to her childhood. She trusted him. She had always trusted him, right from the day he had given her the stone, when she was still unripe, when she hadn't yet bled, and he was already in his manhood. That was the day Cascarina had fallen in love with him.

She'd been sent to fetch water from the river. Upon reaching it she'd heard shouts coming from the pool. Curious, she'd followed the path that led to the pool and when she arrived there she had seen young men diving from the rocks. Often men dived from the rocks, but very few of them dared dive from the highest rock. The reason for this was the narrowness of the gorge. In years past young men had been fatally wounded when, attempting the dive, they had crashed against the rock beneath them.

Sitting on the bank, near the pool, Cascarina had watched Rumicuri leave the other youths and, naked, start scrambling up the gorge. Half way up he paused on an overhang and she thought he was going to dive from there, but he turned and continued up, disappearing from sight before appearing again on the very top. When other youths saw him poised on the highest rock they scrambled out of the pool and sat on the bank near her, staring up at him in silence. She thought he looked like a bird, like a hawk, the way he stood outlined against the sky, so high above that it made her head spin to keep looking.

Then he was in the air. Upwards. He flew upwards. For the merest instant he hung in the air, poised above the gorge, then his body folded in half, his legs came up behind him, and with his head between his arms, straight as a dart, he dived down the narrow channel, missing one of the projecting rocks by a sliver.

The youths cheered when he pierced the diamond clear, sunlit water of the pool. Looking down, Cascarina could see his lean, copper-coloured body swimming near the stony floor. He didn't come up straight away. He stayed there, swimming around, searching the bottom, and to her it seemed like an age before his body straightened and he rose swiftly to the surface in a circle of bubbles. When he climbed onto the bank the youths exclaimed loudly, laughing and cheering, but she remained quiet. Even in those days, as a young man, his expression was hard, unyielding. Without knowing why, she was frightened of him. She ought not to be there, she remembered. Her mother had sent her for water and she had yet to fill the gourd. Grasping the gourd, she made to rise, but at that moment he stepped in front of her, his body naked and gleaming. One of his hands was clenched into a fist and there was a wild light in his black eyes. She feared he was stepping forward in anger, then his hand opened and she saw in the palm of his hand a small stone. He pressed the stone into her own small palm and as he turned it seemed to her that a faint smile softened his countenance.

Later, when she was alone, looking more closely at the stone, she saw that it glowed with specks of yellow. Was it gold? She didn't know, but the stone became precious to her. And when she thought of him standing in front of her in his naked manhood, she felt a quivering ache in her heart. It was an ache that scared her, that was strange – like a longing.

No. When Cascarina became aware of the rumours implicating Rumicuri with Illani, she couldn't believe it. She trusted him. They were like the guarani. Hadn't he said so himself? Hadn't he said they were like the guarani?

One day, not long before the gossip started, when they were in the forest together, sitting by the river, they had spotted a pair of silver-winged, red-crested guarani ducks bobbing on the water, and Rumicuri had said, 'We're like those guarani.' That was all, but it made her happy because the guarani were sacred birds that mated for life. Just to tease him though, she'd asked if this meant he would not take another wife? Not ever, she'd asked him, even after they were married? And he had repeated they would be like the guarani. 'I'm not my father,' he'd said. And she had seen a shadow darken his face. He disapproved of his father. There were not many in the community who didn't. He was the sovereign and the people had to respect him no matter how badly he behaved, but Cascarina knew how women were frightened of being left alone with him in case he tried to seduce them. No woman, not the young ones anyway, was safe with him…

Playfully Rumicuri pushed her onto the grass. Leaning over he said: "When you are pregnant we will marry, little guarani." And she understood what he meant by this, too. For when he became the ruler of his people it would be his duty to father an heir, and were she not to bear him a child he would be obliged to take a second wife…

She hadn't managed to get pregnant at the time the gossip started. She was trying, and she was hopeful that one day soon she would, but she hadn't yet managed it. And this worry, added to the gossip, sapped her confidence. In spite of herself, even though she couldn't believe Rumicuri would do anything to harm her, she began to wonder if it was possible, just possible he was getting tired of waiting for her to become pregnant? This thought, once it occurred, was like a crack in her trust, in her certainty of his faithfulness. And when the gossip persisted, when the rumours wouldn't go away, other doubts began to surface, and she became increasingly anxious and began to recall the things that women said about men: They were weak. Not to be trusted. They were like bulls in a herd, forever ready to mount an available female...

Could it be that he was no different from other men after all? Cascarina couldn't really believe this. She couldn't believe he could be so weak... But what if Illani, with her knowledge of sorcery, had worked an enchantment on him? What if he were bewitched?

Increasingly she came to fear this might be so. And it grew into a gnawing fear. It began to eat her up inside. It gave her no peace. Attacks of panic sometimes overwhelmed her, and at night, unable to sleep, the oppressive darkness robbed her of all enthusiasm, of all belief.

One evening her wretchedness was such that she decided to confront him. She went to his hut and feeling sick, her insides churning, she waited outside, by the door. Just as it was getting dark – the trees black, the sky streaked with violet and pink – she saw him coming down the path, looking tired, and his clothes, his whole body covered in yellowish cornmeal, for he had passed the day helping in the granary. When he saw her, he paused, seeming to hold back, and to her this small gesture was like a fist in her stomach. When he was beside her, she asked him: 'Is it true what people are saying? The things I've heard?' And there was silence. A long silence, and his eyes, those same eyes that so often had blazed with the joy of seeing her, were unrecognisable. They slipped away from her, skittering like tadpoles, furtive, as though trying to hide.

At that moment she knew it was true. He opened his mouth, he began to mumble something, but she wouldn't wait to hear him, she turned and fled as if from her own death.

That was how she found out about Illani. And her anguish was shattering. The world – everything she had always thought so secure and solid – was disintegrating, flying apart like so many shards of pottery. And at night, lying in her bed, she would feel a pain in her womb that was like a blade ripping it. Curled up, hugging her knees, trying to muffle the sobs that racked her body (so as not to awaken the relatives who shared the hut) she would rock herself backwards and forwards...

Even in her bleakest moments, however, she managed not to lose hope utterly. And what sustained her was her belief that Rumicuri had been bewitched. She was ever more certain of this. Illani had used sorcery, she'd put an enchantment on him, so that he had lost his will, he was in a trance, he no longer knew what he was doing...

But Cascarina knew, everybody knew, for she had often heard it spoken, that there was no sorcery in the world that could destroy true love. Bewitchment of the kind Illani had worked were passing things. People said they were like a fever. While the bewitchment lasted a victim was in grave danger, for it took such complete control that the victim became confused and could not act against it. But after a while, if nothing terrible happened, the bewitchment began to weaken just like a fever. Little by little the victim recovered, until one day all was well again and the person looked at himself in amazement, unable to understand what had happened. And so it would be with Rumicuri. Now, for a little, Illani had possession of him. But Rumicuri didn't love Illani. He loved her, Cascarina. It had always been so. The enchantment couldn't last. It would pass. Like a fever it would pass and he would recover his true self and would look at himself knowing he'd been bewitched, wondering what it was he'd ever seen in Illani.

So she waited for the enchantment to pass. But what passed wasn't the enchantment, it was the gossip, because Illani and Rumicuri had stopped trying to keep their betrayal a secret. More to the contrary: Illani, at any rate, flaunted it. Having abandoned her apprenticeship with Amataba, she now spent all her time dressing up in fine clothes, and showing off, giving herself airs as though she were already preparing to become the future queen. More and more they were seen in public together, and the gossip now, if any, revolved around Cascarina, for people wondered what could have happened, what Cascarina could have done to make Rumicuri abandon her.

It was during the celebrations at the end of the corn harvest that Casacarina's diminishing hopes, her fragile defences, finally collapsed. These celebrations were an important event for the community and in years past she had always looked forward to them with joy. So many things happened during the celebrations: People got dressed in their finest clothes and there were feasts and games and dancing, but most important of all was the investiture of the Mother Corn Spirit.

The Mother Corn Spirit was a sheaf of corn that was set aside to provide seeds for the following year's crop. Without this sheaf there would be no good corn, people would go hungry, so the sheaf had to be the largest and healthiest that could be found. For days before the celebrations people scoured the fields in search of it and once it was located it was carried to the main village with great solemnity. Once in the village it was dressed in female clothes and adorned with flowers and ornaments of gold. It was the elders and the nobles who led the procession to the village, but it was the women who dressed and adorned the sheaf. Three women were chosen for the task: The woman who had the most children first and foremost, then the eldest married woman in the community, then a young virgin girl. Attending the 'priestesses' were three other women, one of whom was selected by the sovereign.

For the last few years, since they had been lovers, Rumicuri had chosen Cascarina for this honour. But now, as the whole community got busy preparing for the celebrations, Cascarina heard – not from Rumicuri, not even from him, but from her sister-in-law, Guaneque, that Illani had been chosen!

Up until that moment she had managed somehow to carry on with a semblance of normality. There was so much to be done that for a lot of the time she'd been too busy to think about herself. Sewing clothes, hauling potatoes, slaughtering guinea pigs, helping her sister-in-law and the many women in her extended family, there were times when she felt almost like her old self again. And at moments she'd even joined the unceasing talk and laughter that went on around her. But when, taking advantage of a moment when there was no one else in the hut, her sister-in-law gently told her of Rumicuri's choice, Cascarina turned white, the strength went from her limbs, everything started reeling and she staggered out of the hut not knowing where she was, her mind dazed.

Cascarina went to the celebrations. She put on her orange-brown tunic, embroidered sash, white over-blouse, dark blue shawl, necklaces of beads and silver, large earrings of beaten gold, striped head-scarf... She put on all these things, but numbed, without feeling, as though she were dressing her own corpse.

And when she took her place among the other noble ladies to await the procession she barely managed to respond to their greetings, and she showed no interest in their festive attire (as she would normally have done) or in their light-hearted chatter. Disconnected from all that was happening, she stared down with dead eyes at the parallel lines of people (over a thousand of them, the entire community) that stretched to the bottom of a long grassy slope.

And when the procession appeared in the distance, at the bottom of the slope, with dead eyes she watched the people on either side drop to their knees and touch the ground with their hands, prostrating themselves before the Mother Corn Spirit as it was carried past.

As the procession ascended the slope, drawing ever nearer, with dead eyes she saw Rumicuri appear at the head of it, dressed in his full royal splendour; the gold and precious stones and rare feathers of his costume – a costume he wore only on the most sacred of occasions – shimmering and flashing in the morning sun. Behind Rumicuri, came the elders in their purple garments, and behind the elders, resting on a wooden pallet that was supported by selected men, came the Mother Corn Spirit: A large yellow sheath of stalks and cobs bound with twine.

With dead eyes Cascarina watched Rumicuri grow more distinct step by step, until she was able to see the green glitter of emeralds on his sandals; the black loincloth with red border; triangular necklace of beaten gold inlaid with turquoise; shimmering cape of feathers – green, yellow, blue, red, black, silver feathers from rare and sacred birds; sun-shaped earrings of beaten gold; crown band studded with amber, with topaz, and above the crown band, tall feathers that fanned around his head.

With dead eyes she saw his unsmiling face; his black eyes that stared straight ahead and not once sought her out – not once, even when he was within a few feet of where she was standing.

Like all the other noble ladies, Cascarina prostrated herself before the Mother Corn Spirit as it passed by. When she rose to her feet she joined the crowd that had gathered at the entrance of the granary. There the Mother Corn Spirit was lowered to the ground and no sooner had this happened than the three priestesses came out of the granary dressed entirely in white. Behind the priestesses came the three attendants carrying the flowers and golden ornaments and female clothes with which to dress the sheaf. Illani was the attendant to the senior priestess. But Illani, with her long black hair and beautiful clothes and glittering ornaments, looked like nobody's attendant. Illani, although she stood three steps behind the senior priestess, managed to look more proud and regal than anyone there.

It was now the turn of the sovereign, the elders, the nobles, and in fact the whole community (it had gathered in a compact mass at the rear) to prostrate themselves before the priestesses and their attendants. And Cascarina knew that at this moment, before Rumicuri dropped to his knees, his eyes would be seeking Illani's. She knew this because in years past it had been her eyes waiting to meet his, and it had been her heart which, on this important occasion, had filled with solemn joy.

Only it was Illani who was there to receive him. It wasn't her, it was Illani. And watching them, in the moment before Rumicuri prostrated himself, Cascarina felt the last, tenuous fragments of hope die in her breast. And when the moment came for Cascarina to prostrate herself she dropped to her knees like a stone. And when, with difficulty, she struggled to her feet again, everything looked watery. There were no tears in her eyes, they were dry, there were no tears, but everything looked watery.

After that all became confused for Cascarina. Around her she saw happy faces, colourful costumes, the festive activities of her people, but always they were separated from her by this liquid like water. When people came up to her, smiling, talking, their faces were blurred and she couldn't understand what they were saying. She heard only noises. If someone touched her she could see the movement occurring but she couldn't feel the touch. Nothing. She couldn't feel the ground under her feet or the solidity of a tree or a wall. Time became jumbled in her mind. At one moment she would be in the middle of a big feast (if unable to smell the aromas or taste the food) and at another moment she would be somewhere else, watching the games or the dancing, but always separated from the world by this liquid like water; not knowing how she got from one place to another or how much time had lapsed in between.

The celebrations lasted for three days and nights. In her mind it could've been an hour or a week because she went through the celebrations unaware of time, in a dreadful dream. Then one evening, she didn't know how soon after the celebrations, but one evening when she was wandering without knowing where she was or where she was going, a group of people appeared and grabbed hold of her. Afterwards all she could remember was that when she came to - somewhat groggy, drained, but no longer separated from the world by this liquid like water - she was in Amataba's hut.

Amataba's hut was like no other. The air inside it was redolent with the aroma of herbs – pungent herbs, sweet herbs, spicy herbs that hung in bunches from the rafters. Elsewhere, all around, were earthenware pots of mysterious unguents and potions; the knobbly gajuru stick; effigies carved out of wood or bone; the carcasses of animals, and most frightening of all, the bleached skulls: animal skulls, but as well human skulls.

Amataba herself had a face that looked like a skull. Her cheeks were sunken and her thin translucent skin – oddly unwrinkled – was drawn tight over a pinched and delicate bone structure. But there was little that was skull-like about her eyes. They were intensely bright, often cheerful, quick as a ferret's.

Cascarina was lying under blankets on a bed made of bamboo and cushioned by fleeces, when, not long after she had recovered, Amataba, sitting at her side, began speaking to her in a persistent, sing-song voice.

'When you were brought to me I knew your fickle soul had left you. I went into your mouth and saw your body full of sorrow. Your soul had left you, child, and so I came out of your backside – fu, what a stink!' Amataba fanned her nose with her hand. 'I came out of your backside and then I went in search of your soul…

'Listen. I searched for your soul in the land that lies just this side of the great chasm. In this land that is like no other land all the errant and wayward souls in the world gather with one purpose only, and that's to wait for their bodies…'

Amataba reached for Cascarina's hand and held it between her own two, now stroking it, now patting it.

'Listen child, listen to what I tell you… When a soul leaves its body, the body languishes, it becomes disconsolate, until one day, unable to endure the separation, it goes in pursuit of its soul. This is what happens. And when a body arrives in the spirit land its soul at once enters it, because without their bodies the errant soul can't cross the great chasm…

'Listen. Once body and soul have crossed the great chasm it's almost impossible to turn back. A very few can manage it, but only if they're on the edge of the frontier and are quicker than a blink. But even when those reckless few do manage to go back, theirs is a terrible fate, a wretched fate, because they can never return alive. *Aee, Aee*, those poor creature are the ghosts of the dead that sometimes haunt this world...

'Listen now. Once on the other side of the frontier, vast multitudes of humans, such as you could never count, start marching across the great chasm. And not only humans, plants and animals, too, but we won't speak of that now. But its a strange place, the chasm, because its neither dark nor light and were you to look down you would see there was nothing there: A huge, huge emptiness without end. And the humans who travel across the great chasm are the departed of all the ages, because when a human takes a single step across the great chasm it's as long as a lifetime in this world of ours... So it is, child, so it is...

'And travelling across the great chasm, in the multitudes without name, you can see our proud and noble ancestors, dressed in their magnificent burial clothes of jewels and feathers. And marching by their side, the purinis, yes even our ancestors' murderers... the white skinned demons with their hands dripping blood and hair on their faces and wearing their creaking clothes of metal...

'And to where do they travel? They travel to the far side of the great chasm where shines a wonderful soft blue light. And this wonderful soft blue light is the very entrance to the Holy Source: The father and mother of all creation. The beginning and the end that no living creature, not even the elders, not even they have seen fully, beyond the blue light.

'Listen child... At first, when the vast multitudes cross the frontier of the great chasm, they have bodies like you and me, but with each step, the further they advance, little by little their bodies become like water, so you can see right through them. And then in the far, far distance, as they approach the end of the great chasm, they begin to fade until they vanish altogether. They melt like snow in the blue light of the Holy Source...

'Now listen to what I tell you. Never forget what I'm going to tell you.

'There are many that march towards the Holy Source in peace with themselves, singing and laughing because when they were in this world they faced their destiny without fear. They were brave and noble, and even if they were purinis, yes, even then these humans are blessed.

'But there are others that when they march towards the Holy Source they tremble and drag their feet because when they were

41

in this world their hearts learnt to hate and they became cruel and deceitful. These humans, very many of them purinis, but Indians too, these humans march towards the Holy Source full of terror because they have done evil and they don't know what awaits them once they have passed through the entrance of the Holy Source.

'And there are yet others that march towards the Holy Source meekly, because although they lived gentle lives they weren't brave. These people march towards the Holy Source full of shame and cowardice. This is what happens to them. And thinking of all the opportunities they missed and the true fulfilment that could have been theirs, these poor souls long to return to the world and redeem themselves. But this they can't do. And so they march towards the Holy Source with anxiety and downcast heads, like children pleading for forgiveness...'

After these lengthy words Amataba paused. Finally she said: 'Is that how you want to march, child? Is that how you want to meet the Holy Source? Or do you want to march happy, with an abundance of joy in your heart?'

And then, before Cascarina could answer, Amataba began laughing. Her frail and diminutive body swayed as she shrieked and patted Cascarina's hand.

'*Aee, aee*, what a job I had with your fickle soul! Speak of a rascal the way I had to chase it over half the land of the spirits. And if that wasn't enough for an old woman, you should've seen the airs that haughty soul of yours gave itself! What good is a young and beautiful body to me, said your soul, if it's flooded with tears? But there, I promised your soul I'd make your body healthy again, and so at last your soul agreed to return...

'Listen child, listen to me now...

'You think the sovereign has stopped loving you? This isn't so. Illani is a temptress, and to my regret – it was a mistake, I'll tell you that, it was a mistake – I agreed to take her on as my apprentice. So Illani is a temptress and now she also knows sorcery and that's strong magic. But listen... You've been lost for many days, and while you've been lost the sovereign has been here, sitting where I'm sitting now, watching over you...

'Yes, it's true...

'Listen. The sovereign has been under a powerful spell, and to make matters worse, now Illani carries his child. He'll marry Illani, for he is our ruler and such is his duty. But I've looked into his heart and I've seen your image there as surely as I've seen his image in your heart... Do you hear what I'm saying? *Aee, aee,* men are weak and foolish where women are concerned. Any little sniff of a woman's honey and their poles go straight up! And then they lose all sense and soon they don't know where they are... Be patient, be patient. The sovereign was led astray by sorcery and the scent of honey, and now he wanders lost in a forest of desires, looking, looking for his true path... Stay strong and patient, child, and you'll be like a light in the forest and one day he'll find the path to your heart. This I promise you...'

As usual the women's house was full of activity when Cascarina arrived there. The ten looms, of ancient but effective design, were all in use, and the women who sat at them worked in an intent silence that was interrupted only by the intermittent knocking sound of the shuttles.

In another part of the long room, more women were gathered around large earthenware containers in which they were cold dying different fabrics in bright colours, and because their work was less demanding than weaving, these women made more noise, gossiping and laughing.

Elsewhere, the other women sat on narrow benches along the walls, sewing or embroidering, and yet others just sat doing nothing, waiting for their turn at the weaving or dying.

Cascarina joined this last group, to wait for her loom to be vacated, at such a time as the bad-tempered overseer (an old, shapeless, wart-encrusted woman) decided it was the mid-day changeover. In between watching the overseer taking tally of a stack of finished fabrics, Cascarina half listened to the woman next to her talking about her children. This woman, who was bone thin and had a bad complexion, had yet managed to produce five children. Now Cascarina heard her saying that she thought she was pregnant again. 'I don't know what it is with me,' she was saying. 'All my man's got to do is stick his pole in and I get pregnant.'

Cascarina smiled out of politeness, not to appear unfriendly, but it hurt her to think that this woman could have more children than she wanted when she herself couldn't manage a single one. She was desperate for a child. Often she'd thought that had she managed to become pregnant early on the whole affair of Illani wouldn't have happened. But she had not got pregnant. It was Illani who had got pregnant, who had married Rumicuri, who had given him an heir. And she herself had been trying everything. After Rumicuri had abandoned Illani and returned to her (just as Amataba had predicted he would) she'd tried everything. She'd eaten frogs spawn. She'd fashioned fertility effigies. She'd recited incantations. She'd taken all the herbs Amataba had prescribed. And not long ago she had gone to Amataba's again, at her wits end, pleading with the old woman. Amataba agreed to try something else; a potent form of magic that had rarely failed her, she said, but if it didn't work this time there was nothing more she could do.

So following Amataba's instruction, Cascarina had spoken to Rumicuri and he had agreed to cooperate. The first thing they had to do was abstain from love-making until the next full moon. On that night they were to pluck two hairs each from their respective pubic regions. Rumicuri was to immerse his two hairs in his own seed, and Cascarina was to do likewise with her fluids. After this they were to wait, lying side by side, until Amataba arrived. They were then to give her their two hairs each and she would take the hairs outside and commence a magic ritual known only to herself, but which, Cascarina knew, involved Amataba entering a trance. In the meantime they were to begin making love, and at the moment Rumicuri was about to release his seed he should give a loud shout so Amataba would know the precise moment in which to join the hairs…

So all this had taken place. And it had taken place on the night of the last full moon; too soon to know if Amataba's magic had worked. But the thought that it could have worked, that Rumicuri's seed might already be growing in her womb, was enough to make Cascarina's heart flutter. If only it were true. How happy it would make her. And Rumicuri! She could think of no greater joy than being able to tell him, upon his return from the outside world, that she was carrying his child. But almost at once, no sooner had this hope occurred to her than dark thoughts obscured it. What if the magic hadn't worked? Worse still, what if misfortune were to befall Rumicuri in the world of the purinis?

This last was a despairing thought. It caused her such turmoil that she couldn't remain in the women's house. Abruptly she stood up. Without a word she hurried out of the edifice and headed straight for Amataba's hut, who of all the women she knew, was the one she most trusted to understand her fears...

Amataba's hut wasn't far from the women's house. But as with some others it stood on its own ground, surrounded by bushes and trees. When Cascarina arrived there she stopped outside the door, which on this occasion was half open, and called Amataba by name. When there was no answer she sat down on an upturned log near the door. But after a short while, when there was still no sign of Amataba, she got up and on impulse peered through the gap in the door.

As her eyes adjusted to the dim interior she saw a shadowy shape lying on the bed, and there was something about it that at once sent a shudder up her spine.

A shaft of bright light fell on the bed as she pushed the door open. Disturbed by the sudden light, a cloud of fiercely humming flies rose up. Beneath them Amataba was lying on her back, her mouth and eyes wide open, her right arm dangling over the edge of the bed. Stillness came over Cascarina. She stood without moving, staring at Amataba, at the buzzing flies.

Then a cry broke from her lips. Rushing to the bed she fell to her knees and threw herself over Amataba's body, weeping, wailing...

It was the belief among the Arayana that trees had living, sentient spirits, and the larger the tree, the larger the shade it cast, the more powerful its spirit. Trees were sacred beings. They had to be treated with respect. Should it be necessary to harm a tree, always it was the people's custom to ask its forgiveness.

Smaller vegetation however (unless it had a specific virtue, such as for food or healing) could be treated, if not with impunity, with a lesser respect. For this reason, when, after crossing the bridge, Mountain Trotter unwrapped a bundle of leaves to reveal the six machetes he and his followers had left behind before entering the kingdom, it wasn't the thought of harming the undergrowth that caused Rumicuri to hesitate from taking one. It was rather the fact that the machetes were a purini made tool, and therefore something that was dangerous and alien.

Mountain Trotter saw Rumicuri hesitate, but, useful though a machete was in the jungle, such was the respect Mountain Trotter had for the sovereign that he didn't make any comment. He stood by the open bundle, a white straw hat lowered over his old, sparsely whiskered, gentle face, waiting for Rumicuri to make up his mind.

This Rumicuri did suddenly: he reached for one of the machetes, and as he gripped the wooden handle he felt a strange sensation pass from the handle into his fingers and up the length of his arm, as though the machete were at once bonding itself to his sinews, as though the machete were at once communicating to him a dangerous, seductive power.

After Rumicuri had grabbed the machete, Mountain Trotter replaced the bundle in the hollow of a tree trunk. Next, from the same place he removed an ancient rifle, also wrapped in leaves bound with twine, and after removing the leaves he hitched the rifle strap to his shoulder. Then both men raised the straw baskets, containing provisions, and passed the long straps across their foreheads. Ready now, the baskets resting on their backs, machetes in their right hands, they set off on the arduous trek to the outside world.

There was no path through the jungle. This was virgin rain forest, so dense and mountainous that it might take an Indian with a machete half a day to travel a few miles. Mountain Trotter, however, was no ordinary Indian. The contact with the high kingdom had been a tradition in his family for generations. He, no-one else, was the appointed intermediary between the Arayana and the outside world, and he knew the forest terrain as if it were his own skin. Following Mountain Trotter, Rumicuri had to marvel at how the old man seemed always to know which way to step and where the undergrowth was thinnest – something that was impossible to anticipate by sight alone in this shadowy tangle of tree trunks, of hanging lianas, of branches, of leaves of every size, shape, and shade of green...

Beneath the undergrowth, the uneven ground itself was covered with a detritus of mouldy brown leaves, branches, and rotting logs, but sometimes also with stretches of soft mud. For this reason the men wore their trousers rolled up to their thighs, and after they had crossed one of these stretches they would stop to pull off the black leeches that had fastened themselves to their legs.

Aside from the leeches, the men also had to contend with ants that sometimes got under their clothes and gave fierce, burning bites. A far rarer, though more serious danger, was the presence of serpents. Not the large serpents that could be seen and would slither out of the way; the danger came from the small serpents that hid in branches and clusters of moss, for their bite was invariably fatal and a person could never be sure that he wasn't going to accidentally disturb one.

It had been dry in the forest when the men set off, but as they arrived panting at the top of a steep incline, the shadow deepened and there was a burst of thunder and immediately afterwards came a heavy downpour. Mountain Trotter, with a single stroke of his machete, severed a giant leaf and stood holding it over his head like an umbrella. Rumicuri preferred to let the rain fall on him. After three years of drought in the high ground any rainfall felt good to him. He listened to the gurgling, percolating sound of the rain as it streamed and dripped through the canopy, and lifted his face to better feel the cold wet drops.

After the rain had stopped, with the abruptness it had started, Mountain Trotter discarded the leaf and once again began leading the way through the undergrowth, now and then having to employ short and precise machete strokes against the dense vegetation. From gaps in the canopy above, a strong sunlight was filtering through the leaves and branches, illuminating the undergrowth with a dappled effect and causing steam to rise from the ground as well as from Rumicuri's clothes.

As time passed Rumicuri became increasingly weary. His leg muscles were knotted and his neck ached from having to pull on the head strap that supported the basket on his back. The weariness, however, didn't stop him from being alert to the occasional and always unexpected sounds and sights of the forest: The squawking cry of an alarmed parrot; a beautiful purple orchid blooming bigger than a man's outstretched hand; wonderfully coloured butterflies; huge, delicate, perfectly symmetrical cobwebs, and on one occasion, a clear view of a long-haired, yellowish sloth swinging upside down on a branch.

At last, after the men had been trekking for five, six hours, they arrived exhausted and soaked in sweat at the summit of a ridge. Here, they disencumbered themselves of the baskets. Before sitting down to rest, Mountain Trotter used his machete to hack at the undergrowth until there appeared an irregular hole through which it was possible to get an open view of the jungle.

Standing by Mountain Trotter's side, Rumicuri gazed upon the compacted curly-topped expanse of dark green treetops that under a blue sky covered four steep and sharp ridges lined up one behind the other. These ridges, which were evenly spaced and of similar height, were known to Rumicuri as the Jaguar's Ribs.

The first time he had seen the Jaguar's Ribs was when he was thirteen years old and had made his one and only journey to the outside world in the company of Illapacta and his uncle, Tupaxi. The journey on that occasion had been something of an adventure for Rumicuri, although it had not been intended as one. He had gone because his capricious father, who at that time was already very ill, and had for a change the well-being of his people in mind, had wanted him to: 'As each year passes the purinis grow stronger and advance closer to our land and all we do is hide like a turtle in its shell. So go. Learn all you can, for it may be that what you learn now will one day serve our people...' So the journey was meant to be one of instruction, not of adventure, but he was only thirteen years old (a child even though he had passed the rite of puberty) and thus he set off on the journey with much excitement, and when he first stood here, staring at the Jaguar's Ribs, thinking of the mysterious world that lay beyond it, he felt emotions of wonder, of anticipation, of naive eagerness...

Since that first time he had come this far on perhaps five, six occasions. And on two of those occasions he'd ventured still further; as far as the river at the edge of the outside world. But apart from that first time, beyond there he hadn't gone, and on none of the journeys had he known the drama and excitement that had characterised the first one. More to the contrary, those other journeys had been marked by deep anxiety, for what he had learnt of the purini world did not bode well for his people and always he was afraid that one day he would discover that the purinis had advanced beyond the river...

Having sat down, Rumicuri now opened his basket and removed a couple of custard apples, some dry guinea pig meat, and a kind of biscuit made of corn seasoned with herbs. This food, which was washed down with a gourd of water, he shared with Mountain Trotter. After they had eaten, the men stood up, lifted the baskets onto their backs, and then set off into a terrain that sloped sharply downwards and where the vegetation was so thick and tangled it was like a wall.

No sunlight reached the undergrowth here. This was a place of utter silence and deep shadows; the vegetation so dense that Rumicuri often lost sight of Mountain Trotter even though he was no more than a few yards ahead. And when this happened he would have to examine the undergrowth keenly to ascertain the direction in which the old man had stepped. Unlike Mountain Trotter he wasn't able to guide himself by instinct alone. He had to work hard at 'perceiving' a path.

Another ability he lacked was in wielding the machete. For all its seductive power, on the very few occasions when he tried using it, his strokes were so erratic and clumsy that he only managed to make himself angrier. Then he would look down at the machete with loathing, silently cursing this purini made instrument which, by contrast, in the hand of Mountain Trotter was all fluidity and ease.

After hours of negotiating the inhospitable terrain the men at last arrived at the bottom of the slope, where there was a fast flowing stream. It was evening by then and as Rumicuri emerged onto the bank, looking up, he saw a pink and mauve sky wherein stars glittered.

The men crossed the stream – foaming muddy brown water swirling around their legs – and once on the opposite bank they put down their loads and stood breathing deeply, their dirty, exhausted bodies aching all over. But there was little time for rest as it was necessary to set up an overnight shelter before it got dark.

The first thing they did was to clear a patch of ground. Afterwards they chopped down a good pile of bamboo that was growing nearby; Mountain Trotter using his machete, but Rumicuri, fed up with the purini made tool, employing an obsidian axe he removed from his basket.

Once they had enough bamboo, working quickly, they wove the thinner, elastic shoots into two separate 'floors', just large enough to accommodate their recumbent bodies. These were then skilfully spliced into thicker, upright lengths of bamboo, with the final result of having two separate beds raised about a foot above the ground. Over the two beds they erected a tent-like shelter made of more bamboo spliced together and interwoven with leaves. All this accomplished, Rumicuri got busy building a fire while Mountain Trotter went off in search of a certain plant.

To build a fire Rumicuri employed things he'd brought with him: a narrow length of wood shaped like a pencil which he twirled rapidly between his hands into another block of wood that had a small hole in it. When the resulting friction began to produce smoke he blew softly and quickly into the hole while at the same time pressing against it a small quantity of very dry flax. In a moment the flax caught alight, glowing red, and this glowing flax he placed on the dry tinder of the fire.

Mountain Trotter returned holding a plant he had uprooted. Using his machete he severed the stem, releasing a sticky pungent sap which he rubbed against the bamboo supporting the bed frames with the purpose of dissuading ants and other unwanted insects from disturbing them during the night.

It was dark when the men were able to rest. Sitting on their respective beds, with the fire glowing between them, they shared food and for the first time since they'd set off early that morning they had a chance to talk.

Mountain Trotter spoke of his village, of his fears for his people at the mercy of the soldiers. He wondered if it might not be possible for him to steal into the village and find out how his people were faring and if they had discovered anything more of the soldiers intentions. But Rumicuri was alarmed at this idea. Should anything happen to Mountain Trotter, how would he find his way to his uncle's?

He could get by on his own in the jungle, if not so well as Mountain Trotter, but once in the world of the purinis he would be helpless, completely lost. So he told Mountain Trotter that he couldn't allow it. The old man's face creased with disappointment, but he accepted the sovereign's order. He went on to say that if they were to avoid the village they would need to follow the river further downwards and then past a place the Indians had come to name The Vomit of Death. Rumicuri raised his eyebrows. He had never heard of such a place. What was this place? Why was it called The Vomit of Death? Mountain Trotter didn't know how to explain it very well. Trying to describe it, he said it was something the purinis had made. An abomination that spewed up smoke and a black vomit that killed everything around it. 'Soon you'll see it, highness, with your own eyes,' Mountain Trotter said. Rumicuri fell silent, his face impassive, the dark oppression he felt unexpectedly echoed in a brief shrieking howl that distantly pierced the night.

Later, lying in his makeshift bed, his thoughts turned to Cascarina, for this was the first time in two years he had slept away from her; not, in truth, since he had abandoned Illani.

He had always felt guilty over the things that had happened, how he had hurt and betrayed Cascarina, because he knew how deeply she cared for him and he did not doubt that he loved her.

It was something he'd seen in her eyes that had been the start of it all. She was his relative, a second cousin, but he knew little else about her on the day he'd given her the stone. He hadn't meant anything by the gift. She was a child, not yet in her puberty, and he'd found the stone on the riverbed and had given it to her simply because she was there. But at the moment of placing the stone in her palm he had looked at her and in her eyes had seen, fleetingly, what later he could only describe as a reflection of his inner self.

From then on she was never entirely out of his mind. Sometimes they would meet and he would speak to her briefly. More often he would notice her from a distance, and he would observe little things about her; her easy laugh, how her breasts were developing, the way she walked… Then one day she disappeared to undergo the rite of puberty, which with one thing and another was for girls a lengthy process, and so it was a year before he saw her again.

During her absence he would think of her sometimes, but he couldn't dwell on her because his time was being taken up in preparation for the day when, whether he desired it or not, he would have to assume responsibility for the well-being of the people. Laws had to be memorised, he was given oral instruction in history and religion, and he had to learn how to cultivate fields, tend flocks, build dwellings, calculate harvests, and the many other things he needed to know…

Then, after a year had passed he saw her again. And for a moment he didn't recognise her, she was so changed, so exuberant and beautiful. She and the other girls who had undergone the rites of puberty were, as was the custom, making the best of their release from confinement. They were walking about the main village, dressed in their finest clothes and ornaments, attracting the admiration of young and old alike, but in particular of the young men who had gathered with the sole purpose of watching them.

And he, one of those men, saw a young girl resplendent in her finery, laughing, tossing her hair, looking about her coyly. Then her slanted eyes found him and they became shy, vulnerable.

When he recognised her it was as though an invisible hand had reached into his chest and was squeezing his heart. That's the girl I want; the one I'm going to marry, he thought.

Only in the end it had turned out differently. He loved Cascarina then and he loved her now, but it was Illani he had married because, to his distress, he had discovered that his love for one woman didn't prevent him from burning for another.

He was sure he didn't love Illani. In fact, he wasn't sure he had ever truly liked her, even. She had all the charm of a praying mantis. Her slender limbs, thin features, her sinuous yet high-kneed walk, the way she picked at things with the tip of her fingers had always made him think of her not, as some men said, a cat, but of a praying mantis. And like a praying mantis, too, she had stalked him. There was nothing coy or shy about Illani. She was Cascarina's friend, she knew he was betrothed to her, and yet at every opportunity – with her mocking eyes, with the things she said, the way she positioned her body – she had let him know that she was hungry for him.

For a long time he resisted, but she was determined and it was perhaps this very determination that attracted him to her. Women weren't brought up to be bold. They could be unclothed, or completely naked (as often they were when bathing in the river or for other reasons) and no one gave it a thought. Whether dressed or naked women were expected to behave with the decorum, if not the reserve, that was natural to them. But Illani in this respect behaved like a man. Other women made themselves available, sent out discreet signals, but not Illani. She pursued him, actively, imperiously, and the strength and boldness of her desire was intoxicating.

He found himself unable to sleep, or to concentrate on his duties. He was afraid he would end up like his father: a man of proud intelligence brought low by indolence and philandering. As a child, seeing how his father chased after women without shame or regard for his position (an activity which had ruined his marriage to Rumicuri's mother and had caused strife in the community as a whole) he had resolved to himself that he would grow up with more self-control.

And now he was in danger of succumbing to the same weakness and becoming like his father! His desire tormented him. He took precautions to stay well clear of Illani. When he couldn't avoid her he would stare through her, pretending she wasn't there, or if she tried to approach him he would address her brusquely.

But no matter what he did he could not kill the longing. And then one afternoon it happened that he came across her while walking back from the lower villages. It wasn't a coincidence. She didn't so much as pretend to conceal her intention. Knowing that he would be returning from the lower villages, she waited for him at the juncture were the path divided, one branch going to the river.

When he turned the bend he saw her. She was sitting on a fallen log, wearing a dark blue linen robe, her forearms resting on her open thighs. He stopped, blood rising to his head. She waited, looking at him with an amused, slightly mocking smile. When he came up to her she didn't wait for him to speak. She said straight away, 'I've been waiting for you.' He wasn't yet the sovereign (it would be some months before his father died, finally, from his long illness) but even so her brazen behaviour, as well as the guilt he felt for his own weakness, made him angry. Glaring at her, he said, 'Have you no shame?' Smiling still, she stood up from the log and stepped directly in front of him. Without the least embarrassment in her eyes, she said, 'My cunt is aching for you. I can't help it.' The explicitness of her words flustered him. He made to move around her. But his eyes were bonded to hers, and flustered and angry though he was, he felt a violent, yearning emptiness in his entrails. Then she touched his hand. A shiver went up his arm. His legs trembled. 'Come,' she murmured, pressing close to him, her breath hot on his neck. 'Let's go to the river...'

It was in the first light of dawn that the men set off the next morning. The sky was corrugated with dark, red streaked clouds. Mist was gathered like cotton wool in between the vegetation. All around frogs and toads were croaking loudly. Soon there were flashes, thunder, and it began to pour rain. Unlike the day before, the men did not stop for shelter because they had to cover a lot of ground. The rain, streaming from the foliage, quickly soaked the steep terrain, making the ground underfoot slippery and muddy and much impeding their progress up the first of the Jaguar's Ribs.

The rain fell throughout the morning, but by early afternoon, as they were ascending the last of the Jaguar's Ribs, it abated. After the Jaguar's Ribs they descended to a flatter ground, where the undergrowth became sparser and the trees thicker and taller. Here there were some truly giant trees, with buttressed trunks rising up and up into an immense expanse of foliage that hung with lianas and, interlocking with the branches of other trees, produced an aerial layer of jungle that at times was more dense than the vegetation on the ground. This was warmer, more tropical forest than the one they had come from, and because it was flatter, with thinner undergrowth, they were able to make faster progress.

Late in the afternoon, when the men were only a little distance from the river, they encountered an ant-eater. They came across it unexpectedly. The first Rumicuri saw of it was when he almost bumped into Mountain Trotter, who'd come to a halt. Ahead of them he saw a furry black creature whirling around and rising on its hind legs almost to the height of a man. For a moment it just stood there: tail on the ground, ears erect, a fleshy snout pointing towards them, and its long shaggy forelimbs, which ended in hard, sharp claws, hanging away from its body like the arms of a wrestler. The claws were dangerous weapons. A frightened ant-eater wasn't to be dismissed, so while the animal stood ready to lash out, the men began stepping back. After they'd retreated a few steps the ant-eater lowered its body and with surprising speed it whirled around and vanished into the undergrowth...

The first indication the men had of the river was when they heard a low, steady humming sound. As they advanced the sound became progressively louder until it became more like a roar. Minutes later they came out of the undergrowth and were standing on the riverbank itself, not twenty yards from its crossing point.

The crossing point was on the very edge of a powerful waterfall, for here, after steep and twisting gorges wherein the river tossed and foamed in a succession of impassable rapids, the ground gave way to a broad ledge of solid rock where the water flowed smooth before rolling over the edge and falling like a white curtain to a depth of a hundred or so feet.

It was beyond the waterfall, on the other side of the river, that in Rumicuri's mind the outside world began. Although there was yet a considerable expanse of jungle, little different from the one they had already come through, parts of it were nevertheless known to the Indians and others who lived on its borders, and therefore, where Rumicuri and his people were concerned, it could not be considered safe.

So apart from his one childhood journey to the world of the purinis this was as far as he'd ever ventured. And now as they arrived at the crossing point he had an insistent feeling of unease. Once on the other side there was no saying what incomprehensible dangers they might encounter, and always, for every moment of the day, he would need to be on his guard. To protect himself he had brought a leather pouch containing, among other things, an effigy of the Spirit Condor. After removing the pouch from a woollen bag he carried under his shirt, he brought out the wooden effigy and dropped it into the current, where it briefly bobbed before being swept over the waterfall. By doing this, which was according to Amataba's instruction, he hoped that the effigy would be able to alert the Spirit Condor, whose all-seeing eye would in turn alert him to whatever unknown dangers lay in wait…

The water on the edge of the waterfall wasn't deep, but the stone bed was slippery as ice. Mountain Trotter went first. Rumicuri, following close behind, soon felt the cold water rising to his thighs, tugging hard at his legs as though to deliberately unbalance him. And he was frightened. His heart was knocking against his ribs as he carefully slid his feet forward, for were he to lose his balance there would be nothing to hold on to. In an instant the water would sweep him over the edge of the waterfall, which was less than a yard away, and he would be lucky to survive the deep fall to the rocky, foaming, hissing turbulence below.

Rumicuri was relieved when he saw the other bank approaching. But in order to reach it the men had to avoid a funnel of deep and powerful water by ascending a rocky projection, some two yards high, and then crossing a bare tree trunk which spanned the short gap to the opposite bank.

Considering the load on Mountain Trotter's back, and the burden of his seventy years, he showed impressive agility in pulling himself out of the water and scrambling up the projection. Once there, rather than cross the trunk, he waited for Rumicuri to join him. And when Rumicuri, gasping a little, had done so, Mountain Trotter pointed into the distance and shouted above the roar, 'Over there. The Vomit Of Death.'

Rumicuri saw it. Staring into the distance to where, after a hilly terrain, the jungle flattened into a vast expanse, he was able to make out an uneven, whitish clearing from the middle of which rose a thin column of black smoke. 'Tomorrow we'll pass by it, highness. You'll see the vomit then,' Mountain Trotter shouted.

There were hardly three hours of daylight left after the men crossed the river. Thus, without delay, they climbed down a steep bank to the bottom of the waterfall, then once again entered the forest. Some of the ground in this part of the forest was waterlogged, and these were unhealthy places that stank of putrid vegetation and were a breeding ground for mosquitoes and leeches. The mosquitoes, in particular, were a menace, for they rose up from the mire in fierce clouds that gave the men no respite, savagely attacking their faces as they exerted themselves to get through the bog as fast as possible.

Once on high ground it was better. There were fewer mosquitoes, and the air, though always warm, was less foetid. It was on high ground that the men made their second camp. As on the previous night they erected a shelter and built a fire to scare off unwanted insects. Rumicuri was unaware that the fire also disguised a faint but peculiar smell that occasionally wafted through the forest. The next morning, however, he noticed it.

He'd just returned from washing himself in a nearby stream when he whiffed a strange sort of burning smell. For a second he was perplexed, then his body tensed and his eyes opened wide as in his mind's eye he saw a metal animal come roaring and crashing through the jungle.

Mountain Trotter, who was standing close by, adjusting the straps on his basket, also became aware of the burning smell.

'Smoke from the Vomit of Death, highness,' Mountain Trotter told him.

Rumicuri stared back in confusion. 'No metal animals?'

Mountain Trotter shook his head. 'No. They need big paths to travel on. Soon you'll see them. But not here. They can't come here without paths.'

What Mountain Trotter said was true, Rumicuri remembered. When, as a boy, he'd first seen one of the metal animals, it had come roaring towards him on a wide path. And he'd been so alarmed he had stood unable to move as this enormous thing had borne down on him with unbelievable speed. Then his uncle had yanked him off the path and the metal animal had roared straight past, spraying him with dust and leaving behind a burning smell that was like the one he'd just smelt.

The Vomit of Death was a couple of hours march from where the men had camped. As they approached, Rumicuri tense and apprehensive, it was again the smell that first alerted him: The burning smell of before, but as well a different kind of smell; not so harsh, sweeter, yet far more pervasive. A smell that saturated the air and caught in his throat.

Soon after the emergence of this smell, he noticed how the forest began to look stunted and diseased. Not all at once. There were places where the vegetation looked profuse and vibrant, but gradually, here and there, he started noticing bare patches, places where plants had died and didn't grow again. In these places, which had a whitish hue, he saw brittle stalks without leaves and trees that were losing their bark, that were ravaged with disease, for large parts of their foliage had withered, and where the foliage did grow it looked scanty and lustreless.

Rumicuri had a definite impression of something malignant invading the forest. And the further he advanced the stronger this impression became, until presently he came upon a landscape of such horror that at first his mind couldn't encompass it.

It appeared suddenly, filling the hollows in the ground like pools of water. Only it wasn't water. It was a thick black liquid that glistened with a strange, even gruesomely beautiful, iridescent sheen. And wherever it appeared everything was dead. Everything. It wasn't just the undergrowth that was dead. The great trees – these lofty living beings without whom the forest wouldn't exist – they rose out of the liquid like pitiful skeletons, without bark, without a green leaf, without shoots.

In order to avoid the pools, the men followed the narrow strips of higher ground that lay in between. But even here there was very little that grew; a few solitary trees and plants, their sparse, ravaged foliage somehow making the desolation all the starker. And there was no sound: A silence where nothing stirred, no birds, no insects, no animals…

As they advanced the black iridescent pools grew bigger, deeper, and the bridges of land in between them narrower. The sun, by this time, was high; its hot and oscillating light causing strong fumes to rise from the liquid, so that soon Rumicuri had a severe headache, one made worse by the basket strap pressing against his temples.

All at once, out of nowhere it seemed, a quivering mass of

butterflies appeared. There were so many of them that as they descended through the bare branches of the dead trees they obscured the sunlight. The butterflies had scarlet and turquoise wings. In the greenery of the forest they would have made a wondrous sight. But not here. Here something was terribly wrong, for the butterflies (overcome by the fumes perhaps) were reeling through the air and colliding blindly against the men.

In a matter of minutes the ground was covered with dying butterflies. A few yards away thousands more were falling directly into the black liquid, their wings feebly fluttering as they floated on the surface. Rumicuri was distressed. It was as much as he could bear to see these thousands upon thousands of butterflies accumulating on the liquid, covering it like a rough blanket.

Dazed, he followed Mountain Trotter into the desolation. Eventually the ground began to rise into a hill, and in so doing the liquid dried up and life started returning to the vegetation. However, as they were ascending the hill, Rumicuri now became aware of sounds such as the metal animals made.

The forest was thick on the curvature of the hill and this muffled the sounds. But on the other side of the hill the vegetation stopped abruptly. The sounds came back louder and Rumicuri found himself looking into a huge clearing. Here and there the clearing glistened with pools, but it wasn't this he was looking at. He was looking at a sprawl of oddly shaped edifices surrounded by a vast fence made, he conjectured, of some kind of purini metal. Some of the edifices were square, others were shaped like giant horizontal cocoons, yet others were like short sections of giant reeds. It was from this jumble of incomprehensible structures that the noises were coming, as were the thick black columns of smoke he saw spiralling into the sky.

But of all the edifices the ones that most struck him were two huge sort of frames that stood on their own, some distance from the rest. At their base these frames were wider than many trees placed together; then they began to taper, rising higher and higher, until they ended in blunt points that towered above everything else.

'They say it's from those tall things that the purinis get their vomit,' said Mountain Trotter, pointing to the frames. 'They make deep holes in the earth and the vomit comes pouring out.'

'From *inside* the Mother Earth?'

'Yes.'

'What do the purinis want with it, do you know?'

'Only what I hear,' said Mountain Trotter.

'What do you hear?'

'The vomit makes the metal animals move along the paths. Like it's their food. And it makes other things move as well. Things they call *maquinas*. And I've heard it said the purinis can make many other things out of the vomit.'

Rumicuri was silent. This was a world beyond his comprehension. But one thing he understood with certainty: In this place there was no hope for the Mother Earth. In this place of black vomit and strange edifices the purinis were devouring the Mother Earth. The purinis were tearing into her insides and she was spewing forth black gore. Here, in this place, the Mother Earth was dying.

'Over there,' said Mountain Trotter, pointing to what looked like a thin curving line leading away from the jumble of edifices. 'That's one of their paths; the one we should follow.'

'How long to my uncle's?'

'If the moon favours us… well, perhaps before the dawn.'

Rumicuri had no wish to go. He thought of his kingdom and how at this moment in the late afternoon the air in the main village would be turning crisp, scented with wood smoke. And men would be returning from the fields, tired, their bodies aching, but at peace in the knowledge that they'd secured the livelihood of the community. And the old men, those too old for work, would be standing around chatting while their wives busied themselves with this and that, mending clothes, feeding guinea pigs… And the young children would be running around, making noise, their faces bright, for it was only children who had no fear of the future and for whom time flowed in unceasing abundance.

His own childhood had been like that. Happy. And the world had seemed to him huge and everything in it a source of wonder because fear had not yet corroded him.

It was only after he had passed the rites of puberty that the world had become a different place for him. For three months he and five other boys had been isolated in a dark cavern where the only light came from a fire. And there, watched over by adult guardians, they had cooked their own food, and smeared their bodies with burnt corn ash, and had been forbidden from touching any part of their bodies with their fingers lest they should inadvertently pollute themselves with whatever their fingers might have touched. If they felt the urge to scratch or touch themselves they had to use a special stick.

After three months of purification the other boys had undergone the ceremony of pain. While they knelt naked on the floor fire ants were allowed to roam over their bodies, giving fierce bites that later became inflamed and from which it could take many days to recover. Finally, after four months in cavern, the other boys had their hair shorn and were released. But Rumicuri, because of his position, had to remain in the cavern for a further four months. The men who watched over him were only intermittently present. For long periods he would be alone and he passed the hours alternating between boredom, day-dreams, and at times an all but ungovernable urge to lay his fingers on his body and scratch himself.

When the eight months were up he was so eager to be released that he gladly submitted to his own ceremony of pain, one which was reserved solely for members of the royal line. His hair was shorn and the small finger of his left hand was bound with twine. Kneeling on the ground he placed his small finger on a block of stone, and the elder who was present for the ceremony gripped his finger with one hand, and with his other hand holding a sharp obsidian knife he severed the tip of Rumicuri's finger. The pain made him swoon. Blood gushed from the finger. He became queasy, sweat oozed through his skin. But he managed not to faint.

The nail of his finger was preserved along with his shorn hair, for it was said that the soul, while it was still attached to a person's body and had not yet grown wings, manifested itself externally in a person's hair and nails. Besides endangering the soul, short hair and nails could make a person prematurely old, and this is why the people never cut their hair, and when they rubbed their nails short with a pumice stone why they always kept the dust. And this was why, when the rites of puberty were concluded, Rumicuri left the cavern with his shorn hair and severed nail preserved in a leather pouch slung from his neck.

He hadn't left his childhood behind, completely, after the rites of puberty, or for that matter, not even after his one journey to the outside world. But it was from these years on that he gradually lost his innocence. And with the loss of innocence had come an awareness of mortality, of time, of the peril his people confronted, and these things had spawned a fear in him which might at times be overcome or forgotten but from which he could never entirely free himself.

It was mid afternoon when they emerged from the jungle directly onto the road Mountain Trotter had indicated. The clearing was some distance behind them now and the road stretched ahead of them flat and dusty. Although there was as yet some miles of jungle before the first settlement, the men no longer had need of their machetes and so they packed them into their baskets. With both arms free they were able to lift their hands and pull on the basket straps in order to relieve the ache in their necks and shoulders. And in this way they began following the road with a steady, sort of cantering gait that was slower than a trot, faster than a walk.

After they had been travelling for about an hour, Rumicuri heard a low rumbling sound and a moment later he saw a metal animal appear on the horizon. At once he stopped and stepped back in fright to the edge of the tree-line. Mountain Trotter also stopped, but only after he looked back and noticed that the sovereign wasn't following.

As the metal animal (a green four by four) drew close, in a cloud of dust, Rumicuri waited, tense, ready to flee, unable to comprehend how anything could travel at such tremendous speed. But in fact the metal animal was travelling slowly. It was travelling slowly enough for Rumicuri to see two men sitting in it well before it reached him. And then as the metal animal bounced and rumbled past, one of the men turned to look at him. *A white man.* This was the first time Rumicuri had seen a pure white man.

As a boy, on his trip to the outside world, he'd seen many purinis, but they weren't pure white; they were of mixed blood, some lighter complexioned than others, but all of them with dark hair, dark eyes. So Rumicuri hadn't seen a pure white man before; not like the one he'd just glimpsed, with white skin and reddish hair on his upper lip and eyes as blue as the sky. A white man such as those of legend. For wasn't it said that it was white men who had first come from across the great waters and waged war on his ancestors? It was a glimpse, only a glimpse he'd had just now, but even so in that brief glimpse he'd sensed something about the white man – a sort of aura of power, perhaps – that made an immediate impression on him. Presently, in a mood between dismay and resentment, he reflected that while in his own kingdom he ruled with unquestioned authority, here, in the world of the purinis, he was of no significance at all. He was powerless.

Further along the road he encountered more purinis. They were sitting inside three metal animals. The metal animals were of a different kind, occupying a clearing to one side of the road. These purinis weren't white, they were Indians, or of mixed blood, and the thing that now astonished Rumicuri was the enormity of the metal animals and the ferocity of one of them. This yellow coloured metal animal belched black smoke and made a growling sound that was deafening and in front it had something that looked like an arm with a giant claw.

Rumicuri didn't pause. He and Mountain Trotter went past this place quickly, staring straight ahead, but out of the corner of his eye he could see what the metal animal was doing. It was attacking the forest with voracious ferocity. Its giant claw was tearing up a tree by the roots. The trunk was keeling over and the pale, tender roots were being torn from the skin of the Mother Earth.

The growling sound was reverberating in Rumicuri's ears as he went past, but it wasn't this he was listening to. It was the tree spirit that he heard. A young, strong tree spirit that was resisting its death, making groaning and breaking sounds as it was uprooted and which lingered in Rumicuri's mind long after the growling sound of the metal animal had faded behind him.

Further on, as the flaming orb of the sun sank into the forest, the trees that lined both sides of the road turned black, a flock of squawking parrots flew across the streaked, flushed sky, and then, when it darkened, faintly red and green stars appeared, and a big blue moon came out.

Exhausted, the men took a short rest, squatting by the side of the road and eating the last of their provisions. Having recovered a little they hitched the baskets onto their backs and once more began following the road, which, in the light of the stars and the moon, stretched ahead of them with dim luminosity. And with each step took them closer to a world that, unknown to itself, held in its power the fate of the Arayana.

PART TWO

MOURNERS had been gathering outside Amataba's hut since early morning. Among them were nobles, people such as Illapacta, Cascarina, Punimillo... But whether nobles or commoners the mourners all arrived wearing ordinary work clothes; the plainest attire they could find. And the reason for this, more than an expression of sorrow, was to demonstrate their own worthlessness, and by so doing to further exalt the deceased, who, when she appeared, would be wearing her finest clothes and ornaments.

The women in particular took pains to arrive in unadorned smocks, wearing no ornaments, their hair uncombed, and carrying, in one container or another, a mixture of earth and ashes with which to smear themselves.

But not Illani. When Illani made an appearance her long hair was washed and combed, and while her attire was subdued, she nevertheless wore a colourful waistband and a necklace of silver beads.

Most of the mourners, when they saw her in such attire, were angry. The braver women cast disapproving glances in her direction, muttering amongst themselves, calling her a brazen sorceress, berating her for the airs she gave herself, some even predicting retribution: For Amataba was no ordinary mortal, and though dead, there was no saying what she could still know, or what she could still see, or what powerful spells she could work even from the domain of the dead.

There were a few others, however, all of them men, who were secretly admiring of the fearless way Illani flouted convention. If she could do this, they wondered to themselves, what else might she not dare? And these men gazed at her with secret longing, their eyes dazzled by her svelte, haughty allure.

As for Illani, she was the queen, she saw no reason why she should pretend a humility or sorrow she didn't feel. It was Amataba who had meddled, who had connived with Cascarina, who had stolen Rumicuri's heart and turned him against her. Let them all see it. Let them all know exactly what she thought of Amataba.

Standing among the mourners, clutching the hand of her two year old son, Illani met the hostile stares with an expression of contemptuous defiance.

Inside Amataba's hut, meanwhile, behind its closed doors, unseen by the mourners, a plainly dressed, dour, middle-aged woman was preparing to perform a task that would require all of her courage.

A medicine woman herself – of lesser standing than Amataba, but who now expected to succeed her – Rupuche had already sewn the corpse's mouth and blocked all other orifices with balls of waxed wool in order to prevent the soul from escaping. For even the soul of a powerful medicine woman couldn't be trusted to remain in the body, and were this to happen, were her fickle soul to escape, Amataba wouldn't die properly. She would be condemned to remain in this world as a ghost.

So Rupuche had trapped Amataba's soul in her body, yet ahead of her there remained still another task; one that was more personal and much harder to carry through.

Standing before the naked, emaciated, slightly bluish corpse, she pressed a small and very sharp knife into the corpse's chest. With grim concentration she cut deep into the flesh under the left breast, slicing through muscle, through coagulated blood to reveal white rib bones and a delicate pinkish section of lung. However, it wasn't these she was in search of, so she continued probing, making an ever messier and larger opening, until, cutting under the ribcage, she located Amataba's heart.

After severing the arteries and pulling, cutting the organ out of the body, Rupuche placed the heart in a wooden bowl and with a bone needle she quickly sewed the wound together – partly for cosmetic reasons, out of respect for the deceased, but principally to once again prevent the soul from escaping.

This done, she knelt on the ground before the corpse – her bloodied hands cradling the bowl, her eyes fixed on the raw, purple dark heart – and then she began rocking gently as she murmured to herself: "Your courage, mother, it'll be mine... Your shrewdness, mother, it'll be mine... Your wisdom, mother, it'll be mine..." Over and over Rupuche repeated to herself words such as these while at the same time fighting to suppress her queasiness and to strengthen her resolve to digest Amataba's spirit.

Not her soul. Soul and spirit were two separate entities. A soul could not be assimilated. It could be influenced, but not assimilated, because a soul had a will that was independent of the body it inhabited. A person's spirit, on the other hand, had no separate existence. A person's spirit never strayed from it abode, which was the heart, and when the body died it was said that the spirit died with the body. This, at any rate, is what the uninitiated understood. But a medicine woman knew different. The spirit didn't *have* to die with the body. It was possible for a medicine woman to assimilate the spirit of another medicine woman, and the way to do this was by consuming the dead medicine woman's heart.

Thus, fully resolved now, Rupuche took hold of the knife, cut a small section of raw heart, placed it in her mouth, and swallowed it. At once her stomach protested. She felt sick. She badly wanted a drink of water, but since the ritual forbade this all she could do was to keep her mouth shut. The next pieces were no easier. At one point she feared she was going to retch it all up. But it had to be done. If she was to become a medicine woman no less powerful than Amataba herself, it had to be done. So she forced herself to continue cutting at the heart, eating the pieces one by one until at last it was all gone, the bowl was empty.

This most important and secret task accomplished, she stood up and washed the bowl and her hands with a pitcher of water. With a half-sweet, half-salty taste lingering on her palate, she moved around the shadowy interior of the hut looking for Amataba's clothes and ornaments. Then, having selected the best of these, she carried them over to the corpse.

Rupuche was a terse woman, not much given to expressions of emotion, but strangely, as she began dressing the corpse, it was as though she could already feel Amataba's spirit awakening inside her. A new sort of energy was flowing through her limbs. She felt strong, serene, and her senses somehow sharper, more alert.

Wondering to herself, Rupuche went on dressing the corpse with gratitude, with growing reverence…

It was mid afternoon when the door to Amataba's hut opened and Rupuche stepped out. This was the signal that the corpse was ready for removal. Two young men went into the hut carrying a bamboo bier. When they emerged a little later, Amataba was lying on the bier, her hands clasping the knobby-smooth gajuru stick, her clothes redolent of sweet smelling aromatic herbs, her ears and neck adorned with ornaments, one of which was of beaten gold.

Very slowly the bier was carried in a winding trajectory through the crowds of mourners. Upon seeing the corpse they shed tears. And it wasn't just the women, there were men who wept as well: Fathers whose sick children Amataba had cured, or men who themselves had been saved by her from serious illness. But it was the women who grieved the more fiercely, smearing themselves with a concoction of earth and ashes and releasing high-pitched, keening wails. A few, such as Cascarina, became hysterical. When the bier passed by Cascarina she collapsed on the ground, sobbing, making fearful noises, banging her head on the earth and pulling her hair as though to tear it from her skull.

After some time, once the majority of mourners had an opportunity to view the corpse, the bier was carried into the forest. There a pit had been dug and a large earthenware urn placed in it. While those who had been closest to the deceased – relations, nobles, and others – gathered in a compact mass at the graveside, the two young men who had carried the bier lifted the corpse off it and very gently lowered the corpse, feet first, into the broad opening of the urn. Afterwards they adjusted the corpse into a foetal position, then they stood to receive a gourd of mishqui and a food parcel, wrapped in leaves. Leaning over the opening of the urn, one of the young men placed these victuals next to the corpse for the purpose of providing Amataba with nourishment on her journey across the great chasm. This done, Rupuche tossed a handful of seeds into the urn and then started back towards Amataba's hut.

There was yet much to be done before the funeral was over. The grave had to be filled with earth and stones, and the remainder of Amataba's possessions – her clothes, pots, herbs, the skulls – all these things had to be removed from the hut and destroyed by burning or crushing. Then there was the farewell ceremony that lasted long into the night, when those mourners who wished would gather around a fire outside Amataba's hut to regale each other with wonderful stories about the deceased. These stories were not necessarily true. Often they were exaggerations, even outright inventions, but this was not considered important so long as the deceased was portrayed in a heroic light, and thus, aside from assuming a mythological character, became for the mourners a source of pride, of comfort, of fond memories…

Illani, however, didn't stay for the remaining funeral proceedings. Certainly *she* had no intention of staying behind to say good things about the deceased – that least of all! And so she left early, while the grave was still being filled and mourners had yet to finish clearing Amataba's hut.

Carrying her son on her hip, she slowly followed the path that took her into the main village. Because of the funeral, when she arrived at the main village it was all but deserted. The huts were empty; no old people could be seen gossiping, as was usual at this time of day when the sun was beginning to sink towards the steep hills behind the village. But not everybody was at the funeral. One person who wasn't was the young man called Calchas, the one who had shown the red book to the elders and who had spoken of the Radiant War.

Calchas was standing outside, leaning against the mud wall of the gathering house (the place where the refugees were lodging) when he caught sight of Illani crossing an open space in between the dwellings.

Calchas knew who she was. This wasn't the first time he'd laid eyes on her. And he'd asked questions, he'd tried to find things out because she was a fine-looking woman. Ripe like a sweet melon, he thought, eyeing her waist length hair, her high-kneed yet sinuous walk, and how unexpectedly, while pausing to attend her child, her head turned lingering in his direction.

Was it deliberate? Was she aware of him? After she'd gone, Calchas, his blood turning hot, thought he had the perfect opportunity now that there were so few people about. Yet he remained where he was, irresolute, because it could be dangerous if he was wrong…

But ripe like a sweet melon. And the sovereign's wife! This was the thrill of it… His nostrils flared and his sallow face couldn't help smirking when he thought of the pleasure it would give him to seduce the sovereign's wife… That arsehole had made a big mistake, slapping him, humiliating him…

Leaning against the wall, he casually looked from one side to the other. Making up his mind, he pushed off and sauntered across the open space. When he reached the dwellings he couldn't see Illani ahead of him; he had delayed too long, but he knew where she lived and taking a chance he set off at speed on a roundabout route, hoping to arrive ahead of her.

Illani lived in the best of all the dwellings. Like others it was essentially a mud hut with no windows and a roof of dried leaves. But the hut was twice the usual length; it had a floor of rough stone slabs as opposed to compacted earth; the door posts were carved with intricate symbols; and the dwelling occupied a prime position overlooking the main village, yet was secluded, surrounded by a lush growth of trees and scented flowering shrubs.

When Calchas arrived at the royal residence he knew he was taking a risk. Recovering his breath under a tree, some twenty yards from the door, he reflected that one look was not an invitation. And what if he were wrong about her? He hadn't come here to get himself lynched over a woman. He was an organiser, an agitator; that was why he'd left the guerrillas and gone back to his village. His orders from Chairman Mateo were to convert the villagers to the cause of revolution. But the army had invaded his village before he could get back to the guerrillas. His only chance of escape had been to follow Mountain Trotter. That old fool hadn't wanted him to come, but he'd followed him anyway – out of curiosity and because he had nowhere else to go – and so he'd ended up here. In this place he'd always heard about, for although he was a lowlander he was no *mestizo*, he was a pure blood Arayana.

Oh yes, he had heard about this place often enough. Ever since he was a child, sworn to secrecy, he had been schooled in the history of his ancestors and regaled with stories about the fabled high kingdom. The stories painted the high kingdom to be a paradise where people wanted for nothing, where they lived in enchanted harmony untainted by the corrupt barbarism of the outside world. But what sort of paradise was it? He'd seen it now with his own eyes. It was nothing special. People toiled and quarrelled and got ill here like anywhere else. And all these laws and rules. And ignorant elders. And the royals with fancy privileges and others just plain poor… Bah, it was a rat-hole like any other, and the worst of it was that he couldn't leave. Impossible without a guide. He was trapped here until they decided to let him go. So what was he doing getting himself mixed up with a woman? And the sovereign's wife what's more. It was asking for trouble. If he had any sense he would stop this now, while he still could. But then he kept recalling Illani's languorous walk, how she had turned to look at him, and, without being able to define exactly what it was, he had the inkling that she wasn't quite what she appeared to be…

A ghost. When Illani entered the enclosure, for a second she thought she was seeing a ghost. She thought this because the sun was in her eyes, and what she saw, standing under the tree, completely still, was an indistinct, darkly shadowed figure. The shock stopped her. Still supporting her child on her hip (who meanwhile had fallen asleep) she stood near the door, squinting against the intense light of the lowering sun.

It was him! She was flustered. What was he doing here? How had he got here so quick? Illani wasn't sure how to react. So just then she didn't. She went into the house and put her son down on his bed. After covering him with a blanket she sat down on a low stool next to an open fire, her arm and hip muscle aching. Leaning over, she poked the fire with a stick and tossed charcoal on it from a basket that was nearby.

It was an affront. How dare the lowlander intrude on her like this. Was he such a fool he didn't know she could have him punished? Illani felt she should be angry. It wasn't simply that he was trespassing, it was that had he been seen his mere presence could set tongues wagging, it could compromise her. And a stranger, a lowlander… What did he think? That because she had looked at him it gave him any sort of claim?

She fidgeted on the stool, trying to work up the anger she thought she should feel, but at the same time she couldn't help thinking that the lowlander, if nothing else, was bold.

She had heard about this man. He was the one who had shown the purini object to the elders. And it was because of what he had told the council, they said, that Rumicuri had gone to consult his uncle. There was talk of war in the world of the purinis. She wondered how much the lowlander knew. She wondered what he could tell her, for the outside world, the world of the purinis had always fascinated and intrigued her. And she wondered if any of what he could tell her, might, in some way, serve her…

Sitting by the fire she spun thoughts such as these; a spider spinning a web, and when, making up her mind, she rose to her feet, her breath was shallow not from anger but from excitement.

Calchas meanwhile hadn't moved from under the tree. It made

him nervous to keep waiting, not knowing what she was thinking, but when he saw her step out of the house and holding an empty basket walk across the grass to where some laundry was drying, he knew at once that he'd been right all along. He was safe. She was interested. Why else would she show herself to him? Gloating, Calchas ran his eye over her slim thighs, her narrow waist, her round rump as she bent to gather the laundry.

Once Illani had filled the basket she lifted it to her hip and started back to the house. Deliberately she avoided looking in the lowlander's direction, but she knew he was watching her. Would he approach her? Almost expecting him to, she was a little disappointed when she arrived at her door undisturbed. Going inside she put the basket down, glanced at her son in his bed, and then turned to close the door.

He was there. Standing in the doorway.

Neither spoke, neither moved. For what seemed an endless moment they stood facing each other like enemies before combat: watchful, weary, and with the same mixture of excitement, of fear, of hunger for conquest. Then Calchas' face broke into a lupine grin. He showed his teeth: strong and white. As for Illani, she lowered her eyes and turned away slightly, offering her neck as though in submission, as though unable to resist him, but just as he stepped across the threshold, his hands preparing for her, her eyes rose sharp and mocking.

'Have I given permission?' she said in a husky voice. 'Have I asked you in?'

Calchas stopped, hands dropping, momentarily confused.

'Do I have your permission?' he said presently, the grin coming back on.

Unflinching, she looked him over.

'I haven't decided.'

Calchas leaned against the doorway, nonchalant. 'Take your time,' he said. 'I'm in no hurry.'

'A fool,' she said with abrupt contempt. 'The last thing I have time for is a fool.'

Calchas felt a burn of anger but he disguised it with a laugh.

'Can I come in?'

'My son might wake up. I don't want him seeing you.'

'After dark?' he asked. And when there was no reply. 'I'll come back after dark.'

Illani remained silent.

'No one will see me,' he assured her, as he pushed away from the door.

Bold, thought Illani, watching him go. If nothing else the fool was bold…

Another person who did not stay for the farewell ceremony was Illapacta. Unlike Illani, however, it wasn't for reasons of spite that he left early. He and Amataba had been good friends, more they were cousins; he would've liked to have stayed for the farewell ceremony; he would've liked to tell the young people about Amataba, the many fine things he could remember.

But who was going to listen to him? An elder who had gone funny in the head? And worst of all, he knew, an elder whose disgraceful behaviour had disturbed the people's faith in the holiness, in the invulnerability of his office.

So for this reason he decided not to stay for the farewell ceremony. But it wasn't his only reason. Another was that, walking back from the graveside, his arthritic joints had started aching. A deep weariness had come over him. He felt old, tired, and he feared that if he stayed he might collapse and wouldn't manage to get home unaided.

Accordingly, he set off along the path to his hut while there was still daylight. Wearing his frayed woollen robe, and his white hair, as usual, in disarray, the old man shuffled along a path that circumvented terraced fields, now and then pausing to catch his rasping breath. Or sometimes just pausing to stare reflectively upon this world that Amataba, precious soul, had trusted to the end.

And why not? Who was to say it wasn't for the best? Illapacta could remember how sometimes Amataba had reproved him for his lack of faith. 'Everybody has to believe in something,' she had told him sharply. 'Even when a person believes in nothing he believes in something. So why do you carry on like this, cousin? Why not believe in something good if you can't avoid believing?'

And he hadn't argued. He had deferred to her, pretending his condition came from another cause, an illness over which he had no control, because he couldn't see that it would serve any purpose to tell Amataba what he knew. Not Amataba and not anybody else. Not even his brother elders. Better to let the people think he was funny in the head if that was what they wanted. Better to let them think it was women, mishqui, moral weakness that had been the cause of his undoing...

It was almost dark, the sun having set behind the hills, when he reached his hut. Relieved to have got there he was about to stagger indoors when he became aware of a distant humming sound. Realising at once what it was he stopped outside his door, squinting up at the darkening sky, listening to the sound become swiftly louder. Then it was a roar that was sounding in his ears and looking up he saw the black shape of a metal bird streak low across the sky.

In an instant it was gone, and a moment afterwards the noise also receded, disappeared, so that it was almost as if the incident hadn't happened. This wasn't the first time, however, that a metal bird had been seen flying across the sky. On the contrary, in recent years their frequency had increased; they had been spotted on six, seven occasions, and thus Illapacta remained as he was, listening, squinting at the sky, waiting to see if it returned.

But nothing happened, and eventually, persuaded that the metal bird wasn't going to return he went indoors and gladly collapsed on his bed. For a long time he sat there, aware of his fatigue, of his aching joints, but thinking of the bird, thinking that on past occasions they had flown very much higher, sometimes so high they had made no sound and were little more than specks. But this time the bird had flown much lower. It had looked huge and dark and menacing and it began to worry him that it had flown so low because among his people, aside from Rumicuri, he was the only one to have travelled to the outside world and therefore have any real knowledge of what these birds were.

He knew, for instance, that they were made of metal, and that there was not just one kind of bird but there were birds of many shapes and sizes and uses. Above all he knew the birds were able to carry people in their bellies, and that some of them carried fearful weapons of destruction, and that people were able to look out of the birds and see what lay on the ground.

Troubled, Illapacta wondered if the low flight of the bird had been deliberate? He wondered if his people had been spotted? He wondered if the bird had anything to do with Calchas and the Radiant War?

As if in answer, an image came to his mind of ants seething upon a wounded tapir. It was an image that always came to him when he thought of the purinis. Multitudes upon multitudes of fierce ants seething over the dying body of a tapir. Multitudes upon multitudes of ants eating into the tapir's flesh, relentlessly devouring the helpless animal down to the whiteness of its bones.

Anguished, Illapacta opened a pouch containing balls of coca leaves. Placing a ball in his mouth he chewed on it slowly, releasing an acrid taste that numbed his palate. After a while he began to feel more peaceful, the ache in his joints eased, and with the help of a gourd of mishqui he kept nearby he gradually and willingly slipped into a blank stupor...

Because of the metal bird and his distracted state of mind Illapacta had forgotten to tend the fire after he returned from the funeral. The fire had gone out. It was dark when he woke up. It was so dark that for a moment he wasn't sure if he was awake. He thought it was a dream and he was in the sacred cave again. When he realised he was awake he became aware of the cold, of painful joints, of a throbbing headache. He thought of chewing more coca but for a while yet remained as he was, reminded by the total darkness of the time before he was born, long ago, in the womb of the sacred cave...

The darkness was really only near total because it was rarely absolutely dark in the sacred cave. And in fact from his infancy onwards there was a gradual progression towards light. Not a lot. Always there were deep shadows in the sacred cave. Always there was more darkness than light. But certainly there was more light in the third chamber than in the second. The light in the third chamber came from three father suns high, high up; so high that Illapacta had no hope of ever being able to climb the vaulting stone walls to reach any of these suns.

Illapacta was ten years old when he woke up, mysteriously, in the third chamber. Up until that time he had no idea there was much more to the world than the place in which he was living: the second chamber, because he'd been too young to remember the first chamber clearly. And he believed that beyond the frontiers of his world there was only the mysterious presence of the Holy Source, because this is what the elders had taught him.

In the beginning, the elders told him, there was neither light nor darkness, because in the beginning nothing existed. But then, for reasons that were unclear, the Holy Source had awakened like a person from sleep. When the Holy Source awoke he first opened his eyes and in that instant light was created. After the Holy Source opened his eyes, he yawned, and in that instant air was created. After the Holy Source yawned he looked around, saw that he was alone, and shed a tear of sadness, and in that instant water was created. Then the Holy Source thought to himself, I won't be sad. I will play with what I have created. So the holy Source began to play with light and air and water and in this way he created the world.

When the world was created it was empty. So the Holy Source thought to himself: I will plant a dream in the world. And I will tend the dream and I will nourish it and when the dream has grown I will awaken it.

This is how, long ago, the first elder was created. The elders were dreams that had awoken, and Illapacta was the child dream that had yet to awaken.

The elders told Illapacta that when they left him, when they vanished into the darkness from which they came, they returned to the Holy Source. They told him that beyond the darkness at the entrance of the world (a door of solid wood) there was only the Holy Source, and the many 'mysteries' that the Holy Source had dreamed, such as the food he ate, the bed he slept on, the clothes he wore, all the things, indeed, that gave him sustenance.

So this is what Illapacta believed until he was ten years old. He believed that beyond the door of his world there was nothing but the Holy Source and that he himself was a dream that had not yet awoken.

But one day the chief elder gave him a surprise. It happened after they'd been playing a game of wits on a clay tablet. This tablet was engraved with a design and the idea was to move a small number of stones into a designated area before the opponent could. Illapacta enjoyed this game, he was good at it, sometimes he could beat the chief elder. That day he didn't beat the chief elder, but after they had finished playing, when they were sitting on a mat in a warm shaft of light, the chief elder said to him: 'Illapacta, when I was your age and lived in this world it happened that the Holy Source looked on me kindly and dreamed another world for me. You are doing well. This makes the Holy Source happy. So now he has dreamed another world for you, too.'

Another world? Illapacta's mouth dropped open. He stared at the chief elder – a big fat man with humorous eyes – in amazement. What was he talking about? This here was the world! It was everything he knew. How could there be another world? His head began to spin with the mere thought of it.

The chief elder chuckled. Reaching out he gently passed his plump hand over Illapacta's head. Why was he so astonished? Did he think it wasn't possible? But for the Holy Source nothing was impossible. The Holy Source had dreamed another world for him. A good world. Did he not want to go to this good world?

Dazed, Illapacta asked where this other world was? The chief elder replied, enigmatically, that it was where the Holy Source had dreamed it was. So how would he get there? Illapacta asked, feeling strange, becoming both anxious and interested. How would he get there? And would the elders be in this other world? And how big was it?

But the chief elder wouldn't answer any more questions. He merely chuckled and repeated that it was a good world and he mustn't be afraid. Then he stood up and moved out of the shaft of light. A moment later he vanished into darkness.

Illapacta heard the creaking sound the comings and goings of the elder always made, but he had no thought of attempting to discover for himself what lay beyond the entrance, because from past experience he knew it was impossible to outwit the elders. They always made sure he couldn't slip past them, and was at the required distance when they left or entered the world. And whether the entrance was open or closed its darkness was so total that nothing, absolutely nothing could be seen.

So Illapacta stayed where he was, in the shaft of light, yet in his agitation he jumped up and sat down and jumped up again. He clapped his hands and started pacing about, his mind crowded with questions and thoughts, more excited than he'd ever been.

However, no matter how often he recalled the chief elder's words they revealed nothing more than what had been said. All he knew was that the Holy Source had dreamed another world for him. A 'good' world, the chief elder had said, but 'good' to Illapacta meant only that he shouldn't be afraid (in his world such words as 'good' had simple, restricted meanings). 'Good' didn't describe the other world; much less did it tell him anything about how and when he might get to this other world. When he tried to create any sort of picture of what awaited him his mind fell into confusion. Bigger or smaller, hotter or colder, lighter or darker, this was about as far as he was able to conjecture because just how much of such qualities the other world contained he had no idea.

While he was pacing, the shaft of light faded until soon it became almost totally dark. This is how his days would invariably end. The Father Sun would disappear from what he believed was the sky and it would become dark. It also became colder, chilly, so Illapacta lifted the bowl of food the chief elder had left behind and carried it to his bed of bamboo and fleeces. Sitting down he pulled a woollen blanket over his shoulders and unwrapped the leaves covering the tasengos. Sweet tasengos was one of his favourite foods, and hungry, he soon devoured them.

Not long after he finished eating he felt drowsy – strangely and unusually drowsy. He lay down on the bed wondering if something was wrong with him. A moment later he fell into deep sleep.

When he awoke what he saw was so astonishing that at first he couldn't be sure if he was awake or asleep. With heart hammering and eyes ready to burst he sat up and looked around at the world the Holy Source had dreamed for him.

It was a fantastic world, immensely larger than the one he had left, and with what for him was a dazzling amount of light, for it had not one but two, no three Father Suns! Three shafts of light falling at different angles from a sky that was magnificently vast.

The enormity, the wondrous amount of light, these were the two things that immediately struck Illapacta. But as his eyes adjusted he began to notice the yellow brown formations that in some places fell from the sky and rose from the ground. The tapering formations of rock looked to him like giant wrinkled fingers, their tips in places almost touching, so that in the slanting shafts of light amazing shapes and patterns were created, which Illapacta had no vocabulary to describe but were like vaults and arches.

Overwhelmed, he jumped out of bed, put on his robe and sandals, and step by step he advanced to explore the world the Holy Source had dreamed for him.

And what a world! Hardly had he advanced a short distance than he became aware of a continuous noise in his ears, such as he had never heard before, and somewhat alarmed he was trying to figure out what this noise was when below him, not far in front, he saw something that looked like twining, rippling shafts of light moving along the ground.

Incredulous, he advanced down the slope until he was standing over this thing which after a moment he realized was not light but a transparent liquid like water. Squatting down he gingerly touched the transparent liquid. It was cold and wet, exactly like water. He tasted it. Water! It was water! But not a small amount of it in a bowl, or the brown coloured trickles that in his last world had now and then fallen from the Father Sun. This was to him an incomprehensible amount (how was it possible? how could there be so much water?) making sounds, moving along the ground, bubbling up from a hole in the ground and after some paces vanishing into another hole.

On a playful impulse he kicked off his sandals and stepped into the stream. The sensation of cold water pressing and prickling his bare legs thrilled him. He laughed and kicked his feet, splashing water that glinted in the light of the Father Suns. How much better was this world than he had imagined! And how vast! He was entranced by all the formations that rose up from the ground and hung down from the sky, dividing the world into mysterious lands, some of them nearby, others more distant, shrouded in shadow.

Eager to discover more he left the stream and began walking across the hard yellow lumpy ground until he reached a huge formation. There he stopped, already a little tired, thinking to himself that he had travelled a great distance. Curious, he felt the formation with his fingers, raising his eyes to where, far above, it came to a tapering point. Beyond the formation itself the terrain narrowed and became progressively darker. But opposite the formation there was a low sort of arch that appeared to lead back to another part of the world. He thought he would follow it. Leaving the formation he was about to enter the arch when he stopped.

On the ground he saw a long line of minute moving creatures! At once he recalled the creatures he'd seen in his last world. There had been tiny ones that jumped on his body, and sometimes long brown ones that wriggled on the ground, or others that flitted in the air while making a buzzing noise... Creatures the Holy Source had dreamed, the elders had told him. Sacred beings he could look at but mustn't touch, for such was the command of the Holy Source. More than this he didn't know, but one thing was clear: None of the creatures he'd seen in his last world were anything like what he saw now. For here there were more than he could believe, more than he could count, an endless number of them walking along the ground in a thin line.

Fascinated, and frightened too, he took a hesitant step forward. He bent down, cautiously squatting on his haunches to stare at the moving column of tiny brown creatures. Where were they coming from? Where were they going? He couldn't tell. From where he was squatting he couldn't see the column's beginning or end, but what he could see was how they were moving in two opposite directions, and how, when two individuals met, they would frequently stop and appear to rub their heads together. Another thing he noticed was how many of them coming from one direction were carrying pieces of something or other. Some of the pieces were minute, others were larger than the creatures themselves and when this happened, when the piece was especially large, they would work in unison, two or three of them pushing and pulling the piece along.

Not all the creatures were the same size. A few were larger, almost twice as large as the rest, and these moved on the outside of the column, and looking at them he saw they had a number of legs (he counted six) and as well they had things like two hairs sticking out of what seemed to be their heads.

Engrossed, gradually losing fear, he wondered what would happen if he touched one? It was wrong. He knew it was wrong because it was what the elders had always instructed: he *must not* touch any creatures. But the temptation soon became too strong, he was curious to see what would happen. Driven by an irresistible impulse, he reached out and stuck his finger into the column. At once there was a wild agitation. The creatures closest to his finger scurried back and forth as though confused, and when, startled by the commotion, he removed his finger, he saw there was a creature stuck to it.

Illapacta lifted a finger close to his eyes, examining the creature intently, wondering why it wasn't moving any more? He couldn't understand why it had stopped moving. After a moment, baffled, he picked it off his finger and put it back in the column. The creatures again became agitated, scurrying around their motionless companion, touching it with the hairs on their heads. But still it wouldn't move.

After waiting for a long time to see if the creature would move, he gave up, stood to his feet, and began walking slowly alongside the column to see where it led.

And this was how he came to the elders. Walking slowly along, eyes fixed on the ground, he didn't notice the elders until he was almost upon them. Something alerted him. He looked up and there the three elders were, in their purple robes, sitting cross-legged on a straw mat at the precise location where the column ended.

Illapacta was confused, he couldn't understand what any of it was about, but he was delighted to see the elders and he hurried up to them. The elders responded by cheerfully ruffling his hair, smiling, asking how he liked the world the Holy Source had dreamed for him.

Having no words to express his gratitude he replied in his limited vocabulary that he thought it was a very good world. Then he began plying the elders with questions. Because it was still fresh in his mind, one of the first things he asked was about the creatures. Where did they come from? Why were there so many of them? What were they called?

So the elders told him that they were called ants. They told him that the ants, like all things, had been created by the Holy Source and there was a lot he could learn from watching them. For a while yet the ants would be here and he must observe everything they did, but he mustn't touch them. He must never touch them. Even if he should be lying down and they happened to crawl over his body he *must not* touch them.

Because they were sacred? he asked. Was that why?

Because they were sacred, the elders replied. Everything the Holy Source dreamed was sacred.

But what would happen if he touched them? he wanted to know.

The elders didn't reply at once. Instead one of them (the small frail one who had shown him the emerald and had taught him his name) looked at him keenly, and after a moment said, 'Why do you ask, Illapacta. Have you touched them?'

He was confused. He didn't know how to respond. Then quickly he shook his head. 'No,' he said. 'I didn't touch them.'

And that was the first time he spoke a lie. He had no word for lying, he didn't know what a lie was, but it was the first time he spoke one.

If the elders were aware of it they gave no indication. Instead the same elder said to him, 'Do you know what would happen if you touched them?'

'No,' he replied, lying again. 'I don't know.'

'Shall we see what would happen?'

'Yes,' he nodded, pretending.

So with the elders watching he was encouraged to touch the ants. He poked his finger straight into the column and the same thing happened as before, only this time it wasn't one but two ants that stopped moving. The elders then urged him to try and make these two ants move again, and when he was unable to do so the elders explained that the ants couldn't do so because they were dead.

Dead was a word he hadn't heard before. So the elders explained to him what dead meant.

All that the Holy Source created was called life. Illapacta was life. The elders were life. The Father Suns were life. The water, the rocks, all these things were life. And every life was different. The life of a rock wasn't the same as the life of an elder. But although every life was different, all life had a beginning and all life had an end.

When a life came into being it was called 'birth'. When a life came to an end it was called 'death.' A life was born when it became the thing that it was. Water was born when it became water. Earth was born when it became earth. An ant was born when it became an ant. A life died when it stopped being the thing that it was. Water died when it stopped being water. The water Illapacta drank died when it entered his body and became a part of him. An ant died when it stopped moving and was slowly eaten by the earth. When a life lost its uniqueness, when a life stopped being the thing that it was, when a life could no longer be seen or heard or smelt in its original condition, that was death.

Death itself wasn't bad. Without death there could be no life. If Illapacta didn't drink water he would die. Everything that died was transformed into something that lived. Death was the 'food' of life.

Death in itself wasn't bad. What was bad was a death that came before its proper time, without proper need. This is what had happened with the two ants Illapacta had touched. Everything that lived was sacred. In order to live it was necessary to eat and drink and for this it was necessary to take life. The taking of life was called 'killing'. To kill was necessary, but all life was sacred. Illapacta must never forget this. It was bad to take a life without proper need.

So this was how he first learnt about death. He asked the elders many questions. Some of those questions the elders answered.

Others they avoided or refused to answer, saying that everything had its time, and he must be patient, he mustn't fret, for one day it would all become clear to him, one day he would know all the answers to all the questions.

After the elders had spoken these things, they stood up to leave. Illapacta sat watching them walk away from him. The three elders walked almost backwards, without ever taking their eyes completely off him. They walked in their purple robes through slanting shafts of light, the fingers of rock rising and falling around them, until they disappeared into deepening shadows and then all at once they vanished.

When Calchas was gone, after her son had been put to bed for the night, Illani carried an earthenware container of glowing charcoal to a small shed-like shelter that stood a few yards from the main residence. Once inside she closed the door and emptied the charcoal onto a fire that had already been set in the centre of the floor. The fire flared, then, when the flames died, it began to glow with an intense heat that in turn warmed the fist-sized stones which had been placed in the fire.

While the stones were heating Illani removed the shawl she was wearing, unfastened the sash around her waist, and stepped out of a woollen garment. Dressed in only a sleeveless, knee-length camisole, she placed the discarded clothes in a bundle on top of a stone outside the door. After closing the door again she used something like a wooden rake to pull a portion of the stones out of the fire. Then she divested herself of the camisole. Naked, she poured a thin trickle of water from a pitcher onto the stones. At once there was a sizzling sound and hot steam rose. When no more steam would rise she pushed the stones back into the fire, pulled out others and again poured water onto them. Three, four times she repeated the procedure until steam filled the small space and was hot on her skin. Soon she was sweating. It trickled from under her armpits and in between her small breasts. Then her muscles became heavy. Sitting on a log she sighed to herself, taking pleasure in the intense, debilitating, cleansing heat...

A while later, when she was back in the house, she sat on her bed and in the flickering glow of the fire she rubbed her slender body with the waxy, aromatic pulp of a certain plant. She massaged the pulp into the muscles of her legs, her thighs, her stomach... And it gave her pleasure to do this, to inhale the aroma and feel the smooth, muscular contours of her body. It was a pleasure, she realised, that she hadn't felt for a long time – not since the days before she and Rumicuri had separated.

How could it have happened? It was impossible to imagine how such a thing could have happened except through sorcery. Wasn't it sorcery that had loosened the binding on the effigy? No one else knew where it was hidden or even that it existed. She had made the effigy of Rumicuri in secret and had bound it with twine soaked in her body fluids and had recited the incantations that would keep Rumicuri under her spell. But after her son was born, when things had started going badly between them, she had gone to check on the effigy and to her dismay had found the twine all broken and undone.

And what was that if not sorcery? Powerful sorcery only Amataba could have known how to work. Because that was what had happened. Amataba and Cascarina had conspired against her. That fat stupid Cascarina could never have managed it on her own. It was Amataba who had helped weaken the spell, who had beguiled Rumicuri, who had helped entice him from his rightful home. Rightful, yes! Because he was her husband, he was the father of her son. His rightful home was here. Here with her...

It was above all the lost illusion that hurt. She was haughty, self-serving, she put on airs... She had heard all sorts of spiteful things... But was it wrong to be ambitious? The elders despised possessions but what did they know? They weren't really alive, they didn't have the needs of ordinary people. She had thought she would be happy with Rumicuri; there was no one else, he was the one she had chosen.

Women were not supposed to complain or do anything that wasn't according to tradition. It was the way they were brought up, afraid of saying I want this, this, this... They should demand it. Nothing would ever change unless they made it change. So she wanted a good place to live, a husband who was attentive to her needs, if that was being selfish so be it.

He was the sovereign. It was her duty to obey him in everything. She must put his needs before her own. Mustn't argue, mustn't express her feelings, mustn't be herself... He was the sovereign, yes, but he was also a man. And it was the man who had rutted with her, who'd got angry, who'd told her she was always complicating things, wanting attention, making demands... But was it she who made demands – or he who would not leave his shell? If he wouldn't risk anything of himself how could he know what she was really like? It was an opportunity he had missed. And it hurt her, it made her bitter to think she was like a field that had been cleared and irrigated and planted and then abandoned, wilfully, without ever waiting to discover the bounty it could bring forth...

Life should not be all toil and responsibility. The way he was weighed down anyone would think it was he, not the Holy Source, who had created the world. Life was like a firefly, here for a moment. And if you didn't seize it while you could you ended up with an empty stomach. Dry and shrivelled. She had thought she could make him see this. She had really believed she could teach him to smile and enjoy life...

Thinking of Rumicuri, and that fat infertile Cascarina, and how it had all gone wrong for her, Illani forgot the pleasure of waxing her body. Sitting quite still, her narrow face contracting into a sour, puckered expression, she felt as though her blood were turning to earth.

After a while though she managed, if not to overcome, to suppress her bitter thoughts. She owed Rumicuri nothing. Why should she be faithful to him?

Illani was not exactly sure how the lowlander could serve her. Rumicuri had hit the lowlander and the two men didn't like each other. Rumicuri would like him even less when she took him for a lover. She would flaunt the lowlander. She would mock her husband. He had crapped on her pride. She wasn't going to let him off.

The lowlander was a fool... or was he? She didn't know. She would have to find out. He was bold, though, and not bad looking, and he was a man. She hadn't had a man since Rumicuri had deserted her...

Thoughts turning to the lowlander, Illani began waxing her body again. Her bitterness was replaced by a quickening excitement and with it the expression on her face changed. Her nostrils flared and her eyes narrowed with an intense, cat-like gaze.

When she had finished rubbing her body she rose from the bed. Her long black hair spreading down her back, she padded to the rear of the room where she removed a clean camisole from a line strung between two posts. Once dressed in the camisole she wrapped a thick shawl-like garment around her shoulders and went over to where a number of small baskets were hanging from pegs in the wall. Unhooking two of the baskets she carried them over to the fire and squatting down she removed a pinch of herbs from each basket. Thinking of the lowlander – a bright, predatory gleam coming into her eyes – she dropped the powdered herbs into a container of recently made mishqui that was fermenting near the fire…

In spite of himself Calchas was nervous when he arrived at Illani's. He hadn't forgotten how she had angered him, calling him a fool. Neither could he be absolutely sure she was waiting to let him in. He was afraid of being humiliated again (or worse, of walking into a trap) so before trying the door he paused, adjusting his clothes, smoothing back his hair.

When finally he pushed the door it opened with a creak and half stepping inside he peered into the dim, flickering interior. 'I'm here,' he announced. There was no reply but Calchas wasn't about to back down. He decided to step fully inside. No sooner had he done so than he heard her taunting, husky voice, 'So the fool is here…'

Discomfited, he peered into the dim interior and saw her sitting on the bed with her legs crossed and one hand ready to pass a comb through her abundant hair. It was okay, he decided. She was being haughty but he would soon change that. Quietly exulting, he closed the door and stepped around the fire.

'I have some mishqui. Would you like some?' Illani rose softly from the bed, her manner seeming to change for she gave him an unexpectedly sweet, friendly smile.

He grinned back at her, relaxing, increasingly confident.

'Why not?'

She went over to the fire and returned with a bowl of mishqui. She handed him the bowl and sat down again. He sat down beside her. For a little they remained in silence: Illani slowly combing her hair and Calchas sipping the mishqui, his senses inflamed by her scent, her beauty, the proximity of her body, but in no hurry to let it show; taking his time rather, determined to be the one who conquered.

'You have beautiful hair,' he remarked, breaking the silence, half turning to her. 'You're the most beautiful of all the queens I've met.'

'Yes?' She glanced at him from under lowered eyelids (and, it seemed to Calchas, shyly, which was something that pleased him). 'Have you met many such as I?'

'Oh yes, many,' he teased her. 'There are many in the world I come from.'

'And how is it there are so many? Are there kings, too?'

Kings! Calchas was amused. Rumicuri wouldn't make it as a house servant in the world of the purinis. Over there he was nothing. And for Illani to imagine herself a queen, what a joke; over there any common prostitute would outclass her. How little this woman knew of the outside world; how little she understood, really, just how rich and powerful some of the purinis were.

'Like your husband you mean?' Calchas laughed with light-hearted contempt. He didn't know why but he felt wonderfully relaxed. 'Not when I'm there. I don't know what it is, but when I'm around the husbands all disappear.' He laughed again. He didn't know why but the sound of his own voice delighted him. It had a manly, confident timbre.

She smiled, opening her lips. Her mouth was like a pink and white orchid glistening with dew. 'That must be because you know how to please a woman?'

Stretching his arm he took a little of her hair in between thumb and forefinger and rubbed it with a caressing, proprietary nonchalance. 'Maybe I do...'

'You must tell me about yourself some time. I'd like to know about your world... Shall I get you more mishqui?'

'Why not?'

She took the empty bowl from his hand and went to fill it. He watched her. They way she walked, the sensual flex of her buttocks made him burn with desire. He felt full of potency, like a bull, he thought, and at once, the moment he thought it, he became a bull. His hands were hooves. Mighty horns grew out of his skull. His black gleaming hide rippled with muscular power. He snorted, swished his tail, rose up on his hind legs ready to mount the heifer that was now waiting for him, her head looking back with soft yielding eyes. But at that moment, just as he was about to penetrate the heifer, he became himself again. Just as suddenly as he had become a bull he was again reclining on the bed, and it was no heifer that was beside him; it was Illani, leaning towards him, proffering the bowl of mishqui.

It was strange, yet it had all happened so suddenly, so quickly that he wasn't sure if it had happened at all. He felt peculiar, sort of tipsy; maybe it was only a thought he'd had? But soon, in any case, it was something that ceased to matter for he became aware that Illani had removed her shawl and he became intoxicated by her shapely bare arms, her narrow waist, her breasts pressing with erect nipples against the fabric of her camisole...

Unable to breathe, blood gorging his head, Calchas seized the bowl of mishqui and drank from it recklessly. Illani meanwhile leaned back against the wall. She lifted one leg, bending it at the knee. Her camisole fell back, revealing the smooth flesh of her thigh. Making no attempt to cover herself she turned to look at him with sleepy, teasing eyes, so that he found himself leaning irresistibly towards her. When his lips met hers, when his hand touched her bare thigh, he knew straight away that she was like no other woman he'd known. The sensations he experienced were astonishing. Never had his lips tasted such sweet, seductive succulence, never had his fingers caressed such yielding, silken smoothness.

Dazed, as though from a potion too rich for him, he drew back in order to steady himself. It wouldn't do to spill his seed too soon. Such loss of control would be humiliating. For all her intoxicating allure he was still intending to be the one who held back, who dominated.

When Illani began pulling him down, when she began kissing his neck, when her hands began fumbling under his shirt, Calchas experienced an exquisite thrill of power. With finely controlled urgency he allowed his hand to stroke her hip, gently pushing the camisole up over her thighs. Lightly he passed his hand over the moist fuzz of her pudenda. But almost at once he stopped, startled because now a crackling electricity was shooting up his fingers into his arm. Shifting his body, looking down, he was amazed to see her pubic hair flashing and crackling with countless filaments of white light, as though the hairs were a tangle of miniature lightning bolts. Sitting up with a jerk he looked at the rest of her body, which however was quite normal. She herself was looking at him with puzzlement, as though unable to understand why he'd stopped. He wanted to say something but when he looked again at her pudenda the filaments of light were no longer there. Everything about her appeared normal. While he sat there, puzzled, his thoughts in chaos, she raised herself to draw the camisole up over her head. Completely naked she lay back on the bed. And staring at her, contemplating her beautiful body, he soon forgot his puzzlement. He forgot everything.

Once naked he fell upon her. She was delicious. He couldn't believe how delicious she was: All curves and soft hair. And she was hungry. When he put his hand in between her legs he felt her break open like a ripe mango. This really aroused him. Climbing in between her legs he thrust into her. She received him with a moan. As he began moving inside her she made more moaning sounds. Clear sounds of pleasure which yet became increasingly wild, shriller. At the same time he felt an unexpectedly sharp scratching down his back. It was painful. If it was her nails they were as hard as claws. He thought she must be going wild. Lifting his eyes he looked at her face and that was when he noticed her eyes were a glowing phosphorescent yellow, their pupils narrow vertical slits. Calchas' shock was such that he instantly stopped what he was doing. Was he going mad? His head was muddled. He couldn't think straight. He couldn't understand what was happening here. Her eyes were yellow. They were the eyes of a cat. All at once he panicked, trying to break free of her, but he found that he couldn't move; her arms were immensely strong, as though made of iron. As he struggled he noticed that her nose had turned dark and flat and short yellow-white hair was covering her face. Then he noticed how she smelled different: a strong, tangy, animal odour. Looking further down her body he saw there was nothing human about her any more; it was the body of a huge yellowish cat spotted with black rosettes.

A jaguar. At the moment Calchas realised he was being embraced by a jaguar he heard her making a growling sound and saw her whiskered mouth creasing back to reveal dangerously sharp fangs. He thought the jaguar was going to maul him. Somehow he managed to break free. He jumped up and made an attempt to escape, but inexplicably, no matter which way he turned the jaguar anticipated his every move so that she was always in front of him – a sleek, full grown jaguar, her coat gleaming in the light of the fire, her yellow eyes glowing like jewels, watching him the way a cat watches its prey. This is what Calchas thought at first. He saw the jaguar crouched in front of him – intent, playful, dangerous – and he thought that at any moment she was going to pounce on him. But the jaguar didn't do this. Instead she began purring. Then she padded up to him and rising on her hind legs she placed her front paws against his chest, forcing him to fall backwards onto the bed. As he lay there, breaking into a sweat (even if a part of him was telling him that it must be a hallucination) the jaguar started licking him with a tongue that was like sandpaper. Calchas was powerless. He had no choice but to submit to the jaguar, at every instant afraid lest her rough caresses turn to ripping ferocity. In terror though he was, his penis began responding to the jaguar's tongue. It swelled, it became erect. The jaguar stopped licking him. She positioned herself with her hind legs on the floor and the front ones on the edge of the bed. Swishing her tail she growled softly and stared at him with narrowed, sleepy eyes. Soon he understood what she wanted. The jaguar wanted him to mount her. And how could he refuse? He was powerless, he had no alternative but to mount the jaguar. In trepidation, his whole body trembling, yet his penis fully erect, he stepped up to the jaguar and penetrated her from behind. A dangerous affair. It was a dangerous affair he had got himself involved in. He was much too confused to know how it had happened. But if it was a hallucination such was its hold on him that his doubt quickly passed. The jaguar appeared much too real, much too menacing. He was frightened of her. Were anything to upset her she could tear him to shreds. With every thrust he was putting his life in danger. And after every thrust his gratitude to the jaguar for sparing him increased. It was a perverse, exquisite servility that Calchas began to endure. And the more he fornicated the jaguar the more his servility was bonded to her power, and so the more he began to hate and the more to venerate the jaguar.

Standing under the stars, in the light of the moon, Rumicuri stared suspiciously at the big solid black doors, at the luminous wall (with a fence of metal on top) that stretched from either side of the doors as far into the night as he could see.

While he waited for Mountain Trotter to return, he was thinking that this wall hadn't existed when he had come that last time, all those years ago. He recalled that his uncle had lived in a dwelling which had seemed strangely magnificent, but a dwelling that on the outside was surrounded by bushes, by fruit trees, not a huge wall such as this one; he had no recollection of a wall such as this.

According to what Mountain Trotter had told him, one of his cousins, the oldest of the two boys, had become a warlord of some kind. Much more than this Mountain Trotter couldn't say; they were far from his village and all he knew were the rumours others brought him. But staring at the wall it became clear to Rumicuri that if his cousin had become a warlord he must have powerful enemies, or why erect so massive a fortification?

Presently, from out of the darkness, Mountain Trotter appeared walking briskly.

'This is the same place, highness,' he declared, stopping. 'The wall is new and it's much further forward than the old one. But this is the same place.'

After a moment Rumicuri said, 'How do we get in?'

Mountain Trotter went up to the doors of solid metal. On one side of them he found a button. Hesitantly he pressed it. As he stood waiting two blinding white lights flashed on. Rumicuri was so startled he jumped back and fled along the wall. When he was out of the sphere of light he stopped. Crouching against the wall he stared at Mountain Trotter uncomprehendingly, waiting to see what would happen.

But nothing happened. After a while Mountain Trotter came up to him. Squatting by his side he said he had spoken to a purini and now they must wait. Rumicuri was baffled. 'I saw no one. How did you speak to a purini?' Mountain Trotter tried to explain about the voice – a voice with no flesh, like the voice of a spirit – that came through an artefact on the wall.

Rumicuri was silent. He leaned back against the wall, fatigued, his brow creased in dismayed thought. Was there no end to all the unnatural wonders of the purini world? What had he not seen in the settlement they had passed! Dwellings with walls like clear ice you could see through. The miniature suns, all different colours, green, red, blue, yellow, that became bright and then died and then became bright again. The metal animals with eyes lit up in the dark. A strident jumble of sounds coming from no human form that he could locate – like the voices of spirits as Mountain Trotter had said. And on the pathways in between the dwellings, crowds and crowds of purinis. Everywhere there were peculiarly dressed men and women, milling around him, doing things he couldn't understand, but some of them, it would appear, getting intoxicated on drink and others going in and out of dwellings you could see into and which were stacked with myriad glittering artefacts.

He had been mesmerised. His head had reeled from so many strong impressions. But all the time tense, frightened, and he had breathed relief when they had left the settlement and once again ventured into dark open land.

But how changed it was, too, from his childhood journey, he reflected. On that occasion he had seen only a few metal animals. And their shapes were different. And there weren't so many miniature suns and the dwellings were darker and with fewer glittering artefacts in them. Though as a child the settlement had seemed to him vast, he now realised it had been smaller and less populated than it was today. And it troubled him to dwell on this. It troubled him to think the purini world had expanded. Was there no end to them? Would they not stop multiplying and increasing and devouring the Mother Earth?

A sound interrupted his gloomy thoughts. It was the low rumble of a metal animal coming from behind the wall. The sound died. Silence followed. The men exchanged looks. Soon afterwards there was another, creaking sound. A man stepped out of a small doorway which was framed within the larger solid doors. In his hands he held a squat firearm (a sub-machine gun) and he peered about quickly in the bright light before raising one of his hands to beckon them.

Rumicuri stood up. In uneasy silence he followed Mountain Trotter to the door. The short fat guard stood back and nodded at them to go through. A little way in, on the other side, a woman was standing stiffly beside a metal animal. She was an old woman, wrapped in a loose fitting garment, her arms folded across her midriff and long white hair falling freely over her shoulders.

Mountain Trotter knew who she was but Rumicuri didn't recognise her so quickly.

'Is that you Mountain Trotter?' The old woman spoke in Spanish, peering at them as they approached.

Mountain Trotter understood: He spoke a little Spanish. 'Yes, it's Mountain Trotter. I bring the sovereign.'

Agustina was not Arayana. She was of the purini race and couldn't speak Rumicuri's language. But she was his aunt, she was married to his uncle, and so no sooner had he stepped before her than she greeted him in the way her husband had always said the sovereign of the Arayana should be greeted.

With difficulty, one hand holding onto the car for support, she lowered herself on her knees and placing both hands on the ground she bowed her head.

The short fat guard, standing nearby, looked on in disbelief. The guard thought there was nothing in the world that could surprise him. Never had he imagined he'd see the day when don Federico's mother, the mistress, knelt at the feet of a rustic illiterate Indian, prostrating herself as though he were some kind of saint!

While the guard looked on, Rumicuri reached down and taking hold of his aunt's arm he helped her to stand again. Unable to communicate in words, they stared at each other shyly, both of them pleased and nervous; both of them thinking how the other had changed from the last time they had met all those years ago.

Presently Agustina turned to Mountain Trotter. She took hold of his hands, squeezing them, speaking words of greeting, then she opened the back door of the car for them to get in.

Rumicuri tensed. He resisted getting in, but his aunt reassured him, gently touching his shoulder. Reluctantly he climbed into the belly of the metal animal and sat staring ahead in apprehensive anticipation. As for Mountain Trotter, in his entire life he had travelled in a car only twice, but on several occasions he had travelled by bus, so he could afford to chuckle when the engine started and he felt Rumicuri tense.

'Why are you laughing Mountain Trotter? Do you think I'm frightened of this metal animal?'

'No, highness.' Mountain trotter kept a straight face. But now a rare thing occurred: He saw the sovereign smile. Although it was dark the old man nevertheless caught a glint in Rumicuri's face and he saw the hard features soften.

'You're a liar, Mountain Trotter,' Rumicuri said, the smile expanding. Then it vanished and he gripped the seat with both hands as the metal animal started moving forward. Staring straight ahead he could see the broad flat road unfolding in the white light, and to the sides of the road he could see bushes, fences, patches of ground speeding backwards...

In the front seat next to the chauffeur, meanwhile, Agustina was thinking of all the years that had passed since she had met Rumicuri as a child; she was thinking he still had the grave yet deeply truthful expression which had first endeared him to her. He had grown into a fine looking man. Her own son was also fine looking, but unfortunately he was self-centred, coarse, and it showed in his looks. She wondered what it was that had brought Rumicuri here so unexpectedly? Had he heard perhaps that his uncle was dying? Was that why he'd come?

Agustina's husband, for his part, had felt strong emotions after his wife put the phone down and told him what it was about. Exhausted, ravaged by disease as he was, he had at first been astonished, then joyous at the news that his nephew had arrived. Soon, though, he began to worry. He doubted that his nephew would have made the journey for pleasure alone. And if not for pleasure, why? Could it be he was the bearer of ill tidings? Could some disaster have befallen his people?

After his wife had gone to fetch them, Tupaxo, or Victoriano, to use his adopted Spanish name, struggled out of bed and in his nightshirt he hobbled on unsteady legs to a built-in wardrobe which occupied an entire wall. The space inside the wardrobe was crammed with suits. There were over a hundred of them, all of foreign provenance, all of the best quality, all but a few presents from his son. It was one of his several manias. 'You're going to be the best dressed man in the whole country, papa. I'm going to give you a suit for every week of the year!' his son had once boasted in that grandiose but empty manner of his.

Victoriano had no interest in the suits per se. He was interested in what a suit represented. An Indian in a well-cut suit, wearing a good pair of shoes, could have the status, almost, of a white man. He was not disparaged as was an Indian in ethnic garb or cheap casual wear. But his son didn't know he'd had to learn all this. He seemed to think he cared for the actual suits. In the past, before he became ill, Victoriano had tried to explain to his son the subtle but definite difference between perceived and intrinsic values. Now his son, who had always been wild, had become foolish, but Victoriano no longer had the strength to try to deal with it.

For five years his insides had been slowly rotting. Recently it had become much worse. He was dying. Everybody knew he was dying. He wondered if it was possible that Mountain Trotter had heard of his condition and had taken the news to his nephew? Could that be why Rumicuri had made the journey? As the old man grabbed the first suit his hand fell upon he hoped such was the explanation. It was alarming to think some disaster could have befallen his people. This was infinitely more worrying to him than the thought of his own death. He wasn't afraid of dying. More to the contrary, it was living he could no longer endure. The exhaustion, the unrelenting pain, the knowledge of his own degrading feebleness, made him long for the embrace of death, even as he had once, when he was young, longed for the embrace of a woman...

During his long life Victoriano had desired many women, but he had loved only two. Agustina was one; the other was Rumicuri's mother.

He had always liked Miruaca. She was the first girl of whom he had dreamed. But he was too young and shy to tell her of his feelings. Then, some years later, his brother took a fancy to her. He was five years older and the first in line for succession and maybe that had something to do with Miruaca falling for him because Victoriano couldn't see what other qualities his brother had. He was intelligent, yes, and good looking they said (taller than most and with a nose like a toucan's beak) but he was lazy and arrogant. The affairs of the kingdom had always come second to his carousing, a fact that angered Victoriano, made him envious, because he had believed he was better qualified to rule the kingdom. And yet it was his brother who had become the sovereign and who had married Miruaca.

Victoriano wasn't aware that he loved Miruaca when his brother married her. Somewhere inside him, perhaps, he knew; but he wasn't conscious of it. If he felt anything for her, he told himself it was mere affection. The realisation of his love came later, and much too late, when he learnt of her unhappiness.

Before she married his brother Miruaca had been open and cheerful. Though small and finely boned she sizzled with energy. Her broad and tempting mouth and her lovely eyes were always ready for laughter. But after she married his brother all that changed. Victoriano often saw her looking downcast, and one day when he went to his brother's dwelling he found her crying.

His brother had gone out and she was alone with her first child (Rumicuri's older brother who had died when he was seven). She was sitting on the bed trying to entertain the child but there was weariness and sorrow in her expression, and when she looked up at him her eyes became tearful. Momentarily she turned her face away, wiping her eyes with her hand, but when she turned back to him she saw more tears clinging to her eyelashes.

Victoriano didn't have to ask her for the cause. Everybody knew that his brother had stopped caring for her. Often he was intoxicated on coca or mishqui and he was entangled with another woman. This might not have been so bad were it a case of taking a second wife –

even if he hadn't long been married to Miruaca – but the woman in question was herself married. It was a scandal. His brother was the sovereign. It was his duty to set an example. And not only was he failing his duty, worse, he was taking shameful advantage. The woman's husband was in despair but he had no redress. Who could he appeal to? The sovereign was the highest law in the kingdom. If he, through his actions, caused discord, it was not one or two or three people who suffered, it was the whole community.

Victoriano, knowing these things, and seeing Miruaca's unhappiness, was seized by fury. He wanted to find his brother and shake him by the neck and shout at him: 'Look what you're doing! You're a disgrace! You disturb the tranquillity of the kingdom, you cause discord and resentment, and your callous behaviour is hurting Miruaca. It's destroying the good feelings she has for you! You're breaking her heart!'

And thinking these things, in the midst of his fury, he felt such a yearning tenderness for her that in his mind's eye he saw himself embracing her, consoling her, declaring his love.

His emotions were in turmoil: rage at his brother. A hunger of the soul for this woman. Guilt coming down on him like thunder. And fear. Above all, fear.

This will end in perdition, he thought.

With hardly a word he turned and fled from his brother's dwelling.

Victoriano would not go so far as to say it was because of Miruaca, or his brother, that he had left the kingdom. But from then on his life was never the same. For thinking of Miruaca he could find no peace. And should they chance to meet the very air would become heavy with their forbidden and unspoken longings. What were they to do? Were his brother not the sovereign there might have been a solution. Their situation wasn't without precedent. Had they been commoners she could have divorced his brother. For a divorce all that was required was for the couple to be brought before the sovereign. He listened to their reasons. If he thought they were justified the divorce was granted. But while the sovereign could divorce others he could not himself become divorced. He could take as many wives as he desired but he couldn't divorce them for the reason that there was no authority higher than himself in a position to grant one.

So Victoriano knew it would be impossible for him to establish a legitimate relationship with Miruaca unless his brother consented, and there was nothing to say he would. As for an illegitimate one, it was far too dangerous. Quite apart from the repercussions it could have in the community it would mean defying the sovereign. And to defy the sovereign was to break the law. And for the Arayana there was nothing higher than the law. It was what made them a nation.

Thus Victoriano decided to keep his love for Miruaca a secret. But it was hard on him. His life stopped giving him pleasure, and increasingly he came to despise, resent, and even hate his brother.

Then Mountain Trotter arrived on one of his infrequent visits. As usual Victoriano was among the first to welcome him, because since childhood he had nursed a curiosity about the outside world and he always had questions to ask. Mountain Trotter stayed for two weeks. On the night before he was due to leave Victoriano resolved to go with him. He told himself he was satisfying a long held ambition (which was true) and that he had no intention of staying in the outside world but only wished to see what it was like. But at the same time he also knew, even if he wouldn't openly admit it, that he was going in order to escape from the burden of an impossible love. He told himself he would soon enough return, but when he left he took with him a pouch containing gem quality uncut opals and emeralds inherited from his forefathers and which, Mountain Trotter had told him, could make him a powerful man in the world of the purinis…

At last the car came to a stop. In spite of the novelty and initial excitement, Rumicuri had begun to feel uncomfortable sitting powerless inside it. He was glad when the door opened and he was able to climb out. But almost immediately he forgot the car. Looking up he was now amazed by the edifice that loomed before him. Somehow he had assumed his uncle would be living in the same dwelling he could remember from his childhood. That dwelling had seemed to him extraordinary, but this one was even more difficult to comprehend. It was vast. Not as tall as some of the dwellings he'd seen in the settlement, but vast nevertheless, and it had countless transparent walls, and smooth round posts, and a huge ornate wooden door, and in front of this door, under the glow of a miniature sun, a floor of gleaming stone.

Then, after his aunt opened the door, when he followed her inside, hardly did he perceive the darkness than it was dispelled by a sun which flashed alive as if by sorcery. But he was becoming accustomed to the miniature suns and his surprise was small compared to what followed. There was a transparent wall some steps ahead of them and as they walked towards it the wall, unbelievably, divided itself in two halves, gliding away from each other so they could walk through the open space! And after they had walked through the open space, when Rumicuri looked back, he saw the two halves closing and becoming one again!

Beyond the transparent wall they entered what looked to him like an enormous room but was in fact an imposing hallway. As he was led across it he looked around at some steps that went to another part of the dwelling, and at various baffling artefacts, and at a sun that hung from the ceiling like a giant pendant made of countless glittering stones. Then his aunt opened another door and he was in a room where at once he saw an old man sitting upright in a strange looking seat.

Although he was dressed in purini clothes Rumicuri could see that the man had no flesh on him. His cheeks were sunken, his hair was falling out, growing in patches, and his skin, wrinkled like old leather, was an unhealthy yellow colour blotched with brown spots.

The old man looked nothing like the uncle Rumicuri could remember. The uncle Rumicuri could remember had difficulty getting about even then, but in all other respects he had been a hale, vigorous man; well fleshed, with good complexion, a man who looked younger than his many years.

The old man remained immobile and impassive, but as Rumicuri stepped closer he recognised his uncle from the expression in his eyes. The eyes themselves were rheumy, bloodshot, but in their depths he caught a familiar gleam.

'I'm sorry I can't greet you as I should, highness,' said Victoriano, speaking in a thin, quivery voice.

'It makes no difference, uncle,' replied Rumicuri, standing close to him, trying not to show his fatigue, or the dismay he felt at seeing his uncle so infirm.

'It's been many years,' said Victoriano, 'When I last saw you, you were a sprig and I called you nephew. Now you are a grown man and I call you highness... And our people?' he added after a moment. 'Are they well?'

'For now they're well, uncle.' He turned to Mountain Trotter. 'Tell him what you know.'

Mountain Trotter and Victoriano exchanged greetings. They were old friends, they had known each other for many years, and they were pleased to meet again, but Mountain Trotter nevertheless remained deferential towards Victoriano: because he was the sovereign's uncle, and because he was a powerful man in the world of the purinis, but also because he was older than Mountain Trotter by nearly fifteen years.

Mountain Trotter spoke of the soldiers who had taken over his village. How the villagers were frightened of the soldiers and how he'd managed to escape with others and had gone to warn the sovereign's people. After Mountain Trotter had finished, Rumicuri concluded with an account of Calchas' speech before the council, of his own fear that the war could spread and endanger the kingdom, and of his decision to come and seek his uncle's help.

Victoriano listened in silence, intently, his mind slower than it had once been but not for that lacking the astuteness, even the prescience which in the past had distinguished him from others.

'For now I'm only thankful our people are safe,' he said eventually. 'But these are violent times we live in. Maybe you've good reason to be troubled by all that's happening. Tomorrow we'll see what more can be discovered...'

Victoriano dropped into another silence. Regarding his nephew he felt his heart flood with strong, ambiguous emotions of joy and sorrow, and impulsively, disregarding all protocol, he beckoned Rumicuri closer, and when Rumicuri leaned towards him, he reached out and stroked his cheek. He stroked Rumicuri's cheek as once, many years ago, Victoriano's mother had stroked his.

'A man becomes womanish in his old age, highness,' he muttered.

For some moments more they talked. Victoriano was anxious to know how fared various relations and old friends and he was saddened to learn that many had passed away. When they had finished speaking he exchanged words with Mountain Trotter, asking about the people in his village, saying he would do all he could to help them as well.

Mountain Trotter thanked Victoriano. Presently Agustina said they must be exhausted after their journey and she would show them to their beds. During the last hours the men had struggled against fatigue and now that they had arrived at their destination it was rapidly overwhelming them and it was in a daze that they followed Agustina to a room containing two beds.

Rumicuri recalled that on his first visit he hadn't been able to get accustomed to sleeping on a purini bed, which had been too high and soft for him, so before anything else he pulled the mattress off the bed and onto the floor. Agustina, watching, smiled indulgently when she recalled how he'd done precisely this as a child.

After switching off the light, the men got into their beds (Mountain Trotter had also put his mattress on the floor) and were instantly asleep.

Agustina and her husband didn't go back to sleep. By the time their guests were in bed it was almost dawn, so they stayed up sitting by the window – now and then talking, but mostly silent.

Agustina was sorry that her husband's joy at seeing his nephew should be overshadowed by the troubled news he brought. It was a cruel world, she reflected, that deprived a dying man of solace. Forty-six years they'd lived as man and wife and she knew not a day passed when her husband didn't think and worry about his people.

All those years ago, when he'd first told her of his people she hadn't believed him. Before that he had always lied to her: he told her he came from the jungle region of Barajas. She was a teacher when they met. She taught primary school. Three evenings a week she also gave a literacy class for local adults and he was one of her pupils. He was quite a bit older than her but he soon made an impression because he was different from the others. It wasn't just that he wore western clothes of good quality, it was the way he carried himself. The other Indians who attended her class behaved with self-conscious diffidence, if not gross servility, as though unable to shake off the stigma of belonging to a despised peasantry. But he was proud. Agustina was intrigued. He appeared to be prosperous and there was no doubt he was intelligent, yet there he sat in her classroom more educationally backward than any of them, barely able to speak Spanish, and trying to learn how to read and write with all the halting clumsiness of a five-year-old.

But he was determined. He went to every lesson, did all the work she gave him, and in due course began asking for extra. As a result of the additional work he sometimes stayed behind and then it was only the two of them in the classroom. So that was how they got to know each other. It didn't happen quickly. It was more than a year before they went on a walk together. One evening he said to her, 'Will you come for a walk?' And she said, 'Yes.' Just like that. She was so used to him by then it didn't occur to her that she was going out with an Indian.

He'd told her lies, a whole lot of lies in the beginning. He said he had no living relatives, he said he had done some prospecting in the jungle and had struck lucky. One day he took her to the house he lived in. It was half a mile out of town; a small, flaking, blue house close to a dusty road. Inside it consisted of three rooms, a kitchen, a bathroom. It was through a distant relation of Mountain Trotter's that he'd been able to rent it. Three years for one small emerald. But at the time he lied to her, saying he rented it from a fellow prospector who'd gone back to the jungle. She believed him. She believed everything he said because already she was falling for him.

One of the rooms was piled with books; this was in the age before computers. There were no shelves. Stacks and stacks of books stood against the walls. When she recovered from her surprise he said he bought them. Holding a book (close to his body, she observed; his short strong fingers stroking it with unconscious possessiveness) he said he read the covers and if he thought the book would serve him he bought it. Sometimes he bought one book, other times he bought so many he had to hire a porter to take them all home. He said he wanted to know everything about the world, but he read so slowly and there were so many books, and so there they lay, waiting...

It was four years after they became lovers – four years – before he told her about his people. She was already pregnant with their first child, so perhaps this is what had prompted him? One night he showed her a history book. It dealt with pre-Columbian civilisation and there was a section on the Arayana and their minor empire which, according to the book, had completely disappeared after the Spanish conquest.

But this wasn't exactly true, he told her. The empire may have disappeared, but a kernel of it, unknown to the modern world, survived to this day. She laughed, puzzled. Was he saying this for the fun of it, to make an impression? But when she studied him she saw no trace of lightness in his manner. He was completely serious. She wondered if he was making some kind of political allusion. She asked him what he meant. So that was when he began telling her.

It was true that during the wars with the Spaniards, the Arayana had abandoned their stone cities. And it was true that huge numbers of them had perished at the hands of the Spaniards. But it was false that Ramacapan, the last Emperor, had fallen in battle as stated in the book. It was Ramacapan's younger brother and his household who had perished. The emperor, four of his wives, their children, and an indefinite number of followers had retreated deep into the mountain forest. In time the emperor was joined by more of his subjects. Unknown to the outside world they began assembling again into a community. Another stone city was built, albeit on a much smaller scale, and for the next two centuries they survived undisturbed, following the old traditions. Nobody knew of their existence, not even the descendants of the Arayana who were scattered on the borderlands of what had now become the white man's domain.

As time passed, however, the white man started cutting down the forests, breeding with the Indians, establishing new communities and slowly advancing into what until then had been unknown territory. Alarmed at the prospect of being discovered, the Arayana began sending out spies to keep them informed of events. The spies were loyal, they would die before betraying their people, but how were they to protect themselves against the white man's diseases? A series of epidemics decimated the Arayana. Multitudes died. By the time they built up a resistance there were a scarce few hundred of them left.

Over the next century and a half the surviving Arayana retreated further into the mountain forest as alien civilisation encroached on them. Then, some six or seven generations ago, when they were once more threatened, they split into two groups. The main body, which included the sovereign, moved to their present hiding place. The other group elected to remain in the locality. To the outside world the group who stayed behind appeared no different from the other Indian communities scattered on the edges of the forest. But amongst themselves they retained their language, not a few of their traditions, and above all they possessed the knowledge that the Arayana sovereign and his people still lived in a hidden location that was all but inaccessible to them and utterly so to the outside world.

Since the time of the Spaniards there was much that had changed for the Arayana sovereign and his people. Where once they had been a mighty empire, their number was now little more than eight hundred. The sovereign's power was hugely diminished, they no longer built stone cities, and all that was war-like in their culture – the battle training, the rigid discipline, the human sacrifices, the bloodthirsty war gods, all that had forged the Arayana into an empire – had steadily disappeared. And as this happened, other, more mystical aspects of their culture, which had always been subordinate to the military, began to evolve. With the passage of time the Arayana, through necessity if nothing else, had become a peaceful people whose sincerest wish now was to live in harmony with the Holy Source and the Mother Earth which sustained them.

The Arayana had changed. They had different values, a different system of beliefs to their warrior ancestors. But they were no less Arayana for that. Their heritage had changed but it hadn't been destroyed. So what the history book said wasn't true. The Arayana civilisation endured to this day.

Agustina was astonished by what she heard. She thought it had to be something he had made up. Smiling in disbelief she asked him how he knew all this. 'Because I am Arayana,' he replied, without returning her smile, his dark, deep-set eyes fixed on her. 'I'm the sovereign's brother.'

This was too much! She laughed, convinced he was teasing her. So was it somewhere in Barajas that the Arayana lived? She asked. And hadn't he told her he had no living relatives? He admitted then that he'd lied. He had never been in the jungle region of Barajas and neither was he a prospector, but he'd told her these things because he had no choice. The Arayana depended on absolute secrecy for their survival. The things he'd told her no person from the outside world had heard before. She must understand that were the secret of the Arayana to reach the wrong ears, any number of people for all different reasons could go in search of them; there was no saying what calamity could occur. This was why he'd waited before telling her. He had to be sure he could trust her.

Having heard these things, Agustina began to wonder at last if what he was telling her could be true. It seemed too outlandish to be true. But why would he tell her if it wasn't? He had nothing to gain by telling her such a story. But if it was true, he had everything to lose… Staring at him, she smiled; but it was a diffident smile this time: glassy, defensive, because she began to look at him with new eyes…

Sitting in their bedroom by the window, remembering, Agustina hadn't noticed how it had become brighter. Now a ray of light glinted. Gazing through the glass her eye fell upon neither hills nor trees nor fields, but a low, perfectly flat sheet of mist from which here and there rose thin poles with red and yellow triangular markers. A golf course. The window faced a golf course which her son had built but rarely used. It was just another of his follies. This whole place was riddled with his follies. But what could they do? They weren't the ones in control any more. This was the sad truth. Fifteen, even ten years ago it was different. When her husband had his health there was no one who could stand up to him. It was because he was ill, and his strength was all gone, poor soul, that was the only reason their son had been able to get his way. How could they argue against men with guns? Were they to complain to the army? The police? But he was their son, their flesh and blood, and to them at least he was a loving son. Besides, the authorities were feeding from his hand. In this respect Federico was right when he said all these people – the army, the police, the politicians, were the same as he, only worse, because they pretended to be something they weren't.

Thank heavens, anyway, their other children wanted nothing to do with Federico's business. Their second eldest wouldn't leave the US. He was doing well with his IT business, and their daughter, too, was happy in the capital with her children and the restaurant she and her husband owned. And she wanted them to go and live with her – yes, even now when they were so decrepit. Every time they spoke her daughter brought it up, trying to persuade them to go and live with her. But Victoriano didn't want to be so far away from his people. What if something should happen? He said. What if they should have need of him?

It was odd, but after forty-six years together she still couldn't understand why her husband hadn't returned to live with his people. She could understand why he'd left. He told her there had been a dispute with his brother, Rumicuri's father, and that he was curious about the outside world. But it hadn't been his intention to stay. He only wanted to see what the outside world was like. So her husband had gone always with the intention of returning. This is what he had told her.

But he hadn't returned. Not to live. Although in the years before he got rheumatism, before his legs started giving him trouble,

Victoriano had gone to visit his people on several occasions. And these had been times of much anxiety for her – that first time in particular, such was her fear he would decide to stay, such was her fear she wouldn't see him again.

But she did, he came back, and the moment he arrived was one she wouldn't forget. It was like a miracle. After weeks of worrying she had convinced herself of the worst. And she was desolate, without him life didn't seem worth living. Night after night she lay awake, unable to sleep, wondering how she was going to carry on. Then one day, as it was dawning, she heard a rapping on the window. When she got out of bed and drew the curtains he was standing there, his dark and beautiful Indian face peering at her like a child through the glass. And it was like a miracle.

In those early years it was easy to believe it was because of the love they shared (and because of the children too) that he came back from the journeys he made. But as time passed she began to wonder if this was the only reason, for she'd discovered by then just how much he suffered for being apart from his people. He suffered – but secretly, in silence, and when the children were still little not once did he propose they leave everything behind and go and live with his people. Why not? Hadn't he himself told her that for a woman the journey was arduous but not impossible? And hadn't he told her there was no law as such that would forbid her from living among the Arayana? So why, when it still could have been possible, did he not propose it? Had he been firm with her, had he given her an ultimatum, she didn't doubt that she would have consented. Of course it would've been hard. Not only would she have had to exchange everything she knew for a world that was completely alien, in all likelihood she would never again have had the means to escape from it. That especially would've been hard. The irrevocableness would have daunted her. She would have argued, tried to resist, but in the end she would have gone…

But well, it hadn't happened, and in any case it mattered little any more what her husband's reasons might have been for staying. They were old, their living was all behind them; there was nothing to gain in wondering how it might have been had they gone to live with his people. It was here, in her world they'd made their home and were it not for Federico she would have little reason to complain of the way it had turned out. Federico was her biggest burden, her biggest sorrow. And she felt responsible, she suffered wondering where she'd gone wrong, how she could have failed to teach him a proper regard for the value of human life. In this respect she dissented from her husband. Once, Victoriano had told her that the only people he could trust were his own or someone such as her who had become his own. Everyone else was the enemy. He told her that the Arayana name for the white man was purini, which meant barbarian. This word had originally been given to the Spaniards who had done so much to destroy the Arayana civilisation; but that in reality very little had changed from those distant times. Now there were cars and mobile phones and TV, computers, DNA, rockets going into space, but the people in her world were no less barbarian for that, Victoriano had always insisted. What did she think would happen were his people discovered and found to possess gold and precious stones or have oil under their earth? Would they be respected? No. At worst they would be exterminated, at best they would be cheated and exploited; they would be culturally destroyed, sold into poverty and destitution. And he was to trust such people? He was to call them *brothers*?

When her husband told her these things she could see it was true. But it was true only so long as she looked at it through his eyes. When she looked at it through her own eyes, from her own perspective, it became less true. She could identify with her husband, but not his culture. The only culture she could identify with was the only one she had known, which was her own, and the people in that culture didn't seem to her barbarians.

Of course there was evil. The potential for evil existed everywhere (Were his people so very different? Were they not human?) But because it existed, was she to think her parents, who'd always taught her to be honest and hard-working, were evil? And what of all the other people she knew? Friends, relations, shopkeepers, trades people, doctors, scientists, her colleagues when she was teaching, were all these people evil? No, they were ordinary. Neither entirely good nor entirely bad, just well-meaning ordinary people trying to do the best with what life had given them. No, not then, and not now could she share her husband's hatred of her culture or the modern world.

Her husband was a wonderful man; she could search the world and find no better, but as much as she loved him there were times when she wondered if Federico would have turned out differently had her husband shown greater regard for her modern culture. Federico had always been the wildest of her children, and perhaps for this very reason he needed, more than the others, a strong moral guidance. But her husband hadn't given him one. She wasn't blaming him; she knew it wasn't intentional, yet the truth was that her husband gave the impression of being a man who was ruthless, who cared only for power and wealth and didn't give a fig for anyone outside his family. And really, the worst of it was that their children had no knowledge of Victoriano's true origin. She'd always wanted to tell the children so that they would grow up proud of their father, proud of who they were, but from the beginning her husband had insisted it would be much too dangerous. More than to his children, he said, he had a duty to protect his people – and so they had grown up without knowing, they had grown up with more or less the story he'd first told her: an impoverished Indian from a remote jungle region who'd made his fortune prospecting…

Sometimes Agustina couldn't help thinking Federico would have turned out differently had he known the truth, because he would have seen his father in a different light, he would have seen that his father was a man of real principles. But it hadn't happened, and now it was too late because Federico was already formed and to her grief – loving and generous son though he was – he was like a distorted, exaggerated mirror image of all that appeared to be hard and self-centred in her husband…

Sitting by the window, watching the sun rise over the golf course – the mist on the ground dispersing, floating up like thin clusters of cotton wool – Agustina thought how sadly ironic it was that her eldest son should have turned out to be an embodiment of the very things her husband most loathed and despised about her modern culture.

It was on the second day after his arrival that Rumicuri met his cousin. Rumicuri didn't want to meet him. Concern for his own safety as well as that of his people far outweighed whatever curiosity he may have felt. But his uncle had explained that no one could arrive here without Federico being informed. Federico already knew of his and Mountain Trotter's arrival, he had been asking questions, so his uncle had invented a story.

Victoriano told his son that long ago, when he was a young man in charge of a prospecting operation in unexplored jungle his party had been attacked by a tribe of savages. Rumicuri's father, one of the porters in his employ, had saved his life. The man was long dead but Victoriano had never forgotten the debt he owed him. Then, some weeks ago, the village where Rumicuri lived had been taken over by the army. The soldiers were misbehaving and the villagers were frightened. Rumicuri was a simple Indian who couldn't even speak Spanish, but he knew of the debt Victoriano owed his father, and having nowhere else to turn he had come to seek Victoriano's help…

Federico had been amused by his father's story. Although he could respect its appeal to sentiments of loyalty and honour they had nonetheless seemed to him quixotic, quaintly out of step with the ruthless brutality of his own environment. But at another level – precisely because of the respect he had for loyalty and honour – it had made him feel vaguely inadequate, and because he didn't want to feel inadequate next to this father (a person who in any case he loved and in his present enfeeblement required pampering) he at once volunteered to take charge of everything.

As for Victoriano he had in fact hoped such would be the outcome, for as he explained to Rumicuri, his own influence had become so diminished that it had ceased to count, whereas his son's had grown so much he was now the most powerful man in the region. However, the manner by which his son had gained this power went against the law of the purinis. To protect himself, therefore, his son had resorted to violence. This was why there were guards with firearms. His son was under constant threat from powerful forces which came from many parts of the purini world, but here in his own territory, he ruled like a monarch, almost like Rumicuri himself ruled among his own people. Rumicuri should remember this when dealing with him. For a few days he would do well to forget he was the sovereign. His son had become reckless with so much power but he wasn't stupid. Rumicuri mustn't arouse his suspicions. At all times he must appear servile. When they were introduced it would be a good idea if he kissed his son's hand. It used to be a lot more common in the old days but it was something that might on rare occasions still occur out here in the wilds when a lowly peasant Indian met a powerful benefactor. Such an act would amuse and flatter his son. So long as his son was well-disposed towards him and there was nothing to arouse his suspicions he would do much to help. Victoriano would see to this…

Rumicuri listened to his uncle with a slight frown. Whatever was asked he would try to do, but how was he to go about pretending to be a low caste Indian? He was worried he wouldn't be able to deceive his cousin. Mountain Trotter, who was also present, had no such fear. He was by nature a self-effacing man, who besides had rather more practice than the sovereign in presenting himself as a cap-in-hand peasant.

Thus, when the moment came and Federico entered his father's study (a room of heavy furniture and leather and shelves of books) what he saw was an old Indian who stood scrunching a straw hat in both hands, his face screwed into an anxious, servile frown; and standing beside him a younger Indian (Rumicuri had decided to imitate Mountain Trotter) who was oddly contorted, hunched over like a monkey, and his face twisted into a strange grimace.

Federico – smelling of cologne, dressed in lightweight, cream-coloured trousers and a tropical short-sleeved shirt – didn't know what to make of the younger Indian. Was he taking the mickey? But Federico, fortunately, had too high an opinion of himself to entertain this thought for long; he decided instead the younger Indian was probably scared.

After quickly kissing his parents, both of whom were seated, Federico straightened up and said, 'So this is the son of the man who saved your life, eh papa… Complete with interpreter… Or is it bodyguard?' He laughed at his own joke. 'We'll, aren't you the one who can speak Spanish?' he addressed Mountain Trotter. 'What's your name?'

'Miguel master, at your command,' said Mountain Trotter, giving his Spanish name; then, scuttling forward, stooping low, he swiftly grabbed Federico's hand and kissed it.

Federico was surprised. Lovers had kissed his hand, and once an old woman, pleading for her son; but it still surprised him. Like I'm a bishop, he thought, his short, sturdy body swelling imperceptibly. 'And him?' He looked at Rumicuri. 'What's his name?'

Because Federico was staring at him, Rumicuri guessed his cousin's interest. Deciding to emulate Mountain Trotter he also plunged forward, stumbling in his nervousness, almost colliding against Federico before clumsily grasping his hand.

Federico was amused. His golden-green eyes (inherited from his mother) crinkled. 'Well Miguel,' he said to Mountain Trotter, 'since you're the one who can speak Spanish you'd better tell me how I can help.'

Mountain Trotter began recounting events, limiting himself only to the situation in his village, and leaving out all reference to Rumicuri's people. While he was still talking Federico moved to sit down in a leather upholstered chair. Mountain Trotter faltered; Federico gestured for him to carry on.

Standing next to Mountain Trotter, Rumicuri watched his cousin remove a square shaped object from his clothes. He opened the object and removed a narrow white thing which he placed between his lips. Next he brought out another, smaller, square shaped object which seemed to be made of gold. Then he did something, a sort of flick with his fingers, and a flame spouted from the gold object! Then he lit the thing between his lips and blew a thin stream of smoke out of his mouth and nostrils.

A small block of gold able to spout fire at will. Rumicuri had to marvel at the ceaseless ingenuity of the purinis. Everywhere he turned he discovered new, amazing artefacts of theirs. And he could appreciate how many of these artefacts were of benefit to the purinis; but only the purinis and maybe not all of them at that. What of the low caste purinis he'd seen in the settlement, all crowded together in flimsy, wretched dwellings, the ground stinking of shit, littered with abandoned things?

Mountain Trotter had finished speaking. Federico flicked ash into a tray and began asking questions, his glance occasionally straying inquiringly towards Rumicuri, who immediately looked away, afraid his cousin would think him impertinent or that he might do something to arouse his suspicions. His cousin had been an infant when he had first visited his uncle as a child, so he didn't fear being remembered; nevertheless, they shared the same blood and he was worried that any little thing might make his cousin aware, if not of the similarity between them, then of his similarity to his uncle.

Federico, Rumicuri observed, had his mother's pale complexion, and his hair was wavy, like hers had been before it turned white. He didn't much resemble his father, but Rumicuri knew there were some features of his own which were almost identical to his uncle; features his uncle's great age hadn't managed to erode, such as his sharp bony nose, the square jaw, the large earlobes...

As it happened, though, he was worrying without cause because Federico himself had four illegitimate children that he knew of (all from different women) and God knows how many he didn't. So even had he noticed a resemblance – and he hadn't yet – it wouldn't have bothered him unduly. More than likely he would have assumed that his father, for his own reasons, had lied to him, and the Indian was the result of an illicit liaison.

There was not a great deal Mountain Trotter could tell Federico. He didn't know from what regiment the soldiers came or the name of the officer in charge, or the precise number of soldiers stationed at the village. He'd heard that the soldiers were looking for guerrillas, the Radiant War, but he couldn't be certain as he (and Rumicuri) had escaped without speaking to any of the soldiers…

Pondering, Federico decided that if the army took over a jungle village in this region it could mean one of two things: They were looking for cocaine or they were looking for the Radiant War. He was nearly certain it wasn't cocaine since it was his business to be informed of any such developments. That left the Radiant War; so he would talk to both the army and the Radiant War and both would tell him what he wanted to know – because both took his money: the guerrillas to buy weapons and the army officers to fatten their bank accounts – and in this way he would not only do the Indians the favour they wanted, he would also acquire new and very possibly useful information.

'I'll have to make calls, papa,' he addressed his father. Then to the Indians: 'Maybe tomorrow or in a few days I'll have the information. Then we'll see…' He stood up.

'God pay you, master,' Mountain Trotter thanked him.

Federico started to leave but before he reached the door he turned, saying to his parents: 'I bet these people haven't seen an elephant.'

'What do you want to give the poor souls a fright for?' said Agustina. 'Let them be.'

But the elephant was a new acquisition. It had been shipped from Russia at great expense. He had spent two hundred thousand dollars on bribes alone. He was eager to show it off. He thought it would be amusing to watch their reaction.

'Tell me, hombre, d'you know what an elephant is?' he asked Mountain Trotter.

Mountain Trotter hadn't heard the word before. He had no idea what Federico was talking about. 'No, master. I don't know.'

'Come with me. Both of you. I'll show you.'

'He wants to show us something,' Mountain Trotter mumbled to Rumicuri.

Rumicuri glanced at his uncle, who gave a slight nod. The men followed Federico out of the study. On the metalled driveway outside the house stood a gleaming 1959 red convertible Ford Thunderbird. It was one of Federico's collection of classic cars. Opening the door, he thought it a pity the Indians were too ignorant to appreciate it.

Rumicuri climbed into the rear next to Mountain Trotter and sat down uneasily on the shiny white seat. Although he knew enough now to fear no harm from these particular metal animals he still couldn't make himself trust them.

Federico donned a pair of tinted Raybans. A moment later the engine started with what to him was a low, deep, satisfying purr. Under a blue sky and with the hood down, the Thunderbird glided smoothly along a straight road. Rumicuri stiffened against the breeze that blew about his head. In spite of himself he was excited. He thought it must be like flying the way the landscape on either side of him rushed backwards as they moved forward at a speed that seemed unbelievable.

The landscape to one side of the road, the left side, was little changed from when Rumicuri had come the first time. It was almost a flat terrain, green with pasture, and where here and there herds of cattle could be seen grazing, for it was by rearing cattle that Victoriano had established himself in the purini world.

Cattle rearing was an activity still pursued on the estate, but no longer by Victoriano and not really as a business either. To Federico personally it mattered little whether the cattle operation made money or not; he continued it out of indolence, to placate his parents, and because it was as good a front as any. His real enterprise was not visible from this part of the estate and in fact on the outside it consisted of little more than a discrete bungalow located behind the golf course. The wealth the laboratory in this bungalow could generate, however, was astounding. In less than eight years Federico had catapulted from being the son of a wealthy cattle rancher into a dollar multi-millionaire, and the evidence of such profligate wealth was visible along the right side of the road. What had been grazing land was now landscaped into the golf course, a small artificial lake, fields where grazed thoroughbred horses, and then turning right, they drove through a park with a fountain and a Chinese pagoda until they reached a high white wall with an archway entrance. Beyond the entrance the road forked. A few hundred yards to the left stood a large, modern, terracotta ranch house. This was Federico's own home. It was here he conducted business and entertained girls, but it was the road to the right the car took. After a quarter of a mile they stopped in front of a low white building. Federico got out and with jocular courtesy opened the door for his passengers. Rumicuri emerged light-headed from the journey.

The zoo was the newest of Federico's fancies. It was still in the process of construction and so far the only animal he had acquired was the elephant. But even before he got the elephant he'd built the entrance complete with turnstile because the zoo he had visited in Germany had a turnstile and he wanted everything to look authentic.

After Federico passed through the turnstile he turned to wait for the Indians. Mountain Trotter, who was in front, had seen how Federico had pushed through it, but when Rumicuri came to the bar he stopped, not knowing what to do. He merely stood there and when nothing happened he reached out and tentatively tried to pull the bar. Mountain Trotter returned and told him to push, not pull, but when Rumicuri did so it was too hard and the bars came zipping around. Muttering to each other they fumbled with the turnstile. Federico, watching, grinned with broad amusement.

When finally Rumicuri managed to get through, Federico led them past some building work that was going on. A dozen workers were digging ditches and erecting a wall. They worked by hand, without machinery, because the vet had said the elephant should be disturbed as little as possible after its journey. Rumicuri avoided looking at the workmen.

After walking some distance down a path they came to large, high-fenced enclosure, and that was when Rumicuri felt his heart give a violent thump.

He couldn't believe what he was seeing. Like Mountain Trotter he stood rooted, staring uncomprehendingly at this huge apparition that looked a bit like a strange, giant tapir but in reality was like nothing he had ever seen.

'It's an elephant,' Federico said boastfully, delighted by their expressions of utter incredulity.

The elephant, which stood about twenty yards away, had meanwhile raised its head and was staring at them intently. It was a young female African elephant, not fully grown, but for Rumicuri and Mountain Trotter, huge beyond comprehension. And its snout! Its teeth! Staring at it Rumicuri had to wonder if it was real – a sentient creature like the ones in his own world? Or was it just another of the purinis' creations? And if it was real, where did it come from? How had it got here?

While Rumicuri was pondering, Federico went up to the fence where stood a bucket of ripe bananas. He picked up a banana and pushed it through the steel mesh of the fence. But although the elephant eyed the banana it appeared reluctant to come forward. Only a few days ago it had been one of three other elephants in a Russian zoo. It had been drugged, loaded onto a Russian cargo plane, and flown across the world, arriving some thirty hours later at the airstrip on the estate. Now it was alone in a new and bewildering environment, so it stood eyeing the banana for some moments before it was tempted to come forward.

In fascination Rumicuri watched its ponderous advance. When the elephant reached the fence it stopped, lifted its trunk, seized hold of the banana, and put it in its mouth. He hadn't seen a creature feeding in this odd way before. As he stood watching, his attention was drawn to the elephant's eyes. He thought he saw something familiar in their expression, a sort of bewildered melancholy, and at that moment he knew it couldn't be a mere creation of the purinis. He was now sure it was a living creature – a creature that must have come from some distant land. And in realising this, his wonder was joined by a feeling of sadness, of compassion for the lonely fate of this giant and, he thought, noble creature.

Federico had no such thoughts. Happily he fed the elephant banana after banana, proudly conscious of being the owner of the only elephant in the entire country. And this was just the beginning. Soon he'd have a zoo to rival any in the US. He'd have the largest animals and also the fiercest: crocodiles, tigers, lions, bears, sharks… all the great animals of the world!

It was while Federico was feeding the elephant that two men came up to him. One of the men was wearing a green cotton suit.

He was short and stocky and sported a thin moustache. The second man wore jeans and tee-shirt. A handgun was exposed in a holster on his hip. He was a big man, over six foot, and because he was of Scandinavian extraction he had pale blue eyes and blond white hair.

For the second time that day Rumicuri got a jolt. It wasn't such a jolt as when he had laid eyes on the elephant, but nevertheless: *a white man.* And one so close, so large…

While Rumicuri and Mountain Trotter stood there, their gazes alternating between the elephant and the men, Federico was listening to what they were telling him. Forty kilos of processed cocaine had vanished in Canada. Forty kilos was a lot even here. In Canada it was a fortune. A cock-up? The cops? Treachery? Was it treachery? Federico hoped it wasn't treachery. He liked Carlos. The man had charm… but shit, it was the cunt's job to be *responsible.* Thinking about Carlos, Federico's handsome but already somewhat flaccid face became set and pale.

Federico had done some brutal things in his time. He recognized that the violence had been excessive. And it bothered him; he was ashamed of some of the things he'd done, because he considered himself to be a man of genuine feelings. He loved his parents. Music of a sweet and melancholy kind could bring tears to his eyes. He wasn't afraid of being soft. He was generous. He'd given away hundreds of thousands of dollars to deserving causes. In the town of Calderon alone he'd built a hospital and an entire block of flats to house the dispossessed. No one could accuse him of not having a heart.

But at other times, if he felt he'd been wronged, if his anger was justified, he experienced no remorse at all. People were corrupt. Nature brutal. He didn't hide the shit under any fancy moral facade. If anyone betrayed him they had to pay. Betrayal, even a small betrayal, was the one thing he couldn't tolerate. No one who betrayed him got away with it. *No one.* Once, some years ago at one of his parties, when a man he suspected of treachery had started making passes at his then girlfriend, Federico had gone and got his forty-five and shot the cunt at point blank range, exploding his head like a watermelon…

Federico didn't say a word after the men had finished speaking. All he could think of was getting to a telephone. He truly hoped Carlos hadn't betrayed him.

Federico dropped the banana he was holding and set off at a rapid pace. Going up the path, the two men close behind, he didn't give the Indians a second thought. He'd forgotten all about the Indians.

After he had gone Rumicuri and Mountain Trotter were at a loss, they didn't know what to do. Bewildered by his abrupt departure, they conferred, Mountain Trotter suggesting they remain where they were in case Federico should soon return. While waiting they went back to gazing at the elephant. Rumicuri asked questions but Mountain Trotter was unable to answer them because he knew no more than the sovereign about the origin of this majestic creature.

Half an hour passed, then an hour and still there was no sign of Federico. Finally, after they had been standing there for almost two hours, Mountain Trotter came to the opinion that Federico wasn't going to return at all.

'So what shall we do?' Rumicuri asked.

'If we follow the path of the metal animal we can get back to your uncle, highness.'

Rumicuri agreed. Leaving the elephant they set off, past the building work (keeping their heads low, not looking at the workmen) then through the turnstile. After the turnstile they looked for Federico's car but it wasn't there. More certain now that he wasn't going to return they began following the asphalted road with their steady, half-walking, half-trotting gait.

Outside it was hot and sunny, but Victoriano, perhaps intentionally, as though the things he had to say were so dangerous they required physical confinement, had had the curtains drawn. Inside the study he sat, as usual, in a straight-back chair, wearing a suit and tie, his neck sticking out of his white shirt like a frail twig and his face mummified against the pain of the cancer that was rotting his insides.

Pushed up against his chair was another empty one and after Agustina had left the room, closing the door behind her, Victoriano asked his nephew to sit beside him. Once the two of them were alone in the book-lined study, Victoriano began speaking in his frail, quivering voice, telling Rumicuri the things that Federico had managed to discover.

It appeared the Radiant War was located in deep jungle, a good three days march from Mountain Trotter's village. The guerillas had suffered setbacks. They were short of people and arms. There were internal rifts. And for these reasons it appeared they were in no position to advance against the army. The short of it was that the Radiant War was in retreat. In all likelihood they would head back to their stronghold, a region some distance away, so there was little chance of conflict in the vicinity of Mountain Trotter's village, and really no chance of any conflict at all in the area bordering the high kingdom.

As for the soldiers in Mountain Trotter's village, Federico had spoken to their commander and had been told they would be leaving the area soon. He had also received a firm assurance that any soldier committing an abuse against the villagers would be severely punished. Any villager who had escaped was free to return with complete peace of mind. There would be no abuses and no retributions of any kind.

Listening to his uncle, Rumicuri's face remained impassive but his heart brimmed. For a moment he was far away, anticipating the happy expressions of his people when he told them they were safe.

But then his uncle began speaking again: 'This is good news for our people, yet I fear it may only be a reprieve.'

And when Rumicuri looked at him: 'My soul wants to leave, highness. It won't be long now before I must follow; so it's fortunate you're here. It may even be you've come for a reason that isn't the one you believe.'

Rumicuri waited, perplexed. Victoriano remained silent, as though gathering strength. When he started speaking again he didn't explain himself directly. He started talking about raider ants. Rumicuri knew what these ants looked like, he had often seen the large, fierce ants attacking other nests, but he knew little else. So when his uncle started explaining about the life of raider ants he listened in quiet wonder.

Raider ants were not like other ants, Victoriano said. They were astonishingly clever. When raider ants located the nests of other ants – ants of a different 'race' – they would fight their way into the nest's deepest chamber. They would then steal the eggs and carry them back to their own nest. When the eggs hatched the raider ants would bite the newborn ants in such a way as to infect them with a substance from their own bodies. This substance changed the newborn ants. It made them 'think' they were the same as raider ants.

But they weren't the same. They were a different type, a different race of ant. Although they thought they were raider ants they behaved like the ants from the nest they had originally come from. They went out and spent all their time collecting food which they brought back for the raider ants to enjoy. The raider ants stayed in their nest and lived a life of indolence. They did no work at all. All the work was done by the other ants, who toiled ceaselessly to feed, groom, and look after the raider ants. The other ants had been utterly duped because all the while they laboured under the impression they were raider ants...

Listening to his uncle, Rumicuri wondered how he had come to know so much about the nature of ants. Victoriano, guessing, lifted his hand and indicated the rows of books. All the knowledge of the purinis was contained in these things they called books, he told Rumicuri. Nowdays the purinis had something even more fantastic and incredible which they called the internet, and which was gradually taking the place of books. One day soon books might be a thing of the past, Victoriano said; but until now the purinis had kept all their knowledge in these things called books and for many years Victoriano had been studying their books. His studies showed the purinis, and the white race in particular, to have been the original raider ants. It was now many, many generations since the first purinis, the ones they called Spaniards, had first come from across the great waters. Much had changed since those distant times, but some things hadn't changed. One thing that hadn't changed was their insatiable hunger. The purinis were like a gourd with a leak. No matter how much water you poured in the gourd was never full. When the white men first came from across the great waters it was in search of gold. But no matter how much gold the Indians gave them they weren't content. And when the white men could have no more gold they became hungry for Indian land, for Indian women, for the very souls of the Indians...

Victoriano told Rumicuri he could not imagine just how plentiful and rich and powerful were the white people in their own lands. The white people had long ago discovered that the world was round (Rumicuri had heard this from his uncle before, as a child) and that it was covered by vast lands separated from each other by the great waters. And the different lands in this world were populated by different races. There were five races as defined by colour: black, white, brown, red, and yellow. The white race hadn't always been dominant. And now in some parts of the world the other races were also becoming very strong. But if any of the races could be described as the true raider ants it had to be the white race. From even before the time of the Spaniards the white race had conspired to rule over the other races, and since those times the other races had toiled ceaselessly for the benefit of the white race under the illusion they were raider ants.

Victoriano told Rumicuri the white race had duped the other races by infecting them with their insatiable hunger. Once the other races became hungry everything else became secondary in their obsession to possess all the artefacts and creations the white people had discovered how to fabricate, and continued all the time to fabricate.

But it wasn't exactly as with raider ants. Ants were ants and human beings were human beings. So while it was impossible for a slave ant to become a raider ant, this wasn't the case among humans. Large numbers of people from the other races had succeeded in transforming themselves into genuine raider ants. And in one case, the yellow race, this was becoming true of their entirety. The yellow race was clever and disciplined and they made formidable raider ants.

In this land of their ancestors, as in some other parts of the world, the situation was again different, for the seed of the different races had mingled and created new races. Here, among the purinis, the seed of the Spaniards had long ago fertilized Indian women and created a race of mixed blood. And this mestizo race now largely dominated the original Indian race. But whether of pure seed or mixed, all had succumbed to the white man's hunger. And what was the nature of this hunger? It was for wealth, for riches, because he who was rich in the purini world had *power*. And when a purini had power he became the ruler of other purinis. He became a raider ant.

Victoriano told Rumicuri that in the world of the purinis the desire for power was so all-consuming it made people blind to the living nature of the Mother Earth. For most purinis the earth was no more than a corpse to be plundered. They saw not the injuries they inflicted. They heard not her fearful cries. It could be that in generations to come such would be the injuries inflicted on the Mother Earth that the world itself would die. Then it wouldn't matter if you were a raider ant or a slave ant, a white man, or of mixed race, because it would be the end of everything. It was possible that this world the purinis had created would bring about its own total destruction. This was possible.

On the other hand there was no denying the cleverness of the purinis. And not everything the white race created was harmful. Some of the things they had created were of benefit to people everywhere and even to the Mother Earth. And among the purinis, no matter what their race, there were some more aware than others of the living nature of the Mother Earth. In recent times a change was taking place among the purinis, and even some of the most powerful raider ants among them were coming to see that by inflicting such injuries on the Mother Earth they were courting their own destruction.

But whether the fate of the Mother Earth depended on human beings or not (because no one could know these things for sure) and whether world was finally saved or finally destroyed, one thing was for certain: the world belonged to the purinis. And wherever they lived it was the rich and powerful who ruled among them.

'Listen to me highness.' Leaning over, Victoriano placed a hand, brittle and scaly as a bird's claw, on his nephew's forearm. Rumicuri raised his eyes and for an instant he had the impression that his uncle had shed his years, had become young again such was the passion that now burned through his ravaged countenance.

'Listen to me, highness. In my heart I fear there is little time for our people. Every day that passes, the purinis multiply. Every day that passes, they tear down the forest, build new pathways, erect settlements of one kind or another. One day they will stumble on our people, and if our people aren't prepared they'll be destroyed. This is the reason you're here. I have a feeling that all my years of living among the purinis have been a preparation for this moment.

'When you came the first time you were too young to understand the things I had to tell you. But now my end is near and you've become the sovereign of the Arayana, fate has brought us together. Although I only see it clearly now, this must be the reason I've stayed among the purinis all this long time. It was destined; the reason you're here now: So that my knowledge won't be lost.

'I know you hate this world you see around you, highness. I hate it less because I understand it better, but do you think I wouldn't have preferred to live among my people? I could've returned, even with Agustina, but in the end I stayed here. I stayed because after much bitterness and anger I came to understand that there is no choice. Do you listen, highness? *No choice.*

'Today or tomorrow our people must learn to live in a changing world. Today or tomorrow the Arayana must succumb to the purini's insatiable hunger. For our people there are three fates, and only three: they perish, they become slave ants, or they become raider ants. Which would you have them choose? I became a raider ant because it is the raider ants who endure. The clever among the purinis know this. They know it in their blood. This is why their nations are strong. This is why their nations survive.

'Don't be fooled. The world will never again be as it was in days gone by. You must prepare our people for change. Consult with the elders. If they won't listen, set yourself against them, do whatever you must but make sure our people are prepared.

'This young man who belongs to the Radiant War, get him to start teaching our people the purini language. Or send some of our own to Mountain Trotter's village so they can start learning. Above all make sure that when the purinis arrive – and one day *they will* arrive – our people are wise to their cunning. Our people must learn to meet guile with guile. They must become better purinis than the purinis themselves. This is what I've done and I'm still Arayana. If we become clever it may be that we can fight them with their own knowledge. In this way we might live among them and yet remain Arayana, true to our traditions. This may be, but we must start preparing ourselves. If we don't it will soon be too late...'

When Victoriano had finished speaking, Rumicuri remained silent, wondering at the mind of this dying man who for so long had lived in the outside world.

'I have listened, uncle,' he said, finally.

Victoriano nodded. After some moments his eyelids drooped and his head slumped. Rumicuri was beginning to think he had fallen asleep when his head jerked up.

'Your father and I weren't good brothers,' he said, unexpectedly. 'We quarrelled as children and we quarrelled as men.' The loose, wrinkled skin around Victoriano's mouth folded back in a brief, and, to Rumicuri's puzzlement, ambiguous, even bitter smile. 'But well, if your father were here, listening to the things I've told you, he would know that my only desire is for our people to endure. I may have married a purini woman and fathered purini children but I am Arayana, I will always be Arayana. I can't be anything else...'

Suddenly Rumicuri recalled his father: Tall, loose-limbed, the big nose and a lopsided smile that was both sly and haughty. Fastidious when it came to organizing games, festivities, ceremonies... but moody and soon bored with more mundane chores. A vain, temperamental man, but one who was also physically brave. Even now, years after his death, people talked admiringly of the occasion when he'd rescued Casupu.

It had happened when the bridge across the gorge was being repaired. Casupu lost his balance and fell into the gorge. By good fortune he was halted by the vegetation clinging to the sides, but he was unconscious and there was no apparent way of rescuing him. Then his father, who'd been overseeing the work, tied a rope around his waist and told some men to lower him over the side. Witnesses said he clambered like a monkey down the sheer side of the gorge. When he reached the unconscious man he tied the rope around him and got the men to haul him up. His father climbed up behind him, helping his ascent, on one occasion coming unstuck and holding on by the bare tips of his fingers.

It was a brave feat, and it wasn't the only time he had risked his life in such a manner. Many stories were told of his father's valour, as well as his spontaneous acts of generosity and compassion. But just as numerous were the much less flattering accounts related to his incorrigible philandering and his impatience with people's problems.

Rumicuri's own feelings towards his father were no less conflicting. He could remember the many occasions in his childhood when his father had done something to make him glow with admiration. But also he could recall his resentment, sometimes even hatred, when he saw how his father mistreated mother. Or there was that time when he'd spied his father with his robe high up his back, his naked arse bouncing up and down as he lay in a cornfield fornicating with a young girl barely out of puberty. Or yet other occasions when he was dead-eyed with mishqui and coca, so intoxicated he could barely walk, and when he would completely neglect his obligations and would repel with curses anyone who approached him.

It was in fact mother who, especially in later years, had taken charge of all the day to day duties his father neglected. And it was his mother, not his father, whose resilience, strength of character, and kindness Rumicuri remembered and tried to measure up to in his duty to the people. His mother had been a small woman, with bones so delicate they were like a child's, but she'd had the energy of three. Rumicuri wondered if there was any truth to the rumour that his uncle had been secretly in love with her? Some went so far as to claim it was for this reason his uncle had left the kingdom. Rumicuri himself doubted it. He knew how people liked to gossip and make up reasons for things they couldn't understand. But what was true was that his parents hadn't had a happy marriage. His father had spoiled mother's life. And he could remember how mother, when she was old, had once told him that she was glad his father had taken other wives and mistresses because it had kept him out of her way.

Remembering his parents, thinking of all that they had gone through, Rumicuri found himself reflecting on the vanity of life. The fuss and fury of it. The tangle of dreams and desires and longings. The restless search for something intangible – permanence perhaps? – and then in a moment it was all taken from you. What remained now of his parents? Of his sister who had died in childbirth? Of his brothers? For two of them had also died; one in his childhood, the other in his prime, three days before he was to marry, from a serpent's bite. And what would remain of his uncle when he too passed away? Their lives were so transient, like fireflies in the night. And if it was thus for humans, could it not be the same for their beliefs, their culture? His uncle had said they must learn to think like the purinis, but once they started thinking like the purinis what would become of the knowledge that had come from their forefathers? How much would be lost? Where would the corruption end?

As though guessing his thoughts, Victoriano leaned forward and once again placed his hand on his nephew's arm. 'Listen to me, highness,' he said. 'Listen carefully. With my dying breath I tell you this: prepare for when the purinis come among you. Our people must become raider ants. We do this or we perish.'

PART THREE

ILLANI was quickly tiring of her conquest. She hadn't expected Calchas to cave in so easily. After all he was a stranger, from a world she didn't know, and when he had first approached her he had come across as a young man confident to the point of arrogance.

In the beginning it had given her a thrill. Flesh against flesh, the touch of a man, the first man she'd had since her husband had abandoned her.

Rumicuri hadn't understood her need as a woman. He'd grunted and rutted like an animal. Always with him she'd had the impression it was something he wanted to get over with quickly. He entered her but he wouldn't stay, he wasn't immersed in her when they made love. She had wanted to make him happy, as much as she had wanted to be made happy, but always he was stubborn, he wouldn't let go, all he seemed to care about was his duties and responsibilities...

Was that why he'd gone back to Cascarina? She made no demands on him probably; she lay with her fat legs wide open while he rutted like an animal, and she rolled her eyes and thought it was the best thing that could happen... Stupid woman.

The lowlander wasn't stubborn the way her husband was. He was willing, all too willing... They'd been lovers a scarce few weeks and already she was getting bored. It wasn't turning out the way she had hoped. She knew what she wanted. A man who would assert himself, who would release her from the anger and bitterness she felt. Her husband had hurt her. What better retaliation than a lover who could satisfy her in ways her husband had failed? The best revenge was one that no longer made it necessary. To be able to look at Rumicuri with indifference – if not contempt – her pride restored, happy in her womanhood, that was true revenge.

Only the lowlander hadn't come up to her expectations. He'd called at her door and she had opened it and had let him enter. She had thought he would show mettle, that he would add something of his own to their understanding besides a permanent rutting. But instead he'd crumbled right from the start. He'd succumbed to her world of seduction and sorcery without understanding the real nature of the trap, without knowing that if he was to be conquered and enslaved, he must likewise and conquer and enslave. Only then could he lay claim to her best guarded, most vulnerable possession; a heart which, for the right man, could be loving and tender.

But he had failed. Taking possession of his spirit had been a simple matter; now he hung around her abjectly, grateful for any little attention, even if it was abuse, so that the only pleasure she had left was in seeing how far she could humiliate and degrade him.

And so this is what she did, this night, when Calchas came to see her. Unlike on other occasions, he didn't want to drink the drugged mishqui, but she found ways to make him do it, half cajoling, half enticing him, but in any event letting him know that if he didn't drink what she gave him then he could do without her. So fool that he was he drank it, and afterwards she made him sit naked on the floor while she herself reclined languorously on the bed. Then, to arouse him, she began playing with herself. She allowed her smock to slip back to her thighs and placing a hand in between her legs she stroked herself, not quite allowing Calchas to see what she was doing, but sighing a little, moving her hips a little, until he couldn't control himself and rising from the floor he tried to approach the bed. At that very moment, however, she turned to face him, making a hissing sound, and he at once jumped back in fear because what he saw were bared fangs, long whiskers, eyes that were phosphorescent yellow.

While he stood irresolutely, Illani, appearing quite normal again, ordered him to get down on his hands and knees. Calchas didn't refuse. Because he was afraid, but as well because having lost his pride, having come so completely under her power he now discovered a perverse pleasure in being debased. Once on his hands and knees she ordered him to crawl towards her and as he was crawling she gave a cruel laugh.

When he reached the edge of the bed she dropped one leg over the side and in pitiful gratitude, violently aroused, he seized her foot and began kissing it. For a little she allowed him to kiss her foot, but when he moved up her leg she reached down and grabbed his hair. She forced his head back, pulling hard until she saw his eyes glaze. She liked that. She enjoyed seeing the pain in his eyes. She enjoyed the complete power she had over him.

Calchas wasn't allowed to penetrate her on this occasion. As a final humiliation she sat on his face; not lightly, but roughly, grinding her posterior into his face. And at some moments she was a woman but at others his face was buried under the tail and hind legs of a jaguar. When she climaxed he heard a ferocious shrieking growl and then a paw slashed across him. He hardly felt the slash but when he was sitting up he saw a gash across his chest. Blood spouted. In terror he threw himself off the bed and scrambled backwards under the intent, watchful gaze of the crouched jaguar. However, when he next looked at himself he was perfectly normal and it was only Illani who was sitting on the bed watching him with contempt.

Squatting on the floor Calchas felt hatred towards her. He wanted to make her suffer. He wanted to smash her face in. Yet at the same time, mingled with this hatred was a still more powerful yearning for her. He couldn't help himself. Just one word, one kind word and he would rush into her arms…

But the kind word didn't come. Instead Illani snapped, 'What are you waiting for? Go on, get out!'

Calchas was desperate. He didn't want to leave. He felt an anguished need to be near her. He wanted to know when he could see her again, but afraid lest she tell him that he couldn't, he reluctantly fumbled for his clothes. Once dressed he still couldn't bring himself to leave. He hung back staring at her like a whipped dog.

'Get out! Out!' Illani shrieked.

Calchas slunk away finally, and once alone Illani lay on her bed, one arm flung over her eyes. Men were fools, such fools!

There was no light in the sky when Calchas set off for the gathering house where he was lodging with the other refugees. On previous occasions, after leaving Illani, his emotional turbulence had been such that he hadn't notice the night sky. He had taken the light of the moon and stars for granted. But on this occasion it was so dark he began stumbling straight away and so for the first time in many days he noticed the change in the sky. Looking up for a glimmer of light all he could see was a dense blackness. If there were no stars or moon it could only mean the sky had clouded over. Briefly he wondered if it was going to rain, but the long drought which had assailed the high kingdom was no real concern of his. More than any drought he worried as to how he was going to find his way back to the gathering house.

For some moments he stumbled blindly, then he collided against a tree. He felt his way forward, dazed from the blow, soon tripping, falling into a bush. Increasingly distraught he got up, searching for a way out, but the vegetation had closed all around him and completely disorientated he thrashed this way and that, the hard thorny bushes tearing his clothes and scratching his skin.

But he didn't stop. A frenzy had seized hold of him. Still under the intermittent effect of the drugged mishqui, he lunged at the bushes that weren't bushes so much as the vague outlines of ghosts, the weird shapes of spirits that were neither human nor animal nor vegetable but a disembodied, jumbled mixture of all three.

Leaves with human faces in them, birds with legs that were branches and feathers that were leaves, tree trunks with the bodies of animals, branches that were arms or teeth or claws, human heads that had hair made of flowers and the forked tongues of serpents... He fought them blindly, flailing, kicking, until at last his strength ebbed and his enemies jumped on him all at once, in unison, and knocked him to the ground.

When later he sat up his body was hurting but he was no longer hallucinating. All he could see around him was the total darkness. Sitting on the ground, not knowing what to do, he became overwhelmed by such feelings of wretchedness that for the first time since he was a child tears rolled down his cheeks.

What had become of him? He couldn't really understand it himself, the things that had happened to him. How could a woman have reduced him to this mess that he was? He couldn't understand how a woman could have such power, could make him so needful... Before he joined the Radiant War he'd bedded lots of women. All kinds of women: whores, young girls, married, all kinds... Once there had been a widow and that was serious. She'd cried, begged him not to leave, but he did anyway because he was a man and what he was looking for was something a woman couldn't give him.

That was why he'd joined the Radiant War. The guerrillas gave him hope. There was no hope among his own people. They lived in the useless past. When he was a child an itinerant teacher had come to his village one day a week and had taught him to read and write Spanish. Because the teacher was sent by the government the villagers had to tolerate him. The government teacher wasn't aware they were Arayana. It was a word never spoken to outsiders. The government teacher was under the illusion they were the same as other Indians and so he tried to teach them to believe in progress, in the future. But the villagers weren't interested; they wanted nothing to do with the modern world. They were Arayana and that was all that mattered and the children were urged not to believe anything they were taught.

They were Arayana but among them, of those still alive, only Mountain Trotter had been to the high kingdom. Marvellous things were reported of the high kingdom. It was said they had gold and precious stones and that among them were wise men who knew the meaning of all things and they had a sovereign who was descended from the emperors of old. Calchas had seen men and women become tearful when they spoke of the high kingdom. It was for them a source of ancestral pride; something they could dream about, a sort of promised land.

But a promised land for whom? They, his own people, weren't allowed anywhere near it! It was all a big hoax; it had nothing to do with the real daily hardship his people had to endure. Calchas hadn't been taken in by the myth of the high kingdom, he couldn't see how it was going to help him or anyone, and as he grew older he came to care less and less about his roots. If he remained in the village he would marry and father children and then his fate would be sealed. It would be like being buried alive because the village wasn't going to change. He didn't want to grow old like his parents, like all the others who toiled ceaselessly from dawn to dusk and dreamed of a futile, sterile, vanquished past. They were drowning in the past, and he didn't want to drown, he wanted to take possession of the world – the changing world, the modern world, the world the government teacher had told them about.

So he left.

For three, four years he roamed the country. He moved to the capital where he saw such wealth as he would not have believed. He saw great houses, glittering department stores, cars driven by beautiful women, fancy restaurants and banks and offices, all the fanfare of modern life, but with no opportunity himself to be a part of any of it. He worked as a lowly porter in a marketplace. On his back he transported everything from sacks of potatoes to mattresses and once even a piano. He was an Indian, and used to physical labour; even so it was a back breaking job for which he was paid a pittance. City people were stingy and selfish, and the wealthier the stuck-up housewives were the more they haggled, the less they paid him. He grew to hate them: these rich people with their airs and graces who treated him like shit, these rich people with their cars and fine clothes and grand houses and he breaking his balls for them, going home to a tin and cardboard shack in a slum that was built on a rubbish dump and where every day he saw people dying, if not of hunger, of neglect and disease...

After the capital he lived on the coast. It was better there. Because he spoke Spanish he was able to get work first as a porter in a run-down hotel and later as a street hawker selling ice-cream. The ice-cream job was the best. It was a small beach resort and every day he would tramp the brown sand with a box of ice-creams packed in dry ice. He liked looking at the undressed bodies of the women. In the evenings after work he would usually go for a bathe in the tepid sea. Later he might get together for a beer with the other men who worked the beach. In some ways it wasn't a bad life. He had friends, sometimes a woman, and he had enough money for food and a dingy room in a cheap boarding house. It wasn't a bad life but only because he had known much worse. His poverty and the prejudice he encountered never let up. The government teacher had told him the modern world was full of opportunities. But for whom were these opportunities? The privilege and wealth of the modern world was like the high kingdom of the Arayana. It was inaccessible; it was something a poor and uneducated Indian such as himself couldn't hope to possess.

It was while he was an ice-cream vendor that he first heard of the Radiant War. A bomb had blown up a car transporting a government minister and the Radiant War claimed responsibility. He read about it in the newspapers. He was proud of being able to read; he read newspapers others had discarded whenever he could. He also discussed politics with an old hawker he knew. This man was a communist who said he would have joined the guerrillas himself were he thirty years younger. Calchas didn't know anything about communism but he liked what the old man told him. Vaguely he began to wonder how he might learn more about communism and the Radiant War.

It happened when he got the sack. The ice-cream racket was controlled by hoodlums. He got into a dispute with one of them over payment and they gave him a hiding and told him to get lost. He had no plans, nowhere to go, but as he was leaving town he came across the hawker. The old man said he could pass the night in his shack. They stayed up until the small hours talking. Finally the old man said he knew somebody who knew somebody, if he was seriously interested...

Joining the Radiant War was like entering a monastery. Once through the preliminaries he was taken to a training camp in the jungle. His head was shaved; he was given a khaki uniform and was assigned a bunk in a segregated dormitory. The recruits rose at four in the morning. They underwent military training in the dark. At daylight men and women came together for a study period which lasted until midday. They were taught to memorise the works of Marx, Mao, and Chairman Mateo. After lunch there was more military training. In the evenings there was more study. They turned in at nine at night.

It was a disciplined life. Alcohol and drugs were prohibited, as was intimacy between the sexes, unless they were married. But Calchas was happy. After he joined the Radiant War it became his whole existence. He no longer had to question his reason for being. He was no more one of the nameless, despised poor who counted for nothing. The Radiant War gave him hope, it gave him a place in the world, it gave him a mission.

There were people of many different backgrounds in the cadres of the Radiant War. But Calchas stood out among them on three counts: he was an Indian who could read and write; he originated from the very area the guerillas had plans to control; he showed initiative. For these reasons he was selected to become an agitator.

It was Chairman Mateo personally who gave him his instructions. The headquarters of the Radiant War consisted of a bamboo dwelling with a palm roof. Chairman Mateo sat in mottled sunlight behind a makeshift desk. In stature he was almost a dwarf. He had short arms and an oversized head which, placed as it was on his small body, made him look like an ant. A mestizo in his fifties, with nicotine stained teeth, thin hair combed meticulously in order to conceal baldness, and thick spectacles, Chairman Mateo was nothing to look at but he was revered. For Calchas it was an honour to be summoned into his presence. He invited Calchas to sit in a canvas chair. Coffee was served; Chairman Mateo lit an American cigarette (the first of many) and began speaking in a smoky voice that was almost a whisper, so soft Calchas had to sit on the edge of his seat and lean forward in order to hear what he was saying.

He spoke softly but his pale eyes glittered behind his thick spectacles and the words that fell from his lips had a ferocious beauty. He said the flames of revolution were invincible. He said they would leap up and turn into lead and from the din of battle would come the light, from the dark luminous glow there would be born a new world, a new society. He said they, the Radiant Warriors, were but fragments of time, mere flickers, but their deeds would last through the centuries. He said the revolution was small, in its infancy. But the voice of the oppressed masses was thunder roaring and soon it would roar over the whole country, the whole continent...

Chairman Mateo said many beautiful things and not once did it occur to Calchas to wonder about the things he did *not say*. Chairman Mateo did not mention the revolution's victims, the blood of the innocent, and unlike certain other more romantic revolutionaries, he did not say they must become hard without losing their tenderness. And Calchas never asked about such things because, as with all the other recruits, the words he heard gave him certitude. Chairman Mateo had this knack, to fill his followers with certitude. When Calchas left his presence, a glow imbued his being. There was a plan. A new and brighter order would arise from the ashes of revolution. And he was a part of it. He had the certainty...

But now as he sat in the dark, brooding wretchedly, it was as though it had all happened to someone else. He felt disconnected, unable to recapture the person he had been before he arrived in the high kingdom. The Radiant War didn't matter anymore. Nothing mattered. Illani was all there was. She had entered his body and stolen his spirit. He could not understand how else it could have happened. All this Arayana sorcery he'd heard about as a child, and had grown up to despise (for what self-respecting communist would believe in the supernatural?) now seemed to him to be true. And it wasn't that she had given him drugs; it was that she had somehow used these drugs to deprive him of his will. She had bewitched him. He was lost in an erotic compulsion for her that he couldn't shake. He couldn't free himself. The whore had got hold of his balls. She sat and laughed at him, mocked him!

The thought made him shudder. He hated her, truly hated her, and he felt horror at himself, at what he had become.

At the very moment Calchas was sitting with his head in his hands, feeling sorry for himself, Cascarina awoke with a start. Almost at once she realised something was different. It was the darkness that was different, close and strangely heavy, and then, as she lay wondering, there was a white flash and a moment afterwards she heard thunder. She heard it come from afar, a cracking sound that grew louder as it advanced until it passed over her in the darkness like a stampede of hooves.

Cascarina hurried out of bed and went to open the door. At first it was so dark she couldn't see anything, but as she stood in the doorway hugging herself against gusts of cold wind more flashes appeared and in the black sky she saw lightning spreading like roots. More thunder followed, great sonorous peals of it, as though the whole sky were laughing. Smiling herself, Cascarina had to marvel at this wondrous event.

For three years it had not rained. For three years they had watched the snow vanish from the mountain and the pasture wither and the spring and streams diminish to mere trickles. For three years every dusk without fail the four twin children in the community had performed a rain making ceremony for it was believed that twin children had the power to make rain. Every dusk for three years these children had danced and smeared their bodies with mud…

Cascarina did not know what had caused the change, whether it was the twins, or the bones of the dead that had been disinterred and sprinkled with water, or the effigies of frogs and toads, or the bloodletting ceremonies when volunteers flayed themselves with thorns, or whether it was something entirely different, but whatever the explanation she had no doubt it was going to rain.

And this it did. A single drop of wetness fell on her head and then another on her hand, and then it fell in a tremendous drumming torrent. Rain! Rain! Laughing, overcome with joy, she stepped out into the open and with her face uplifted she stood turning slowly while huge drops of rain lashed down so strongly on her they stung. She didn't care. She thrilled to feel the rain stinging, running down her face and neck, drenching her clothes, turning the earth under her feet to squelching mud…

It was only after Cascarina had retreated inside again that she became apprehensive. Having changed into dry clothes she sat huddled by the warmth of the fire listening to the rain fall in a relentless barrage until it began seeping through the palm leaf roof and she heard water trickling onto the floor. Visions crossed her mind of the roof caving in or the walls dissolving, and so she stood up and after lighting a torch in the fire she moved about the hut locating the trickles and placing earthenware containers under them in order to collect water.

Not long after she had finished and was sitting huddled again by the fire, there was a rattle at the door and she heard voices outside. Swiftly she went to unfasten the peg that held the door. When it opened her brother and his family came hurrying in. They were all soaking, splattered with mud, and before the parents could speak the two children started babbling, saying their house had collapsed. Collapsed? Cascarina looked at her brother, Capayambe. One of the walls had gone, he said. They were lucky it wasn't next to the beds. He was going back to see what he could rescue. His wife, Guaneque, wanted him to stay. She said they should wait until daybreak but he replied there might be nothing left to rescue by then.

After he left, Cascarina found what clothes she could – some of her own, some Rumicuri's – and gave them to her sister-in-law and the children to change into; then she got busy preparing warm food. Meanwhile Guaneque chattered nervously, making light of her misfortune, saying what did it matter if their house had caved in because it was a small sacrifice to make for all the wonderful rain. Cascarina agreed: The important thing was that nobody had got hurt. Yes, replied Guaneque, it was lucky no one was hurt and houses could always be rebuilt but only rain could replenish the bounty of the Mother Earth.

They were sitting around the fire, eating bowl of food, when Capayambe returned, his plump body covered all over in mud and carrying a bundle on his back. He placed the bundle on the floor, saying he was going back to see what else he could retrieve, but the women insisted he stay for a bowl of food. Capayambe crammed the food down, without sitting – a short, rotund, energetic man – and immediately afterwards he departed.

The women opened the soiled blanket that made up the bundle and with the children watching they sifted through odds and ends.

Everything was covered with mud. Guaneque was pleased with some of the things but there were others she couldn't understand why her husband had bothered to rescue. Just like a man, she said, holding up a silver ornament. What use was this to her? Better if he had rescued her pots.

While the women were occupied a wan light had been spreading into the darkness. Going to the door Cascarina opened it and looked out. In the dawn twilight the rain poured down ceaselessly, like a shimmering curtain, from a sky that was the colour of charcoal. Everywhere was the sound of water, thudding, pattering, dripping, gurgling, and from a distance came a sound she knew must be the river; swollen, roaring with a violence such as she couldn't recall.

Guaneque appeared behind her carrying a pot of water. She said the pots were overflowing. Cascarina went to get a pot herself. As they were emptying the pots Capayambe appeared through the sheet of rain carrying another bundle. Once inside he dropped the bundle and said he was going straight back to get the guinea pigs he'd managed to rescue and put in a basket. Capayambe was gone a couple of hours and Guaneque was beginning to worry when at last he appeared with the basket of guinea pigs. By this time he was so covered in mud it lay on him like a solid wrapping in which only the whites of his eyes were visible. Peeling off his clothes, he said he had gone to investigate. Two other dwellings had collapsed. Word had it the fields were flooded and the river had burst its banks. At all costs the granary had to be protected and he was going to consult with others. Guaneque asked him what he was going to wear. Capayambe managed to laugh. He said he'd go as he was – naked.

Day and night, night and day it rained without pause. After three years of drought everybody was happy it was raining, but mixed with their happiness was also apprehension as there were some among them who began to wonder if it would ever stop.

Apart from the terraced fields there was little flooding as such, for the mountainous terrain was too steep to retain water. On the other hand this steepness created another problem in that water rushed down the slopes with great force. In the main village in particular, where the dwellings were built close together on a slope, the water funnelled between them in torrents which threatened to erode the mud walls. A number of dwellings were in danger of collapsing. In order to avert this it was necessary to dig channels and redirect the flow away from the walls. It was a considerable task which involved a large part of the community. Men – naked because there was no point in wearing clothes – went out in squads and with their simple tools began digging ditches, laying stones, doing whatever was needed to spare the dwellings. The women meanwhile were busy preparing food for the men, or some of them had been recruited to help in the granary where a quantity of corn was being shifted to the weaving house as a precaution.

Cascarina herself was asked to oversee the distribution of food to the squads of men. For this purpose the gathering house was used. Women brought food, or some of it was prepared on the spot, and was then served to the men who arrived in shifts for it was an operation involving well over a hundred men and they hadn't the facility to feed them all at once.

It was in the gathering house that Cascarina noticed Calchas. She noticed him because he sat by himself in a corner doing nothing. All the other lowlanders were helping; the women working in the granary preparing food, the men joining the squads, but Calchas did nothing. He sat on the floor, dressed in torn, dirty clothes, his hands clasping his knees, staring at everything that was going on with a haughty, scornful grin, or so it seemed from a distance, on a first impression. But Cascarina knew, everybody knew, the lowlander was behaving this way because he had been bewitched. When Cascarina examined him more closely she noticed there was a glazed, refracted expression in his eyes, as though at any moment he might start crying. It reminded her of her own despair when Illani had stolen Rumicuri from her. She was sorry for the lowlander. On impulse she filled a bowl of warm food and took it to him.

'It'll pass,' she told him. 'See how it's raining when we thought it wouldn't rain ever!'

Calchas regarded her blankly.

Cascarina smiled at him, placed the bowl on the floor, and returned to her work. Soon she was so busy she forgot about him. Later, when it was getting dark and she had finished for the day, she remembered and turned to look at him. He was sitting in the same position, leaning against the wall hugging his knees, the bowl of food beside him untouched.

She couldn't think what else she could do for him. But the same night, when she was in her hut, her thoughts turned to him, and to Illani, wondering at the bitterness that must be poisoning her heart. Because why else would she want to ruin the lowlander? She didn't have to be cruel. The things that had happened in the past had nothing to do with the lowlander. Illani could use as much sorcery as she liked. She could ruin all the men she wanted, but it wasn't going to bring Rumicuri back to her. He had no feelings for her. He said it had been a mistake, he hadn't realised how demanding she was, thinking only about her own needs. He was the sovereign, he had to consider of everyone, the whole community, he couldn't pass all his time trying to please her. This is what he had said...

Reclining on her bed, the ceaseless rain drumming on the roof above her, Cascarina wondered if one day Rumicuri would decide to take another wife? Although the idea was upsetting to her, she could see how it might happen because men didn't think about women the same way women thought about men. Some elder women had young lovers, it was true, and it was also true that some women said it was wrong a man could have more than one wife while a woman had to make do with only one husband. They complained and protested but she wondered if given the opportunity they would actually want more than one husband? It would only mean a woman would have to do double the work and make double the effort to keep both husbands happy. Men were different. They could have two or three or even four wives and instead of doing more work they did less! The few men she knew who had more than one wife were like that. Lazy. It was the women who looked after them, and it was only because there weren't enough women that most men had to content themselves with one wife.

But Rumicuri was the sovereign. In the time of his ancestors there were emperors who'd had more wives and concubines than they were able to enumerate. Now of course it was all different. The sovereign's first duty was to father an heir. It was no longer thought important how many wives a sovereign had. Yet when Cascarina thought about it she didn't know of any past sovereign who'd been content with only one wife. Rumicuri's father had enjoyed three. The last one he married not long before he died, a young girl hardly out of puberty. Cascarina wasn't sure she approved. But he had been the sovereign, he could do what he liked, and anyway all men were the same: bulls in a herd, always ready to poke, and the older the men got the younger they liked their women. And what was there to make her think Rumicuri was any different? After what happened with Illani she no longer saw him the same way. It wasn't that she loved him less. He was her whole world. She couldn't imagine life without him. It was just that after Illani she came to realise that he was no different from other men: easily tempted, a bull in a herd...

But why was she thinking about this? How could she know what the future was going to bring? If anything was certain to spoil a person's happiness it was thinking and worrying about the future. Maybe that was what the elders meant when they said a person should strive to live each moment as though it were the only one on earth... *Aee, aee*, how difficult life could be. So complicated and difficult... but it could be pleasant, too. Good, happy moments that made you forget all the sorrow. And she had good reason to be happy now...

Musing, she could picture the joy it would give Rumicuri when she told him she was pregnant. She could see him smiling – he who so rarely smiled. But when she told him she was pregnant he would smile. *Aee*, could it really be true? Was she pregnant? When she had missed her cycle she wasn't so sure, but it was already seven weeks and what could that mean if not that she was pregnant?

It was a fine gift Amataba had made them before she died. For so long she had been trying to get pregnant but it was Amataba's magic that had made it happen. And now it was inside her, a tiny little dream because all life began as a dream. That was how the Holy Source had created the world. And it was the same with humans. The child inside her was a dream that had yet to awaken. So when a woman was pregnant she had to be careful not to disturb the dream. There were some who believed that if a woman was unhappy when she was pregnant then when the child was born it would grow up to be of a melancholy nature; or if the woman was angry, when the child was born it would have tantrums or grow up to be bad tempered... So she wasn't going to become sad or angry, she would be patient and she would try to be happy although it was so hard now with Rumicuri being away from her, in the world of the purinis... How she missed him. How she longed for his safe return. He could arrive at any moment, today or tomorrow, at any moment. It was all she could think of. It was as much as she could endure not knowing where he was, if he was safe, waiting for him to return... It was as much as she could endure...

It had stopped raining when Chotavalo, the youngest of the three elders, emerged from the sacred cave. But as the rain ceased a white mist descended, so thick that Chotavalo could scarcely see a few feet in front of him. Not to be deterred, he continued at a slow but resolute pace down the steep mountain slope – a swarthy, chubby man dressed in a purple robe and with dark eyes that conveyed an impression of staunchness, of humour, above all of a sort of vibrant, fearless serenity.

Further down the mountain the mist became still thicker, so dense that Chotavalo was unable to see his way when he reached the main village. It was only the appearance of mushy footsteps in the shin-deep mud that told him where he was, but even then he wasn't sure of his precise location and making a turn he walked into a solid wall. He stepped back, rubbing his face, then broke into laughter. While he stood laughing a door opened and an old woman peered out. Not seeing anybody, she stepped around the side of the house and in the mist managed to discern the purple of an elder's robe.

'So it's you, Tura,' Chotavalo remarked, when he became aware of the old woman. 'Now at least I know where I am.'

'It's this mist, *tata*,' the old woman replied respectfully. 'Nobody can see anything. Have you come all the way from the sacred cave?'

'I have,' replied Chotavalo. 'I bring good news. This rain augurs well. Preparations are to start at once.'

The old woman's face, wrinkled as a walnut, creased into a smile that showed wide gaps in between her teeth. 'How life goes by, *tata*! It doesn't seem so long ago when we were preparing for your own birth.'

'Pass the word around, Tura, preparations are to begin at once.'

'That I'll do,*tata*.'

When the old woman went back inside she sat down on a stool by the fire next to her husband, and told him of Chotavalo's announcement. The old man didn't reply at once. Without looking up he went on warming his gnarled hands over the fire. After a long silence, he said, 'There'll be flowers.'

Tura understood what her husband meant. After three years of drought the rain would bring precious life to the soil. On the parched slopes of the mountain flowers would bloom and when a new elder emerged from the darkness of the sacred cave he would see the world being born in all its pristine glory. Tura smiled as she sat thinking of the birth of the world, because for her, for all the Arayana it was not simply the arrival of a new elder that was celebrated, it was the renewal of their whole world. In olden times this renewal had been celebrated with human sacrifices, but not any more, now they had more peaceful ways to celebrate…

Arriving at Illapacta's, Chotavalo stopped outside the door and called to announce his presence. When there was no answer he pushed the door open and peered in. Illapacta was lying in bed, snoring. Chotavalo clicked his tongue and stepped inside. The hut was in a mess. The fire had gone out. Water had saturated the packed earth floor, turning it to mud. Pots, a spare robe, bits and pieces were strewn about carelessly. There was nothing Chotavalo could do about the mud, but without waking Illapacta he got busy building a fire and tidying what he could. When the fire was going he placed a thin slate stone on it and foraged among the baskets hanging from pegs in the wall. Into a bowl he placed some water, corn meal, ground nuts and spices, which he kneaded into dough, shaped, and cooked on the hot stone.

Whether it was the aroma of fresh food or something else, Illapacta awoke just as it was ready.

'You have a good nose,' Chotavalo remarked.

Illapacta sat up groggily. His white hair was dishevelled and his robe filthy. He struggled up from the bed in his bare feet, and ignoring the mud, which squelched between his toes, he stumbled to the door. Standing in the doorway he lifted his robe (giving Chotavalo a view of bony shanks and spindly legs) and farted and urinated into the mist and mud.

'I know what you're thinking,' Illapacta said, once he was seated on a log stump across the fire.

With a wooden implement Chotavalo lifted the pancake from the stone and held it out to Illapacta.

'So it's been decided?'

Chotavalo nodded. 'The rain augurs well…'

Illapacta munched on the pancake. When he'd finished eating he said, 'I'm sure Cuspi will make a fine elder.'

Chotavalo was silent. He was thinking he himself hadn't known a finer elder than Illapacta. When he was a child in the womb of the sacred cave, of all his teachers Illapacta had been the one he most loved and admired. He had been like a father to him, and when

137

he was in need, like a mother too, and after he emerged from the sacred cave it was from Illapacta he had sought further instruction in the path of elderhood. In those days Illapacta (although always somewhat slovenly and eccentric) had been an elder of tremendous ability and understanding; to Chotavalo's mind he was the most enlightened of all.

So what had happened? Chotavalo didn't know. Nobody knew. Some believed it was a sickness that had entered his body, others wondered if it was not something that had occurred on his journey to the outside world. But it was only speculation, nobody knew for certain because Illapacta himself gave no clue; not once had he spoken to anyone about what aggrieved him. Chotavalo knew only that some four, five years after he returned from the outside world there had come a dramatic and inexplicable change in him. Almost overnight, it seemed, Illapacta had began to completely neglect his appearance and to lose all interest in the affairs of elderhood. More and more he shied from company, confining himself to the solitude of his dwelling where he would consume such quantities of coca and mishqui as to pass into a mindless stupor. Chotavalo had been shocked to witness this swift and unfathomable dereliction in the man he revered, but disturbing though it was, he had never been so perturbed as to fear the vision itself had vanished in Illapacta.

From his own experience Chotavalo knew that no one who had seen the world being born could escape from it. The impact of this event was such that it became as much a part of a person as the flesh on his bones, as the air he breathed. The experience of seeing the world being born was fused into a person's consciousness, the two became one; it was unthinkable to imagine how an elder's vision could be harmed unless the very fabric of his consciousness underwent an irreversible corruption.

Had this occurred to Illapacta? Chotavalo did not believe it had. For many years now something had been affecting him; his access to the vision was obscured as clouds obscure the sun, this much was clear to Chotavalo, but it was not to say he had lost his reason. There was nothing wrong with his memory, his speech, his intellect. And except for when he was in a stupor all his faculties were intact. Chotavalo didn't know where lay the true cause of his problems, he simply did not know, but he hadn't lost the hope, even the expectation of one day seeing his old, beloved teacher recover his former serenity.

'I was wondering,' Chotavalo ventured, 'If you would consent to be present?'

'I don't know young Cuspi. He was never in my charge.'

'But you're an elder all the same...'

Illapacta regarded Chotavalo thoughtfully. 'If I understand you correctly,' he said after a while, 'what you're asking isn't what you appear to be asking... Why would I consent to be present?'

'Why not?' responded Chotavalo. 'It would please the people. It would please me. Unless, of course, you've lost all regard for the vision?'

'That's my affair...' Illapacta frowned, but then seemed to change his mind. 'Let me think about it. I don't know. I suppose it isn't every day a new elder is born...'

Chotavalo didn't persist. The fact that Illapacta had agreed to consider being present was in itself a sign. Hopefully, he wondered if it was possible that after all this time Illapacta was at last beginning to mend?

After Chotavalo had departed Illapacta's first impulse was to see if there was any mishqui left, but then he changed his mind, for once resisting the impulse, deciding this wasn't the moment for self indulgence. And in fact, Chotavalo's visit, his announcement that a new elder was soon to be born, caused Illapacta to recall the circumstances of his own birth with such intensity that for a timeless instant it was as though he had not aged, as though the years hadn't passed and he was back in the sacred cave...

It was a cruel deception the elders had played on him, all those years ago, in the months before he was born. Always the elders had exhorted him to be patient, assuring him that one day he would know all the answers to all the questions. Another thing they told him was that the time was approaching when a great event was going to happen. The elders didn't tell him anything more, they would not elaborate on what they said, but he was given to understand that the event was going to be something incalculable that would transform his life forever. So when the deception occurred he was in no way prepared for it. He was expecting something wonderful to happen and instead it was something unforgivably cruel that happened:

One morning, when Illapacta was fourteen years old, he opened his eyes and thought he must be dreaming because he wasn't where he should have been and everything was different. The three Father Suns that had shone for him every morning when he woke up were nowhere to be seen. Instead there was one very small and feeble sun in a sky that was utterly dark and seemed much, much lower. Dazed, then sitting up in violent confusion he rubbed his eyes thinking it must be a sleeping dream. He rubbed his eyes but nothing changed. It wasn't a sleeping dream. He was absolutely awake and what he now did was turn his head this way and that in wild anxiety trying to make sense of his surroundings. Where was the soothing, rippling stream of water? The beautiful rock formations? The high sky? The vast spaces? All the pleasant and familiar surroundings of his world? All he could see in the feeble light was a laden darkness beyond which was a still deeper darkness and then beyond that a wall of such blackness he knew it must be where space ended. A clammy dread came over him. In the past, every time he had awoken in a new world it had been bigger, brighter, better than his last world. But now he feared it was the reverse and that he was back to the beginning, to the mean, cold, dark world he could first remember. Was this the great awakening the elders had promised? Or was it something else? Had he perhaps done something to displease the elders? And where were the elders? Why was he alone?

Rising from his bed (the same bed, the single object that was instantly familiar) he moved around in agitation, somehow still hoping it was a sleeping dream, or if not, that something would happen to make this horrible world go away. Then another thought occurred to him. Was it possible the elders were playing a trick? It would scarcely have been the first. In the past the elders had played all sorts of tricks on him. Might they have moved him during the night to a part of the world he hadn't been able to discover, which the elders had kept secret from him? He wished it might be so, even if it was against his better judgement, for he knew the world intimately: In years past he had explored every nook and cranny, every surface, every frontier of the world and (unless he had been transported to the place the elders themselves inhabited, whatever and wherever that was) he couldn't understand how the elders could have concealed such a world as this from him. What this world sort of resembled, although it was even darker, he thought, was the first world he could clearly remember (the second chamber) but he was too frightened to want to believe this; that he was back in that world

140

of long ago. Instead he tried to tell himself that it was a mere trick, a test of some kind, and so he plunged into the blackness hoping to discover a way out.

Almost as soon as he penetrated the blackness, however, he came against a cold hard surface beyond which he could not go. Feeling the surface with his hands he began following its contours, at each instant hoping it would lead him to an exit; but there was no exit, all the surface revealed was the alarming smallness, the suffocating confinement of the space he was in. He had almost gone around the whole space when, without warning, he heard from close by, the voice of the chief elder: 'If it's a way out you're looking for, Illapacta, I don't think you'll find it.'

He stopped, startled, his emotions in confusion, peering to locate the chief elder. "Why am I here?' he cried, distraught when he spotted the large, melon-shaped form of the chief elder sitting under the light of a very feeble Father Sun.

'Come, sit down,' said the chief elder.

Illapacta sat down beside him on the hard ground.

'So what do you think of this world the Holy Source has dreamed for you?'

Feelings of bitter anger surged over Illapacta. 'Why am I here?' he protested. 'Why has the Holy Source dreamed this world for me?'

'That's something we can't know,' said the chief elder. 'The mind of the Holy Source is beyond understanding. Only he knows why he dream what he dreams.'

This answer did not satisfy Illapacta. It was all wrong. Nothing the elders had done had prepared him for this change in his circumstances. They had always assured him that one day something wonderful would happen. And dreaming of the wonderful moment when he would know all the answers to all the questions he had imagined himself passing through the door of the world and coming into the presence of the Holy Source. Beyond that his imagination didn't reach except to anticipate it as a moment of fulfilment, of complete bliss.

'But you said I could know all the answers to all the questions,' Illapacta protested. 'So how will I if the mind of the Holy Source is beyond understanding?'

'A good question,' said the chief elder. 'Only one thing is necessary to know all the answers to all the questions and for that it isn't necessary to know the mind of the Holy Source.'

Illapacta was silent. His trust in the elders, in the Holy Source had been broken and in its place he now experienced an emotion for which he had no words, because it was an emotion he hadn't fully experienced before. Anger, yes, but this was more than anger, it was intense sullen hatred. And he had no word for hatred, but vocabulary or no vocabulary his heart turned cold and his vision red when he looked at the world he was in and thought of how the elders had tricked him.

'You aren't happy? You don't like it here?' said the chief elder, and when there was no reply, 'There's nothing I can do about that. I have no power over the dreams of the Holy Source. But there is one thing you *can* do.'

Still no reply.

'Listen, Illapacta. If you really wish to escape from this world you don't like, and if you really wish to find all the answers to all the questions, then what you must do is this: Find the answer, the only answer to the one question that will provide the answer to all the other questions.' The chief elder paused. 'The question is this: What is the Holy Source?'

Illapacta was now thrown into confusion. How could he know what the Holy Source was? He'd never seen the Holy Source. All he knew were the worlds the Holy Source had dreamed. That's all he knew. And hadn't the chief elder said the mind of the Holy Source was beyond understanding? He was playing tricks again. It was an impossible question!

'How can I know what the Holy Source is?'

'That's exactly what you must find out.'

'But *how*?' Illapacta cried.

'That's what you must think about. There won't be many distractions here in this world the Holy Source has dreamed for you. Doesn't it occur to you that the Holy Source may have placed you here just so you can answer this one question? Think about it… Be angry if you like but that won't help you. What you must do is trust us elders and never stop looking for the answer. What is the Holy Source? Answer this one question and you will know all the answers.'

'And what'll happen then? How do I know it won't turn out to be just another trick?'

The chief elder stood up. 'Listen Illapacta, You're asking questions now and that's good, that's what we've taught you to do. But when you know all the answers you'll know it won't be a trick because you won't need to ask any more questions. That's all I'll say...'

And so it was that Illapacta found himself pondering the answer to the chief elder's question: What is the Holy Source?

When he awoke each day it was the first thought to enter his mind and he would continue to ponder it, almost without pause, all through the day up to the moment he lay down to sleep. In fact, he became so obsessed he couldn't stop, and the more so because often the answer seemed to be tantalizingly near.

Quite a number times he felt so close to the answer that a shiver went up his spine and his body trembled with the effort of trying to break through. On one occasion he was sure he had. All at once his body became light, as though it were held to the ground by no more than a thread, and as well he felt insubstantial, as though he were separated from his surroundings by no more than a layer of skin. It seemed as if everywhere there was an invisible but palpable something connecting him to the air, to the light, to the ground, to the blackness that was the frontier of his world... Was this 'something' the Holy Source? Illapacta became sure it was. It struck him that all life was merely different manifestations of the same thing, and that this 'sameness' all life had in common was no other than the Holy Source. It seemed a brilliant discovery. It was a discovery that suddenly overwhelmed him, vanquishing all his doubts and filling him with a happiness so irrepressible it spilled out of him in bouts of giggles and laughter. It seemed that he had never felt so complete, so certain.

However, this discovery did not persuade the elders. When the three elders, seated on a mat in the feeble light of the Father Sun, asked him to answer their question, Illapacta found that he couldn't.

How to explain what he alone was able to perceive and had no words to describe? Illapacta tried to. He said, 'The Holy Source is –' After a silence, one of the elders asked, 'Is what?' At once at the back of his mind Illapacta sensed he was being led into a trap, but such was his eagerness to express his understanding that he blurted, 'The Holy Source is everywhere.' And when this reply elicited no response, too late, he added, 'I am the Holy Source, you are the Holy Source, this world is the Holy Source.' Again they were silent. Finally they stood up. 'If all this is the Holy Source, and all this is all there is,' announced the chief elder, 'then you'll have no more questions. You'll be happy to remain here.' And with that the elders stepped into the darkness towards the door of the world.

As they disappeared from view all of Illapacta's certainty crumbled. Instead of the happiness what he now felt was an abrupt panic. Come back! he wanted to shout. Don't go! Don't leave me! But they did go. He heard the creaking sound of the door being opened and closed and then he was alone again. In his distress, for some moments losing all self control, he rushed after the elders to the door of the world and for the first time ever he dared attack it. In the past, in this world as in his others he had felt the doors with his fingers, and although forbidden had even tried to pull them and open them, but he had never dared attack one with all his strength. But this is what he did now. He rammed the door and kicked it and tried to pry it, but no matter how hard he tried the door would not budge. It was solid. He could make the door move a little but it was much too dark for him to see what he was doing and he couldn't get it to open. At last, giving up, he returned defeated to the dim light of the Father Sun.

Sitting down on his bed, he was assailed by feelings of failure, of wretchedness, of deep depression. At that time all he knew about death was what the elders had told him. Death occurred when something stopped being the thing that it was; and if he hadn't been right after all, if all things weren't the same, then he wished he could stop being the thing that he was. He wished he could die. He wanted to be dead.

But when the elders returned and saw how despondent he was they made a fuss over him. They brought him tasty things to eat, they joked and laughed and encouraged him to persevere with his quest. Before they left they gave him words of instruction: They said that if he wanted to know what the Holy Source was he should spend the first part of each day, just when it was dawning but before it was full light, sitting on the mat staring at where the Father Sun was due to appear, so as to strengthen his eyes. They also said he must do double the amount of exercises he did every day in order to further strengthen his body, and likewise, in order to strengthen his ears, he should double the amount of time he spent beating the rumi drums. All these things were necessary, they said, because when the time came to know what the Holy Source was – and if he persevered he was certain to find out – such would be the power contained in the answer to all the questions that he would need all of his stamina to withstand it.

So this is what he did. Each day he would sit on the mat staring up at the dawning light. After that he would ponder the question the elders had given him. Later he would do his exercises. When he had finished his exercises, he would return to his pondering. When the light of day began to fade he would turn to the rumi drums, beating the rhythms and chanting the songs the elders had taught him. At last, when it was dark, he would eat again and then he would retire to his bed, his mind once more focused on the one question whose answer alone could bring about the transformation the elders had promised...

A hoax. A huge, methodical and deliberate hoax. Sitting by the fire, recalling that distant time when he had been sequestered in the sacred cave, Illapacta knew that were it not for seeing the world being born there could be no justification for what the elders had made him endure.

From the time of his birth, for fourteen years the elders had remorselessly plundered his childhood. They had not permitted him to know his parents. He had not seen a tree, a bird, a flower. He had not known what it was to swim and run free and gaze at the stars. Apart from the elders and the mysterious memory of his mother, he had no knowledge of other human beings existing, not to speak of children. He hadn't looked at girls, taken part in games, indulged in any of the innocent pastimes of childhood... It had all been taken from him. Stolen. Everything. The elders had stolen his entire childhood.

And in exchange for this most precious of gifts that life could bestow on a human being, the elders had given him lies and lies and lies! With neither compassion or pity, with absolute ruthlessness the elders had fabricated an artificial world with the sole purpose of depriving his senses and of distorting his whole perception of reality.

It was a cruel deception to inflict on a child. And yet, Illapacta knew, in all the generations of elderhood, among the multitude of elders who had existed since the time of their forefathers, there was no memory, no rumour of a single elder having cause to regret his fate. And what made this so was the world being born. The elders

145

referred to this experience simply as 'the vision', because there were no words capable of describing what happened when, after fourteen years of isolation in the sacred cave, the door of the fourth chamber was opened for the novice elder to venture through.

So it had been for Illapacta. For three months they had confined him to the cramped darkness of the fourth chamber while he struggled relentlessly to answer the chief elder's question: What is the Holy Source? But this too was just another deception, for they hadn't expected him to be able to answer it. No elder ever had. The real reason it had been asked was in order to confuse and exhaust his mind to the point where, unable to go further, he was on the brink of abandoning the search, of giving up altogether, and thus his mind became, if not blank, passive.

And it was when he was at this precise juncture – strong in body, empty in mind – that the elders arrived early one morning.

Handing him a purple robe, the chief elder said, 'Go and wash. Put on this robe. We'll be waiting for you at the door of the world.'

Immediately, upon hearing these words and seeing the purple colour of the robe, Illapacta was alerted. He sensed that something very unusual was about to happen. Yet from past disappointments he'd learnt caution, and so he tried to restrain his agitation as he went to a place where in the faint light he squatted over a hole and defecated. Afterwards he threw handfuls of earth down the hole from a pile that was nearby and then he stepped over to where stood a large earthenware container of water. Standing naked on a stone slab he used a bowl to scoop water and in this way he washed himself. Once he had washed and dried himself with a cloth he returned to the straw mat by the bed and put on the purple robe the elders had left for him. Ready now, he advanced into the blackness where stood the door of the world.

When he reached the door he heard the chief elder say, 'Illapacta, we'll now open the door of the world. I'll go first. After I go, you follow. My brother elders will follow behind. But ask no questions. Say nothing. Only know this: Soon you'll see what you've never seen before. When you come upon the vision so much will happen at once that you'll need all your strength to withstand it. A fear such as you haven't experienced will overwhelm you. Many are the elders who upon first beholding the vision have wanted to return to this world you're in. *But there is no return.* No one who beholds the vision can ever go back. We will be by your side until your fear passes. For it will pass, Illapacta. And when your fear passes, slowly you'll begin to understand. Slowly a great peace will fill your being. Slowly you'll come to understand all the answers to all the questions...'

After saying these words the chief elder turned around and opened the door of the world. In trepidation Illapacta stepped after the chief elder, but immediately beyond the door there was only a familiar total blackness, and so narrow that on both sides of him he could feel stone brushing his shoulders. With his heart sinking, prepared to be disappointed once again, he followed the chief elder step by step, twisting and turning until they came to another door. They opened this door and passed through. There was more darkness, and then quite abruptly it became much brighter. A moment later Illapacta found himself in a place that had rock formations and a high sky. Another world? It was similar to the second world he had known, but much smaller and also it had no Father Suns. Instead the light came from a place low down, directly in front of where he was standing. The light was white, intensely bright, brighter than any light he'd ever known and were it not for the exercises he'd done every day, staring at the Father Sun, this light would have blinded him. As it was he was able to stare into the light and as he did so his breath came short, his heart started pounding, and his stomach felt queasy because he had the impression of great emptiness, of something incredibly vast opening up beyond the shaft of light.

The elders did not speak. Instead the chief elder touched his shoulder, then turned and stepped towards the light. With weak legs, trembling all over, Illapacta followed him. He walked straight into the light...

All this had happened many years ago, but even after all this time Illapacta had no words to describe to himself what had happened from that moment on. To emerge from the sacred cave and contemplate the world being born at the same time as being born himself was something unimaginable. It was something that to this day was still inside him, so fused into his consciousness that no matter how he tried it could not be erased.

And Illapacta had tried. How he had tried! To this end he had turned his back on elderhood, had endured opprobrium, had drunk and drugged himself. And to the degree that he'd managed to dull his senses he'd managed to dull the vision; but to erase it completely hadn't been possible, it was always there, somewhere in his consciousness, and when he was sober any little thing might cause an involuntary change in his perception of the material world.

If he was walking along a path, for instance, and happened to notice a particular plant, it might suddenly leap out at him with transformed clarity. He would see not merely the plant's overall shape and colour, but as well the serrated edges of the leaves, their grooves and ridges, the many shades of green, the patches of yellow, the spots of brown, the hairs on the stem… all these things he would see at the same instant, with vivid intensity. And at the edges of the plant he would see the rainbow coloured aura that surrounded it and blended into space that was not yet space, air that was not yet air, for this also he would perceive, with vividness, as something that had density, that was almost like a thin transparent liquid.

But this liquid wouldn't be transparent everywhere, nor would it be static, nor would it have uniform density, for in reality this liquid that was not yet liquid, that was perhaps more like a membrane, was a vibrant extension of the things it surrounded. And he would perceive this. He would see the plant that then became an aura that then became the light of the sun that then became the terraced fields that then became the rasping sound of his sandals as he took a step along the path, for sounds and smells, no less than sights, would also be intensely present, intensely clear…

And so it would be for everything: A butterfly cavorting across the path would gleam and shimmer like a fantastic jewel, and he'd see not only the ripples the butterfly left in its wake, he'd also hear the fluttering sound of its wings. And if he stared down at the path, the cracked earth, the dust, the small stones would dance before his eyes in richly coloured, ever changing patterns…

Such were the perceptions that could affect him at any moment when he was sober. Yet this material change in the substance of reality was only one, relatively small aspect of the vision. An elder's apprenticeship didn't stop on the day he emerged from the sacred cave. On that day it was said a novice elder would understand all the answers to all the questions because he would come into being at the same moment the world was being born, and consequently, in this experience of total becoming, total being, all questions and answers would cease to have meaning. But as with an infant newly born so too was the novice elder helpless after his own birth. The elder had been born, now he must grow or perish.

After a novice elder had emerged from the sacred cave, therefore, he embarked on what was called 'the path of elderhood'. The path of elderhood was the complete opposite of the deception a novice elder had endure in the sacred cave. There the intention was to make him believe in an entirely artificial reality so that when he came into contact with the actual world it would produce an irreversible transformation in his consciousness. Once the transformation had been attained, however, the intention was to strip the vision of all trace of artifice or deception, honing and purifying it until the novice elder was able to penetrate beyond the material substance of the vision to an immaterial and internalised understanding of the Holy Source.

When an elder attained this knowledge he stopped being an apprentice. He became a full elder, able to summon or dispense with the material vision at will, for now it was no longer necessary for him to contemplate the vision in order to be aware of the Holy Source. The Holy Source was in his sinews, in his blood, in his bones. Everything about him, his every thought, his every action, reflected the certainty of his own immortality. A full elder reposed inscrutable and serene in the knowledge that nothing really died, for whether through a natural cause or an act of violence, everything was undergoing a continual process of change. Nothing existed in isolation. At the moment a plant, a clod of earth, or a sentient creature began to disintegrate, at that moment it was already becoming part of the thing that was consuming it. A person died but didn't vanish. A person's flesh, which was the coarsest part of him, returned to the Mother Earth, there to be broken down and dispersed in a world that was forever being born. But a person's soul, which was the most rarefied part of him, was able to pass beyond the substance of the world being born. A person's invisible soul was able to cross the great chasm, it was able to reach the essence of the Holy Source, that which the elders named the father and mother of all creation, the pure knowing…

But what if an elder should turn his back on the pure knowing? What if an elder should perversely make up his mind that he no longer wanted to be an elder?

In all the history of elderhood such a thing had not happened before. To an elder the idea was an absurdity, if not an impossibility, for how could he deny the vision, the pure knowing? It was like denying the existence of the heavens, of the Mother Earth herself. It was like denying the reality of one's own blood and bone and flesh. This was why when Illapacta was sober the vision was liable to come flooding back without his being able to control it. In order for him to summon or dispense with the vision at will (as he had once been able to) he would first have to stop attempting the impossible. If a person recognised that he had a body he could become forgetful of it. But if a person spent all his time denying he had a body, then the body would take control. The person would not be able to escape. The presence of his body would torment him in the same way Illapacta had become tormented by the vision.

It was Illapacta's journey with Rumicuri to the world of the purinis that had been the cause of his undoing. He had gone in ignorance, believing that his knowledge made him invulnerable, believing that the vision answered every possible human need and therefore there wasn't anything in the outside world that could harm him. But the things he'd seen in the world of the purinis had entered his body like a sickness. It was a sickness that had lain dormant inside him for five years, so that he was hardly aware of it, but then had overwhelmed him.

One night he woke up with such a start it was as though he had received a blow. Dazed, baffled, he lay in darkness feeling an inexplicable dread. Then as abruptly as he'd awoken an image came to his mind with such force that for a moment he forgot where he was. The image that came to him was of marching ants swarming over the body of a wounded tapir. The tapir rolled its eyes, it bucked and stomped in an attempt to shake off the fierce red ants that rushed up its legs in a seething, humming mass. In a matter of instants the ants had reached the tapir's flank and belly, their minute yet voracious jaws stripping skin, tearing into flesh, so wounding the tapir that its legs buckled and it crashed to the ground. In another few instants the ants had covered the tapir; a seething blanket of ants swiftly and relentlessly devouring it, until there was nothing left, not a strip of skin, not a piece of flesh. A bare white skeleton.

The image vanished but not the feeling of dread. Illapacta couldn't understand any of it. What did he have to be afraid of? And why had this image come to him? He had seen marching ants before, he had seen tapirs, but he couldn't recall having seen a tapir being devoured by ants. So why should it occur to to him? What significance did it have?

Then, as he lay pondering, without knowing why, he found himself thinking about the world of the purinis. Memories came back to him. He recalled the metal animals – the ones that not only moved along the ground but the giant mouths that had devoured the Mother Earth. And he recalled the settlement with its dwellings all crammed together and the many strange artefacts. He recalled how the purinis had crowded around him, hurrying from one place to another, and he, feeling isolated and threatened in their midst, had wondered if they had souls, if they were real human beings, such was the emptiness and hardness he seemed to sense in them...

He recalled many things from the world of the purinis, but what he recalled most sharply was the occasion Victoriano had taken him inside one of the purini dwellings. Before they left for this place (Rumicuri hadn't on this occasion accompanied them) Victoriano had made him dress in purini clothes, saying he would only attract scorn and ridicule if he went in dressed as an Indian. After he'd changed into these clothes they travelled in the belly of a metal animal until they came to a dwelling. Here Illapacta found himself inside a huge room illuminated by miniature suns hanging from the ceiling and where there were rows of seats all facing an enormous wall of yellow cloth. A number of purinis, some alone, others accompanied, were occupying the seats, but a lot of the seats were empty. Victoriano took him to a row and they sat side by side on the seats. More purinis entered. Presently the light dimmed. The wall of yellow cloth parted in two, astonishingly, as though a spirit had done it, and the two halves rolled back to reveal another wall that was entirely white. Before Illapacta had time to wonder the room went dark and a shaft of white light illuminated the wall. Illapacta glanced behind him and saw that the light was coming from a square hole, high up at the rear of the room. An instant later he heard loud sounds and looking again at the wall he was astounded to see moving, dream-like images appear on it!

While he gazed at the coloured images in startled bewilderment, Victoriano leaned towards him, whispering, 'This is one of the many ways the purinis have of telling a story. The story is about two purini nations at war...'

Illapacta stared at the wall unable to comprehend how they could create such sorcery. It appeared on the wall like a dream: a world of moving images where purinis appeared wearing peculiar clothes, doing things whose significance utterly eluded him but which nevertheless led him to reflect that the purini ability to create an artificial reality made what happened in the sacred cave seem like the crude work of children.

Victoriano didn't explain anything more of the story that was taking place. Nor was it necessary, for even Illapacta, bewildered as he was, came to realize that the images were of destruction. A destruction of such violence and intensity that he was numbed by it. He saw enemy bands cutting each other down with firearms as though they were blades of grass. He saw metal animals rolling over rough ground, pointing with things that stuck out like thick spears which roared and spat fire and smoke and where the spears had pointed the Mother Earth would burst open and purini soldiers would collapse dead or wounded. He saw metal birds flying in the sky that from their bellies dropped things that looked like big stones. But when the stones fell on a purini settlement they would cause roaring bursts of smoke and fire that totally destroyed the dwellings, leaving only heaps of rubble...

How long this dream-story of destruction lasted, Illapacta had no opportunity to find out because it was still going on when Victoriano whispered, 'We have seen enough.' Then he stood up and Illapacta followed him in the dark to the door of the dwelling.

Outside they didn't speak. They got inside the belly of another metal animal and sat in silence on the journey back to the place where Victoriano lived. Later that night, however, when they were alone together, Victoriano said he wanted to show Illapacta the power of destruction that the purinis possessed. That was why he had taken him to see the dream-story. The dream-story was not real, it was an illusion, an ingenious artifice of the purinis, but there was nothing artificial about their power to destroy. All those fantastic weapons Illapacta had seen *they possessed in reality*.

'Our people are blinder than a pig's arse,' Victoriano told him. 'They think that because the mountain and the forest protect them they're safe. But these barbarians don't need to travel with their feet. They have metal birds armed with weapons that can kill our people in a moment, without putting a single purini in danger. If our people are safe, Illapacta, it isn't because the purinis can't reach them, it's only because the purinis haven't noticed them. But from the day they arrive amongst our people, be it through the forest or from the air, from that day on it'll be the end of the Arayana.'

Lying in the dark, stricken with a sickness that was inside him like a premonition, Illapacta recalled something else Victoriano had told him. He said: *The purinis will fall upon our people like marching ants upon a wounded tapir.*

So this was why the image had occurred to him. This was why sickness had invaded him, why he had such a deep feeling of doom... But why now? Why should it strike him now, five years since he had come back from the outside world?

Pondering, Illapacta realised that the truth of the matter was that after he had returned to his people he had buried all that he had seen deep inside of him. And if he had done this it was because being and elder had taught him that it was sufficient to *be*. An elder took account of the past and of the future only in so far as it served an attainable objective; he didn't worry over what he couldn't control. Other people worried and fretted over their safety, other people were tormented by impossible desires. An elder contented himself with being. For him it was sufficient to exist.

And if this was sufficient, why therefore the dread? Why, lying there in the dark, thinking of the world of the purinis, was he assailed by this sense of doom?

Illapacta was unnerved. Like a man who suddenly sees a chasm opening under his feet, he turned away, scrambling for the safe ground of his former certitudes, at that moment lacking the courage to confront the terrible knowledge the question implied. But although at that moment he would not confront the question, this nevertheless was the first crack in the flawless unity of the vision, this was the beginning of his undoing...

Outside, the thick early morning mist had dispersed and the orb of the sun had risen over the forest. It was a beautiful morning; one as had not been seen since before the drought, for the mountain was heaped with sparkling snow, and further down in the kingdom, among the dwellings and fields, the earth was a dark moist brown, the grass glistened with dew, the air smelt fresh, and everywhere the vegetation seemed to come alive with a renewed greenness and the delirious song of birds and insects...

As with the birds and insects and other creatures, the people too felt a need to celebrate. Soon they began emerging from their dwellings with happy faces, laughing and exclaiming at this unexpected end to the drought. The drought had weighed on them. For three years they had lived in tense expectation, their spirit depressed, wondering what they could've done to so anger the Mother Earth that she should deprive them of her bounty.

But now, if angry she had been, it was an anger that appeared to have passed. The people felt as if a burden had been lifted. They gathered here and there in groups to chatter and with not much thought of working that day. Children played, youths flirted, and older folk gossiped, or talked of what could be done now in the fields, or of things to do with the celebration for the birth of the world...

One of the very few people who did not go outside to enjoy the morning was Illapacta. And the reason for this wasn't so much that he didn't want to participate as that it hadn't yet occurred to him. After Chotavalo had departed Illapacta had become so absorbed by his reflection on the events of his long life that he hadn't stirred from his seat by the fire. He'd sat there without moving, not even to tend the fire, and now as he continued sitting there, an odd intuition began to form in his mind.

Who knew why? Who could say why it had taken so long? Sometimes it was the simplest truths that were the hardest to discover. But perhaps it was Chotavalo's announcement that a new elder was soon to be born that had prompted it. Or perhaps it had been there all the time, growing like a seed that one day breaks through the soil. Or perhaps it was just that he was exhausted, tired of all the torment... But whatever the reason, Illapacta was of a sudden struck by the realisation that it was not the vision that had let him down, it was not the vision that had proved insufficient.

For such is what had occurred. His undoing had begun at the moment when he'd discovered that the ultimate reality, the immutable certainties of the vision, were not enough to console him in the knowledge that his people were going to be destroyed.

And he had no doubt they were going to be destroyed. For five years after returning from the outside world he had buried this terrible knowledge. But then it had overwhelmed him like a sickness. All he had seen in the outside world had indicated that his people were doomed, that the purinis, with their vast numbers, with the power of their artefacts and weapons, would one day descend upon the Arayana.

And it was a knowledge that had so assailed Illapacta that he had found no solace. Everywhere he looked he had seen remorseless and inexorable destruction. Should his eyes chance to fall upon a group of children innocently at play he would see purinis cutting them down with firearms. Where men were working to build a dwelling he would see stones of fire falling from metal birds, killing people, reducing the dwellings to rubble. Everywhere he turned he would hear the terrified cries of women and children. Everywhere he looked he would see his people succumbing to the implacable ferocity of the purinis.

His people were doomed. And it wasn't only that they were going to die, it was that they were going to vanish from the Mother Earth. Their whole history, their whole culture would vanish. There would be no more elders, no sovereign, no laughter, no dreams. Everything would vanish. The purinis would destroy them totally. They would disappear *as if they had never been.*

Illapacta hadn't suffered so much for himself, for his own death, he had suffered for his people. And the vision hadn't been enough to reconcile him to what he knew must happen. His brother elders saw a world being forever born, where one thing was transformed into another, and where nothing really died. He also saw such a world, the transformation in his consciousness would not allow otherwise, yet it was as though behind the world that was forever being born he had encountered another world, *a world that was forever dying.*

But now, sitting by the fire, he wondered if over the years he had become so tormented that he'd been unable to see through his own torment. There was nothing that would save his people, but was he therefore to abandon them?

Like a gleam from a dark horizon it struck Illapacta that there was a simple truth he had failed to perceive. And this was that if it was the fate of the Arayana to vanish as though they had never been, and if there was nothing he could do to prevent it, then he, as an elder, had the duty to show his people the only thing that was left when all hope was gone.

Why should his people not laugh and smile? Why should they not work the fields, make love, dream of good things? Why should they not celebrate the birth of the world? When the end came it would come.

Pondering, he looked up from the fire and turning his head he noticed the shafts of sunlight that penetrated through the slats of the bamboo door. Slowly he struggled to his feet. With aching joints he hobbled over to the door and opened it. Squinting into the flood of warm golden light, he saw the sun shining in the sky, and in the distance, beyond the nearby tree tops, he saw the mountain covered with snow.

It wasn't that the vision did not suffice, because whether the vision sufficed or not wasn't the issue. What he'd failed to apprehend was that without courage it made no difference what a person perceived to be the truth. With courage the vilest falsehood could be made to seem worthy, but a truth without courage would always be worthless. It wasn't enough to have courage alone, but neither was it enough to possess a truth without courage...

An elder without courage is like a person who won't open his eyes. Does that mean the world is different because a person refuses to look at it? Does that mean the vision is flawed because an elder won't accept it for what it is? No, all it means, thought Illapacta as he stepped into the flood of light, is that an elder without courage isn't worth a monkey's fart.

PART FOUR

CASCARINA liked geckos. Almost every hut had one or more of these slim, delicate lizards which lived in the crevices of the roof and would emerge at all hours to stalk the walls and roof beams for unwary insects. Besides being useful, the geckos were largely unafraid of humans and they had beautiful translucent golden-brown skins. But what most intrigued Cascarina was the way they were able to walk along the walls or upside down on the roof beams as easily as if it were flat ground.

When Cascarina awoke on this fateful dawn the first thing she noticed was a gecko poised upside down on a roof beam directly above her. It stood in a shaft of early sunlight slowly moving its head. Sleepily she lay watching it, the silence punctuated only by the slight snoring sound coming from her brother in one of the beds opposite, for he and his family were staying with her while their own rain-damaged hut was being repaired.

While watching the gecko, vague images drifted through her mind, the remnants of a scarcely remembered dream, then she became aware of an uncomfortable tender feeling in her breast. Immediately she was wide awake. This was something new. There could be no doubt about it now, her body was changing, even her middle felt different, a little fuller, rounder... Cascarina smiled to herself. She still hadn't got used to it. It seemed amazing to her that after all this time of trying she was pregnant at last. Why was nobody awake? Turning her head, seeing her relatives asleep, she wished they were awake so she could share her joy with them... But no, let them sleep. They needed it after all that had been going on, and was still going on now with all this work that had to be done in preparation for the arrival of the new elder. She herself would have to go out this very morning and gather plants for the dyes. But it would be enjoyable. She didn't mind the work because preparations for the birth of the world were a time of happiness. All that was missing now was Rumicuri. If only he would get back in time!

As she lay pining for him, wishing he were beside her, Cascarina became aware of a distant droning sound. She was puzzled. What could it be? A purini bird? She listened, suddenly tense though without being unduly alarmed, waiting, expecting the noise to pass as it always had on the few past occasions when a purini bird had been heard or sighted.

But not this time. This time the noise grew rapidly louder – a strange, frightening noise that appeared to descend from the sky like reverberations of thunder.

She sat up. Her relatives were all at once awake, their heads rising with torpid, bewildered expressions. As they did so the thunder-like reverberations started receding. Cascarina exchanged looks with her brother, Capayambe, who by this time was sitting up. Nobody spoke. The noise had almost disappeared when there was a flash and an instant later a sound such as they had never heard. A sound so loud and solid it made the walls and floor tremble as though it were an earthquake. And just as it began to peak there were two more rapid orange-edged flashes followed by another two bursts of sound that merged into a single blast of such magnitude, of such impact that a wall cracked and a roof beam came crashing down and mixed with the swirl of dust an immediate, strange burning smell.

Cascarina was so stunned she had no thoughts, no feelings, but as the reverberations of sound diminished and the dust dispersed she saw across the fallen beam the children's faces shrieking soundlessly.

Capayambe was the first to move. He got up staggering, his body naked and his eyes wide open. Without a word he did something strange because he ignored his children, he ignored everybody and instead foraged about until he found his robe. He put it on and then with a frenzied, wild look, he croaked, 'Stay here! Stay here! Don't move!' Then he turned and opened the door and rushed out.

After Capayambe had gone the children began crying. Guaneque stood up, her naked body shaking all over so that even her teeth were chattering. Scrambling over a beam she sat down next to her children who huddled against her and cried, 'What is it, mama? What is it? Is it the purinis? Is it the purinis?' Guaneque did not respond. She sat motionless, her face drained of colour and her eyes staring across at Cascarina in mute terror.

Cascarina's own response was to pass from being stunned to feeling herself being engulfed in a vortex. Her head spun. She couldn't breathe. She had no control over her mind. It was fragmenting. Her consciousness was breaking up...

How long she remained in this state she didn't know. But at the worst moment, just when she feared she was going to lose her mind completely, lose all control of herself, some distant part of her began to recover, as though in acceptance of the inevitable. Against the bafflement and blank incredulous terror there was now a feeble but increasing sense of resignation. Slowly it overcame the worst of her panic. Her mind recovered and space stopped spinning. Panting, drenched in sweat, she began to gather herself, not quite sure for what, but if it was to be death then she did not want to die shamefully. She wanted to die fully aware.

So she waited. She waited while the strange burning smell wafted stronger, and now, through the incessant crying of the children she heard the droning sound returning in the distance. The sound of the purinis, she was sure. The sound of certain death – quick and merciful death. This was all she could hope for...

But why? Why did they have to die? Her brother had told them not to move but the forest was only a little distance away. It was a chance. Suddenly she was sure. She must save herself, save her baby, save anyone she could.

Scrambling off the bed and stepping over the beam she began shaking Guaneque's shoulder. 'Quick! Hurry! We must leave, the forest, quick!' Guaneque looked at her uncomprehendingly. Cascarina became rough. She pulled Guaneque's arms apart and seized the children, yanking them to their feet. 'Hurry! The forest!' The children understood but they didn't want to leave their mother. When they saw Cascarina shaking their mother they too began pulling on her.

Near the door, as if waking from a trance, Guaneque twisted free and grabbed a blanket and some clothes.

Once outside Cascarina looked around in dread of seeing purinis, but there was nobody on the ground. Only a foul smelling dust that lingered in the air and high up in the sky, above the trees that separated the hut from the rest of the village, two purini birds – closer and different from others she had spotted in the past – hovering with a whining roar like ferocious giant wasps.

Cascarina turned towards Guaneque and the children. 'They're coming again! Let's go. Hurry!' Together they began running down the path, away from the village. As they reached some fields there was another flash followed by another blast. Still running, Cascarina glanced behind her and saw what looked like an orange glow, the glow of fire rising from behind the trees. Moments later they left the path for the trees that surrounded the fields. Once in the forest they kept running, deeper, deeper into the shadowy undergrowth; tripping over logs, crashing through branches until they became so breathless they had to stop.

'Are we safe here?' panted Guaneque's eldest child, a girl of ten, as they squatted naked on the forest ground.

Guaneque had managed to rescue some of her children's clothes and now, as though in protection, she got them to put these clothes on. To Cascarina she gave a smock, and for herself there was the blanket, which she wrapped around her shoulders.

'I don't think they can see us here,' said Cascarina, though none too certain, afraid that even the forest wouldn't be able to protect them.

Guaneque's youngest, a boy of six, began crying. He made no sound but he sucked in breath and his eyes filled with tears.

'What are we going to do?' said Guaneque.

After a moment Cascarina said, 'The river cave. We'll be safe there. Go to the river cave, Guaneque. I'll stay and tell others.'

Guaneque was alarmed. 'The purinis will see you!'

'I'll be careful, but I must get to the low villages before the purinis, I've got to warn them.'

Guaneque's eldest daughter was staring at her with imploring eyes, her shoulders were shaking, but there wasn't a moment to waste. Without another word Cascarina turned and swiftly pushed through the undergrowth.

When presently she came to the edge of the forest she concealed herself behind a tree, breathless, peering towards the path in between the terraced fields that ascended a slope like irregular steps.

There were no sounds. The sky was empty. She couldn't see any purini birds in the sky. Everything was eerily quiet. It gave her an impression of unreality, as though nothing had happened and it were all a bad dream. Very quickly, however, this impression was dispelled by a harsh, bitter, burning smell that wafted in the air and also by a slight haze of smoke she noticed rising from behind the screen of trees at the top of the fields. Where were the purini birds? For an irrational moment she dared wonder if they could have gone? And such was her anxiousness to believe this, it crossed her mind to sneak up to the screen of trees, not far beyond which was the main village.

Almost she was tempted, when, as she stood undecided, three purinis appeared on the path that came out of the trees. Cascarina froze. The men wore green clothes and in their arms they carried things that looked like short fat sticks. As soon as they came out of the trees they stopped, their heads looking around with quick sharp movements. Cascarina flattened herself against the tree, not moving, one eye just managing to see the men, who, after scanning the terrain, turned around and quickly went back into the trees.

No sooner had they gone than Cascarina retreated into the undergrowth. Coming to a decision, she began hurrying in a direction parallel to the downward trajectory of the path. But the undergrowth was impeding her progress. Every passing instant was critical, so even while she knew she would be taking a risk she came out of the undergrowth and ran along the uneven strip of terrain which separated the fields from the forest.

When she arrived at the bottom of the fields, rather than take the path she decided to go back into the undergrowth and approach the nearby cluster of huts under concealment. Yet hardly had she veered towards the undergrowth than she saw four of her people, four men following the path out of the trees. They too saw her, and came hurrying over.

She stepped back into the undergrowth, beckoning them as they came closer. When they were all concealed in the vegetation she spoke to the men with agitation, asking if they'd been attacked by purinis? The men replied with equal agitation. They'd heard sounds, terrible sounds, and they'd seen a purini bird, a strange bird fly past them low down, but they didn't know what was happening, they were on their way to find out.

Words poured out of Cascarina. The men listened in horror. Three of the men were young, the fourth man was older. One of the young men, tall and long haired, rolled his black eyes. 'We should separate and save who we can.' His companions agreed without hesitation even if their faces remained stricken. The older man said he would stay with Cascarina. Having agreed, the three young men departed, hurrying to wherever there were dwellings, hoping to arrive before the purinis. Cascarina and the older man, Tusuma, ran to the nearby huts. There were six of them scattered amongst the trees but the huts were empty because their occupants had come together after they had heard the sounds and spotted the purini bird and were now huddled under a tree close to the forest. This group, which numbered some twenty people, consisted mostly of women and children, although there were a few older people as well.

When Tusuma and Cascarina reached them there was a commotion. One woman began shrieking. Tusuma – a squat man with an ugly face – became angry. 'Be quiet! Do you want the purinis to hear? Make for the river cave. Hurry!'

'Not without my father. No. I'm staying. I'm not going,' said a big fat woman.

This woman's father was old and blind. He sat on the ground, his varicose, ulcerated legs sticking out of a frayed robe.

'Don't be a fool, woman,' he said, staring out of blank grey eyes.

Tusuma had no time to wait. He started walking and the distraught party followed him into the forest. But Cascarina lingered behind, as did the fat woman's husband and their two plump adolescent daughters.

Cascarina grabbed the woman's arm. 'Do you want to die? Do you want your daughters to die?'

'My life's done. I'm ready to die. I'm not afraid of the purinis,' interjected the old man. 'Are you here, Jamauna?'

'I'm here,' said the woman's husband.

'Then what are you waiting for? Don't stand about. Take her by force.'

Jamauna was a short skinny man. He was much smaller than his wife. How was he going to take her by force? He looked at Cascarina helplessly, then lunged at his wife, his small hands grabbing one of her bulky arms. The two daughters and Cascarina joined in. Between the four of them they managed to drag the sobbing woman away from her father.

As they reached the forest Cascarina glanced back. The old man was sitting alone where they'd left him and she felt fear and sorrow for him. But they must escape while they still could…

The first thing Calchas noticed, when he opened his eyes, was a segment of roof beam no more than a few inched from his face.

I'm alive, he thought.

Immediately he recalled how an unusual sound had awoken him and as he sat up he'd seen the others from his village scrambling out of beds, hurrying towards the door of the gathering house. In a flash it had crossed his mind that the sound was being made by approaching aircraft – helicopters? – but that was all because even while he was thinking, and before he could get out of bed, there had come a blinding light. No sound. Only a blinding light.

Staring at the beam Calchas tasted gritty earth in his mouth and he became aware of a weight on his body. Moving his head slightly he was able to look down and see that he was covered with earth and rubble, but as well there was a wide light-filled gap from his waist down.

Tentatively he tried to extricate himself. His right arm came free but his left arm would not move. Turning his head again he saw that his left arm was trapped under the beam. Making a greater effort he tried to twist sideways and move his legs. As he was doing this he heard sounds, voices. Instantly he stopped. The voices were in Spanish.

'Áca no hay nada. Here there's nothing.'

'Pues estarán enterrados. Well, they must be buried.'

Calchas heard the heavy, crunching sound of approaching footsteps. Seconds later a shadow obscured the sunlight. He held his breath, not moving, but it was no use, he'd been seen, for abruptly a voice said, 'There's one here.'

Soldiers. As they began clearing the rubble he saw their boots and patterned green trousers. He thought of playing dead, then decided it wouldn't work. Better to pretend he had no understanding of Spanish, play stupid… A face appeared in the gap above his waist: a lean young face under a floppy jungle hat. Dark Indian eyes regarded him curiously. 'He's alive,' the soldier said, turning to his companion. 'His left arm looks trapped. Let's clear this shit.'

It took the soldiers some minutes to remove the obstructing earth and rubble. Then both of them took hold of one end of the beam and managed to shift it sideways. Earth fell on Calchas' face. The soldiers removed more rubble, then they reached down and with unexpected care lifted him to his feet.

Calchas stood giddily, the soldiers holding him. He noticed his right arm was caked with a mixture of blood and earth. But as yet he felt no pain.

The soldiers started lifting and pulling him. They wanted him to walk. Calchas decided there was no point resisting. He stumbled forward. Pain flared in his arm. After some thirty yards they approached a large group of survivors guarded by a two armed soldiers. Beyond the group were heaps of rubble or partially destroyed huts, some of which were smoking. And to one side of the group, on a slight rise, an officer was standing by himself. In one hand he held a radio transmitter. The soldiers brought Calchas to the officer.

The officer was plump and middle aged. He had puffy cheeks, a small black moustache, a frowning brow, and eyes that regarded Calchas with neither anger or indifference, but to the contrary had an expression of anxiety, even distress. Calchas, who had learnt something of military insignia, decided he was either a Captain or a Major.

'Did you ask him?' The officer addressed the soldiers.

'No sir.'

The officer studied Calchas.

'Do you speak Spanish?'

Calchas remained silent.

'You don't speak Spanish? Nothing?'

When Calchas remained silent the officer sighed in exasperation. Then the radio transmitter crackled and a voice came through. The officer placed the transmitter to his ear. The voice on the other end was audible though unintelligible to Calchas. He could, however, hear the officer. He heard the officer say, 'How many?' Then: 'Any who speak Spanish?' Then, as if in reply to a question: 'No. I can't make them out. The devil knows who these people are.' The officer sighed. Then: 'I suppose we'd better have them all in one place, just in case... Very well, Captain, when you're finished get them up here... Over and out.' Lowering the transmitter, the officer studied Calchas again, sighed, then said to the soldiers, 'Okay, put him in with the rest and carry on your search.'

'Yes sir.'

The soldiers escorted him towards the survivors. As they passed by a demolished hut Calchas saw the mangled corpse of a young woman sticking out of the remains of a roof. Further on there was another corpse. It was a man. His tunic was in shreds, his flesh burnt, and one of his arms was all but torn away.

But more disturbing than the dead were the wounded. Guerrilla though he was, Calchas had little experience of battle, and he recoiled now when he arrived among the survivors and saw the wounded: An older man cradling a younger man and both soaked in blood. A woman sitting on the ground, moaning, her hands covering a big wound across her belly so as to keep her entrails from falling out. He turned away, sickened, but no sooner had he done so than he saw a severely burnt child screaming, running to this adult and that but no one daring to touch him for fear of making it worse. And elsewhere a woman lay on her back shaking with violent spasms while a man (her husband?) knelt beside her, holding her arms, his clothes all torn and one side of his face smashed to a bleeding pulp. And everywhere, in the eyes that stared back at him, there was confusion and fear when not outright terror.

But then came a surprise. Calchas saw medics. He saw two medics moving among the wounded, applying bandages, giving injections, doing what they could to alleviate the suffering.

It must be on the orders that officer, he thought, bewildered. But why? A wave of pain flared up again in his injured arm. When the worst of it had passed he went back to his thoughts. Maybe it was some kind of mistake? The Radiant War? Was that it? Could it be possible? Why not? If his comrades had moved closer to this part of the jungle, maybe they'd been mistaken for guerrilla... Was it possible? Calchas had very little knowledge of aircraft. He knew enough to distinguish a helicopter from other aircraft, but since he'd never been in the air himself he had only a vague notion of what could be seen from above. Still, no other explanation seemed to fit. Why would the soldiers bomb them and then try to help them unless there'd been a mistake?

A glimmer of hope, if only for his own survival, began to strengthen Calchas. Speculating that the worst had passed, maybe, and he might yet come out of this alive, he remembered Illani and dared wonder if she was alive.

He gazed around, scanning the nearby crowd, the unwounded standing or sitting on the ground. Not seeing Illani among them, he went further into the crowd, searching for her, picking a path through the hundreds of people that were gathered, as submissive and as uncomprehending of their fate as wild animals in a hunter's trap...

One of the huts that had escaped the bombing was Illapacta's. When he had awoken to hear the droning sound, and instants later a roaring blast that made the walls tremble, he among all the Arayana had been the only one to understand what was occurring.

The purinis, Illapacta had thought. They've arrived.

After the first shock and despite his arthritic bones he had jumped out of bed, quick as a hare, but he hadn't immediately left the hut. Instead he'd done something he had avoided for many years: He put on his purple robe, his official elder's attire. And he tidied his hair, drawing it back and tying it behind his neck. Only then, when he'd smartened himself as best he could, had he left his dwelling and started hobbling along the path to the village.

Soon a foul burning smell invaded his nostrils and he saw black smoke rising beyond the nearest trees. Getting closer to the main village he abruptly saw three purinis hurrying towards him along the path. Calmly, without hesitation, Illapacta carried on towards them. The purinis came up to him dressed in greenish clothes and they carried firearms. He had seen this type of purini once before, on his only journey to the outside world. Warriors, he thought. Purini warriors; the ones they call 'soldiers'.

The soldiers started making signs and speaking to him in their own language. Their expressions were alert, watchful, but as well detached, as though they were not so much looking at him as through him. When the soldiers realised he couldn't understand them, one of them gave him a gentle shove and gesticulated that he was to walk. When he started walking two of the soldiers went on ahead, while the third soldier walked behind him, close on his heels.

Going from hut to hut the soldiers collected more people. Some of the people appeared on their own, others were afraid to come out and these the soldiers removed, if necessary, by using force. One old man fell to the ground as he was being hurried out of his dwelling and one of the soldiers gave him a prodding kick in order to make him stand. Had Illapacta been a younger man he would have rushed the soldiers, because he wanted to lash out at them even if it meant dying. But he was old, his strength was gone, so all he could do was hobble over and disregarding the abusive soldier he helped the old man to his feet.

But on the whole the soldiers weren't violent, no more than necessary for their ends, and Illapacta was at a loss to explain it. How could the purinis arrive with such fury, destroying their dwellings, and now not kill them? Why were they being herded together? What did the purinis want?

The soldiers marched them through dust and smoke, past the burning ruins of the main village, all the while collecting more people. Some of these people were burned and wounded and there were some among them who couldn't walk. Illapacta knew what he had to do. He started reprimanding some younger men near him, telling them to show courage, telling them to behave like human beings, until, shaken from their stupor, the young men began to help carry those who needed assistance.

Finally they went past the smouldering ruins of the granary and arrived at a field where they were all being gathered. Presently a chief warrior appeared among them, now giving orders, now going over to one Arayana or another and making signs, talking, trying to communicate.

But at that moment it was more than Illapacta dared to hope that any good could come of it. How could he know what the chief warrior wanted, what evil intent he had in mind? He'd never doubted that when the purinis arrived it would be the end for his people. He was all but convinced the warriors were rounding them up only to make it easier for them to be killed. So when he saw women clutching their children, some so scared they stood in their own urine, their legs streaked with piss and dust, he spoke to them, saying, 'Are you frightened because of these miserable purinis?'

'Are we going to die, *tata*? Are the purinis going to kill us?' a woman pleaded.

'And if they do? Are you afraid? I tell you, it's a wonderful thing when you cross the great chasm. You have nothing to fear. The Holy Source won't disappoint you; trust me when I tell you these things…'

But then, even while he was speaking, Illapacta noticed the medics. Unlike Calchas, he didn't know they were medics, but he saw a soldier doing things to the wounded. Perplexed, he watched the soldier stab a young, injured girl with something he held in his hand, and afterwards he took a roll of thin white cloth and gently – yes, this was the confounding thing – gently he wrapped it around her thigh.

After the soldier had finished and moved to another wounded person, Illapacta came up to the girl and while her family looked on in confusion he started questioning her.

The girl didn't know what the purini had done to her. All she could say was that he'd made the pain go away. She felt funny, drowsy. What did it mean? she asked. Was she going to die? Illapacta put his hand on her head, but he was unable to reply. Leaving the girl, he started following the soldier to the next wounded person, but then he sighted Calchas standing not far away and at once he hurried over to him.

'Why are these purinis going to the wounded?' Illapacta asked.

Calchas looked at the old man.

'I know what they're doing. I don't know why.'

'What are they doing?'

'Helping them.'

'*Helping them?*'

Calchas, in pain himself from the wound in his arm, said again, 'They're helping to heal the wounded.'

Illapacta opened his mouth, closed it, then turned to look at the soldier in the near distance, then returned to Calchas. 'Why would they help the wounded if they're going to kill us?'

'Maybe they aren't going to.'

'Not kill us? Is this possible?'

Calchas was silent.

'So why have they destroyed our dwellings? What are they doing here if they aren't going to kill us?'

'I've just said, I don't know.'

'But you speak their language, you know the outside world. Why do you think they're here?'

'It could be a mistake. That's all I can think of.' Calchas paused; then he ventured, 'Maybe they're looking for the Radiant War.'

'The Radiant War?' Illapacta frowned. 'If they know we're not these people you speak of they'll go away, they won't harm us. Is this what you're saying?'

Calchas shrugged.

'Speak!' snapped Illapacta. 'This isn't the time for silence.'

'Yes maybe, but I don't know for certain, not yet.'

'But you speak their language. Do they know you speak their language?'

'The chief soldier asked me if I did, but I pretended I didn't.'

'We've got to get the advantage,' said Illapacta. 'Do you understand?'

Under different circumstances Calchas might have answered with sarcasm, but the situation was too critical. He said, simply, 'How?'

'If you spoke to the chief soldier now what would you say?'

'I don't know. But he'll know I lied to him.'

'You could tell him you were frightened. That's why you lied.'

'He'll ask questions.'

'Yes, and you can answer them.'

'Do I tell him the truth?'

'You can't tell him we're Arayana. Think of something else.'

'I could tell him we're Yombris…'

The Yombris were a tribe of Indians so diluted and widely dispersed in the outside world the term had become generic. Beyond the fact that they were Indians there was no particular culture associated with the Yombris. So when Calchas, Mountain Trotter, or any other Arayana lowlander was asked by the purinis to what tribe they belonged they habitually answered that they were Yombris.

'If they believe we're Yombris,' said Illapacta, who was aware that this ploy was sometimes used by the lowlanders, 'they won't harm us, they'll go away?'

Calchas screwed his face against the pain throbbing in his arm. 'I can't be sure. They didn't leave my village… But if they know we aren't the Radiant War I think we'll be a lot safer. I'll tell them we're Yombris…'

The wounded, the burning dwellings, the dead… how could it be stopped now? In his bones Illapacta feared that the end he had foreseen, and which for so long had unmanned him, could not now be averted. But even if it was so, even if it had to be, did that mean he shouldn't try to stop it? No, no, they had to fight to the end…

'Speak to the chief soldier,' said Illapacta. 'Tell them we're Yombris.'

Arayana though he was, Calchas felt no profound loyalty to Illapacta's people. He cared even less for them than he did for the people in his own village. But the soldiers were his enemy – the Radiant War's enemy – and he had his own skin to think about… and Illani's, too, if he could find her, if she was alive…

'I'll go with you,' said Illapacta.

'What is it sergeant?' The Major glanced at the two Indians the soldier had escorted to him. One of them was an odd-looking old man in a purple robe. The headman? he wondered.

The soldier indicated the young Indian. 'This one, it seems, speaks a little Spanish, sir.'

The Major's eyes opened wide.

'Spanish? You speak Spanish?'

'A little,' said Calchas, then reluctantly, 'Señor patron. Master sir.'

'I'll be dammed! Didn't I speak to you not long ago?'

'Yes, sir.'

'Why didn't you tell me you could speak Spanish?'

Calchas remained silent.

'How many of you speak Spanish?'

'Only me.'

'What? Only you?'

'Well, there were some others, but they're dead,' Calchas lied.

'Are you telling me that among this entire multitude you're the only one who speaks Spanish?'

'Well, there's one or two more maybe, but I don't know where they are.'

The Major sighed, indicated Illapacta. 'Who's this man?'

'He's our elder.'

'So who are you people?'

'We're just poor Indians, master sir, that's all we are.'

'I know you're Indians. I'm not blind,' said the major, irritably. 'What do you call yourself? What tribe?'

'No, we don't belong to any tribe. We're just poor Yombris... poor Yombris working the land, that's all we are.'

'Yombris, eh?... Aren't you a bit far away for Yombris? There are no roads around here; nothing. What are you people doing here in the middle of nowhere?'

'Working the land, the way we've always done, that's all we're doing.'

'That's all, eh?... With no roads? And only you speaking Spanish? How long have you people been living here?'

Calchas hesitated. 'I don't know.'

'You don't know?'

Calchas spoke to Illapacta in Arayana. 'I told him we're Yombris. I think I can make him believe us.'

'Doesn't he believe us, then?'

'Not yet. Say something more, anything, make a sound.'

'What do you want me to say?'

'Our elder says we came here in his father's time,' Calchas told the major.

'What about you? Were you born here?'

'Yes, sir.'

The Major narrowed his eyes. 'So how is it you speak Spanish if you've lived here all your life?'

'No, I was born here, but we've got other relations that live in a village near Rioloja, near where the oil is. That's how I know Spanish. I was living with our relations and there was a government teacher.'

'Hmmm... So there's a path through the jungle? No road, but there is a path? Is that what you're telling me?

'Not a good one, but we Yombris are used to it. We can find our way.'

The Major was silent. Abruptly, watching Calchas, he said, 'Have you heard of the Radiant War?'

'I don't know. What's that?'

'The Radiant War. Guerrillas. You know what guerrillas are?'

'I don't know. I've heard the name...'

'So you know what guerrillas are? What *rojos* are?'

'I don't know. Only what I've heard.'

'What've you heard?'

'Some people, bad people that go around with guns making trouble for poor Indians, that's all I know.'

'That's all, eh? Where do these people live, do you know?'

'In the jungle, I've heard. And in other places. But I don't know where.'

'Around here? Have you seen or heard of any that live *around here*?'

'Here?' Calchas pretended to look baffled. 'No we've never seen anybody like that around here. We're just poor Yombris working the land. We've never seen bad people like that around here. Thanks be to God,' he added for good measure and quickly crossed himself.

The Major fell silent. His bottom lip nibbled at his short black moustache. He wasn't happy. Damned colonel. *No civilian population*, he'd said. My guess is the bastards have a secret base here, he'd said, stabbing the map. And there were the reconnaissance photographs, too; aerial, taken not long ago, better than satellite. Some showed quite clearly a Radiant War encampment that wasn't so very far from here. The Major wished it had been him instead of Casal who'd been sent there. But there was another photograph. The colonel had shown it to him, indicating what appeared to be evidence of human habitation. He'd checked, the Colonel said. He'd even asked the Geographic Institute. It was supposed to be virgin forest. No one knew of any humans living there. No uncontacted savages even. Nothing. The Colonel said if this was the case then it could only be the Radiant War. Looking for deeper hideouts in the jungle. And the structures looked pretty solid, there appeared to be cultivated fields; it could even be their major base, the Colonel said... Still, it could've been worse, the Major thought. The attack chopper had been too fucking hasty. Too damned fucking hasty. He would put it in the report: didn't wait for orders. Why should he carry the can? No, he'd stopped the attack as soon as he realized. Somehow it just hadn't seemed right: the terraced fields, the layout of the huts...

'Sergeant.'

'Yes sir.'

'Take the old man back.'

'Yes sir.'

'You,' the Major said to Calchas. 'Stay here. I might need you.'

The major walked off and sat down on the remains of a wall. Wearily, he passed a hand over his face, and then lifted the radio transmitter. He was too far away for Calchas to hear what he was saying. Calchas thought of Illani. If she was dead he would try to get back to the Radiant War. But what would he do if she was alive? He didn't know. A part of him wanted to fall at her feet, but another part of him wanted revenge, wanted to hurt her...

Suddenly the Major was coming back towards him. He didn't look the same. He looked angry.

'Stay with me,' the Major said, brusquely.

Calchas was confused. Something had occurred. He could sense it from the major's abrupt change of manner.

The Major called the Sergeant over. The Sergeant went back to the survivors and in his place a soldier arrived.

'Walk in front of us,' the Major ordered Calchas. 'I'll tell you where to go.'

They set off. The Major and the soldier behind Calchas.

Indications of guerilla activity, what the devil did Echiveira mean? The Major unfastened the safety strap on the canvas holster on his hip. Difficult man Echiveira. Don't care for him, not one bit… Slippery as an eel. A manipulator. Crude, too. Wouldn't trust Echiveira in a tight spot. But cunning. If there's any credit coming out of this he'll be after it…

'Hey you! Turn this way… Yes, yes, this way.'

Funny clothes these Indians wear. Don't know what it is. Something doesn't quite fit… A path through the jungle, but this is virgin territory; in the middle of nowhere for God's sake. How the fuck do they get to market? Or maybe they don't? How is it he's the only one who speaks Spanish? And what if they're not really Yombris?… Guerrillas? The Radiant War?… No, don't think so… Too many women, children, old folk. But maybe the guerrillas have been here, got a few sympathisers, that's always possible… Could be a justification, officially, so far as the report –

'Not that way! Where are you going?'

'I don't know, sir. Where do you want me to go?'

'Up there. See the helicopter. Up there,' said the Major, pointing beyond the ruined huts and smoke to where the blades of a helicopter were visible.

The helicopter was in a flat field, which, Calchas realised, wasn't far from Illani's dwelling. He wondered if the house was standing.

'This way, sir,' Calchas said, gesturing.

'Well, okay, you show the way. But careful, no tricks…'

'No sir, no; why would I?'

I've blasted your village, thought the Major. That's why. And he was sorry. He wished it hadn't happened. He himself had a daughter in a wheelchair, paralysed from the waist down after a car crash. He could understand the pain and fear these people must be enduring. And he was a military man. Not a murderer. It was easy to forget these things when fighting the Radiant War. They were criminals, butchers. This Mateo cunt couldn't give a damn how many innocent people he killed. He was a fanatic; you couldn't pussyfoot with the reds… Still, he regretted the casualties. His orders to the attack chopper should've been clearer. They should've waited, taken a chance, checked more closely…

In a grass field – verdant after the recent rain – stood a large, armed, troop carrying helicopter. And standing nearby was a tall, stick-thin officer dressed, like the major, in green and khaki jungle fatigues. Behind him, in the open hatchway, the pilot and another crew member were lounging.

The thin officer, Lieutenant Echiveira, had large ears that stuck out of a floppy jungle hat, and a long oval face with large nostrils and thick lips. He had a comical, monkey face, the lips held in a permanent rictus that passed for a smile. Yet oddly, it wasn't a good humoured face. Calchas himself was quick to notice this, even if he couldn't say what exactly it was that made him instantly wary.

'Well Echiveira, what is it? Where's this evidence?'

'I'll show you, sir. Who's he?'

'He talks Spanish,' the major said. 'The only one I've found, so far.'

Echiveira looked at Calchas. There was a flicker in his small, close set eyes.

'This way, sir. It's in the hut over there.'

Echiveira led them away from the helicopter with long, bowed strides. Coming to the end of the field they entered a grove of berry bushes and small fruit trees and now Calchas' heart quickened because Illani's dwelling lay beyond the grove.

Why? Was Illani there? And what did this man want to show the Major?

Illani's hut had not been bombed. It was intact. A soldier armed with a sub-machine gun was standing guard. Echiveira, with a quick, almost imperceptible glance at the soldier, went in first. The Major stood aside, ushering Calchas before him. Calchas was fearing the worst, but the moment he stepped inside he saw Illani huddled on the bed clutching her child in her arms. Their eyes locked and Calchas, in spite of all the resentment he bore her, felt himself come alive. And Illani, too, was overcome; if not out of love, at least for being reunited with someone she knew, who was close to her. And more, someone who knew the ways of the barbarians.

It was her child who had delayed her escape. In the last few days he had become unwell. His shit had turned liquid and he was feverish. She'd been up with him half the night and was in exhausted sleep when the purinis came. The first thing she knew about it was when she was awoken by sounds so sudden, so completely strange and frightening she was unable to move. The dwelling shook as though an earthquake had struck, or as though the earth around her were bursting open. Then, even while she was wondering and as the blasts of sound faded, she heard another sound – a roaring hum descending from the sky above her dwelling. And it was at this moment it occurred to her to think of the purinis.

At once she jumped up and rushed to her child. But when she picked him up he was soaked in sweat. Her whole being was screaming at her to flee, but her son was feverish and she couldn't bring herself to leave without first gathering dry clothes, food, a gourd of herbal medicine she'd prepared.

It took her no time at all to get ready, but it was nevertheless a fraction too long because as she paused outside her hut (her child on one arm, a bundle in the other) trying to decide which direction to take, she saw two purinis emerge from the bushes and start running across the grass towards her.

The purinis didn't harm her. Although almost they did. One of them, the one now guarding the door, pushed her back inside and started shouting at her in his language. She stood shaking while the two purinis started throwing her belongings around, pulling the cloth bags from the walls and emptying them on the floor, smashing pots, poking here and there, and then they stopped.

While one of the purinis looked on, the other came up to her. He pushed her violently onto the bed. As she lay clutching her child the purini pulled his pole out of his clothes and then threw himself on her, forcing her arms apart, shoving her child aside as though he were not human, as though he were some unwanted artefact. Her son fell to the floor. He was screaming. She could hear his pitiful screams as the purini lay on top of her, his foul breath on her face, and one of his hands ramming itself between her legs, forcing them open. She didn't resist further. She surrendered. She went limp because all she could think of was saving her child.

But before the purini could penetrate her, another one appeared, the thin one with the monkey face. He spoke something and at once the purini got off her, adjusting his clothes.

Illani snatched her son from the floor. She cowered on the bed as the purinis talked amongst themselves and then the monkey faced one sent one of the purinis away. The other one stayed behind, the one who'd tried to violate her, and the two of them began looking around, not throwing things about like before, but more carefully, and that was when he found her ornaments – gold, silver, the pouch of precious stones – and the red artefact Calchas had given her one time…

The soldier by the door stood at attention as the Major went inside.

'So what is it? said the major, giving Illani and her surroundings a cursory glance.

'I found this, sir,' said Echiveira, stepping up to the Major.

The major recognised the book at first sight. Chairman Mateo's piece of crap. Frowning he opened it and thumbed through the pages.

Calchas, standing close to Illani, experienced a sinking feeling. The strength went from his legs. He had forgotten all about the book, he'd forgotten that one evening to impress Illani, after telling her about the Radiant War, he'd shown her the book and left it with her.

What could he do now? How could he explain its presence without making them suspicious? He didn't want to think what might happen... Trying not to panic he scoured his brain for a plausible story.

'Is this all you've found? Anything else?' said the Major.

Echiveira hesitated.

'There's something else, sir. Take a look yourself. It's under the bed.'

The Major moved forward. Echiveira was now standing behind him. As the Major bent down Echiveira slipped a revolver from his holster. The major stuck his arm under the bed. His hand felt something. He'd just started to pull it out when Echiveira placed the barrel against the back of the Major's head.

A cracking sound. The Major slumped to the floor. No emotion showed on Echiveira's face. His expression didn't change. He glanced down, saw blood and brains seeping through the Major's hair, and then stepped up to Calchas.

'On your knees.'

Calchas knelt on the floor. Echiveira placed the revolver against his temple. I'm going to die, thought Calchas, and all at once everything became extraordinarily clear. Without turning his head he was able to see everything around him: The Major dead on the floor. Illani frozen on the bed, pale, staring with uncomprehending eyes. This monkey's arse who was going to kill him... Any instant now his life would be over, finished. And he felt a profound regret for all that he would not live to experience, for the life he would leave behind, incomplete, unresolved. But more than afraid, he was resigned.

'Are you with the Radiant War?' Echiveira asked.

'No,' Calchas heard himself saying.

'What is this shit? If you're not with the Radiant War who are you cunts?'

'Yombris.'

The Radiant War. Yombris. Some lost tribe. A heap of shit. What the fuck did he care? It was all the same to him.

'You know what's under the bed, don't you? Gold, silver, emeralds... Is there more?'

Now Calchas understood. As immediately as the calmness had come it deserted him. His being leapt with obscure hope. Should he tell them?

'*Is there more?*'

'If I say, you'll let me live?'

'It's your only chance.'

'And her, too. This woman?'

'Only if you tell me the truth. You help me and you can both go.'

Something warned Calchas not to believe it. But now that he'd been given a glimmer of hope he couldn't let it go. Life was everything.

'There's more.'

'Where?'

'In the dwellings.'

'What d'you mean? I'm talking about a whole lot more you son of a whore; mines, treasure, *the whole lot.*'

'No. There's nothing like that. It's from our ancestors. There's only what's in the dwellings.'

'What dwellings?' said Echiveira, after a moment. 'All the dwellings?'

'Not every dwelling. But some have a little. Some more.'

'Stay where you are. Don't move. I'll be watching you from the door.'

Echiveira went and spoke to the soldier guarding the door. They spoke in low voices so that Calchas couldn't hear what they were saying.

'I think he's telling the truth,' Echiveira said. 'It isn't what we thought, but if there's as much in the other huts it'll be plenty.'

The soldier grinned tensely, showing a gold tooth. 'What do we do now? Do we cut Jimenez in?'

'Sir. I'm sir to you, pisshead. Don't get ideas...'

'Yes, sir.'

'I'll get the Indian to talk to the woman, tell her to show us where the best huts are. I'll get Jimenez over now. We'll have to cut him in. He can guard the woman's kid. She won't try anything if we've got her kid.'

'What about the Indian?... Sir.'

Echiveira went back into the hut. They would collect the treasure and transport it to the chopper in ammunition cases. No one would suspect. More worrying was Maldonado. Maldonado (a captain and Echiveira's superior) had on the major's orders taken a chopper and troops to the other dwellings further down. He'd be occupied for a few hours yet, rounding up the Indians. They'd have long enough unless Maldonado was inclined to contact the major. That could be a problem. But Echiveira was confident he could handle Maldonado. Unlike himself Maldonado came from a privileged background and had been promoted unjustly. He was weak. And he was young. Echiveira was neither weak or young. In fact he was old for his lieutenant's rank. But that didn't mean he didn't have brains. He had more brains than Maldonado. He'd think of something to keep the nancy boy out of his way...

The fat woman was distraught at having to abandon her father. She lagged behind, weeping, stumbling and tripping and on one occasion she fell to the ground, bruising her body. When at last the group arrived at the river, she flopped down on the bank exhausted. Seeing that she wasn't ready to enter the river, her scrawny husband and two teenage daughters resolved to stay behind until she recovered. 'You go ahead,' they insisted to the others.

The river was swollen from the rains of a few days before, but like most of the Arayana, Cascarina had known how to swim since childhood. So she took off the robe she was wearing, left it on the bank, and jumped off a rock into a long narrow pool. Though the water was deep and cold the current was not particularly strong and she swam with relative ease to a waterfall that fell foaming and thundering for a distance of some three yards.

At the base of the waterfall, to one side of the cascade and a couple of feet under the water level, there was a rock ledge. Using the ledge as a step she was easily able to rise out of the water, then, ducking her head, step through the cascade into a small cave. At the rear of the cave was a narrow tunnel opening. She crawled into the tunnel. The rock walls were close, so close they brushed her arms and thighs, and further in it became dark. It was many years since she'd been in the tunnel, not since she was a young girl, but when she came to a place where the tunnel widened, branching into two further tunnels, she remembered to take the one on her left, away from the river. As she crawled along this tunnel the sound of the river diminished into silence, a smell of smoke reached her nostrils. A moment later she heard low, intermittent sounds, and then a voice: 'Who's there?'

'Me. Cascarina.'

A hand reached out to help her. She raised her head, twisted her legs around, and lowered herself over the drop. When she was standing the yellow flame of a flare appeared. The flame wasn't bright enough to illuminate the immensity of the cavern. What she saw instead were shadowed figures huddled around two small fires (the cavern had always been stocked for emergency).

A man with an ugly face came up to her. It was Tusuma.

'Where are the others?'

'On the bank. They're coming. Is Guaneque here?'

'Yes… Come to the fire.'

A space was made for her by one of the fires. She sat down close to it, shivering, peering at the red-tinged outlines around her. Then a hand touched her shoulder. It was Guaneque. Cascarina shifted to make room for her sister-in-law. Guaneque sat down.

'I saw three purinis. And I found some people. Is Capayambe here?'

Guaneque shook her head. It was what she was going to ask Cascarina: if she'd seen her husband.

'But why have they come. *Why*?' a stricken voice made itself heard.

No one knew how to answer, what to say.

'I keep thinking this must be a bad dream. This isn't happening,' another voice said.

Again no one answered, but it was something they all felt. Cascarina herself felt like this. Although she was able to recall everything it yet seemed distant from her, as though touching only the surface of her mind, less real even than a dream because she had no emotion now. It was strange…

It was about an hour after the fat woman and her family had followed Cascarina into the cavern that two other groups arrived, one soon after the other. These were the people that the young men, who Cascarina had warned, had managed to gather. They numbered some eighty people. Like everybody else they came in cold, wet, and naked (their clothes and other things would be hauled in presently).

It became noisier. Some infants were crying, as well as a few women. Other people began speaking of the things that had passed: A small group had stayed behind in the forest to look after a woman who'd gone into labour. An old man had managed to reach the river but had drowned in the pool and they'd hidden his body in the undergrowth. Some other men had refused to come to cavern and had gone to see if they could find and warn yet others before they were caught by the purinis…

But there was one thing no one there was able to tell. And this was the fate of all the people who'd been caught by the purinis. They couldn't speak of this because so far there was no one there who'd been caught by the purinis and had subsequently managed to escape. So there was no one who actually knew what was now happening in those places were the purinis had control. Then another group arrived, about twenty people. These came from the remotest dwellings, those that were located near the last cultivated fields on the edge of the jungle that led to the gorge. It appeared that a purini metal bird had landed near them. However, unlike in the main village, there'd been no destruction. But the purinis had burst into the dwellings and they'd chased others who tried to escape. The ones who were now here had managed to flee even so. And once in the forest, they'd found each other and waited to see if others would join them. But when no more joined them they decided to come here. Whether more from their area would arrive presently, they didn't know.

Eventually words dried up, everything was said. A group of men got busy fetching the things that had been left on the river bank and some women were attending people in need, but mostly they sat in the darkness, each with their own thoughts, some showing more fortitude than others, but not one them willing to voice the one thing they most feared, that was touching them all like the breath of Tomacha:

Tomacha, the dream that did not satisfy the Holy Source and had learnt selfishness and awoke itself before the Holy Source could un-dream it. Tomacha, the bloodthirsty god of their ancestors. Tomacha, the destroyer. Tomacha, the source of all that was cruel...

Hours passed. Another sixty people arrived. Some who'd escaped from the lower dwellings, others who'd been located and warned in time by the men who'd gone searching. One of them, a young man, had ventured close to the main village. This man had climbed a tree. From there he was just able to make out the ruins and had seen what appeared to be crowds of people in a field, watched over by the purinis. Coming down from the tree, he had started moving closer to the ruins but then a purini had seen him just as he was crossing an open bit of ground and so he'd fled. The purini had chased him, but he'd managed to get away.

This young man aside, however, none of the others could add anything more about the situation than was already known.

Then, around mid-afternoon, it happened.

Four people arrived in the cavern. When they stood in the flare of the light there fell a hush more ominous than any commotion, for these people were known to be from the main village. One of them was Cocuma, a half-brother of the sovereign. It was he who spoke first. 'Dead,' he said in a whisper. Then louder, 'Dead! Dead!'

There was an echo in the cavern, and the words multiplied, bouncing off the walls. People started rising to their feet. Cascarina and Guaneque were among the first. In silence the people came forward, gathering around Cocuma and his companions, all of whom seemed to be in a state of profound trauma. Abruptly Guaneque rushed forward, grabbing Cocuma's arm. 'Did you see my husband? What happened? Tell us!'

'Dead,' Cocuma said. 'Everyone is dead.'

But then, one of his companions, and older man spoke up. 'No, not everyone. Not everyone. Some are only wounded. Many others ran. I saw them.' His voice broke, his chest heaved.

'Tell us,' said Cascarina, her limbs trembling. 'Was there more fire. *Tell us*.'

'It fell from the sky, from the metal wasp-birds.'

'Illani tried to warn us. I saw her,' said a youth. 'She came running when the purini birds were in the sky. Yana! Yana! Run! Run! But for many it was too late.'

There was a sound at the cavern entrance. A single woman appeared. She had also escaped the purini fire. Then more started arriving (the cavern was huge so there was no lack of space) and with each arrival more of the catastrophe was told:

All day the soldiers had gone from place to place, capturing everyone. Even the low villages hadn't escaped. The people from there had been carried, ten, fifteen at a time, in the belly of the metal bird and brought to the place in the main village where everybody was being gathered. But nobody knew what was going to happen. Early in the day Illapacta and the lowlander Calchas had been seen with the chief purini. Then the chief purini and Calchas had gone away and Illapacta had returned. But not the chief purini. Illapacta had returned guarded by another purini. No one knew what was going to happen. In the afternoon many of the purini warriors guarding them had retreated, they had hurried towards the top of the village. But not all left. Others had stayed behind, guarding them. Some of the people had spoken of escaping, and given more time they would have, but then they had seen one of the birds appear over the trees. Then two other birds had appeared. They went up into the sky, but the one above the trees had moved over the field and stayed low. It had hovered over them. Something was dropped from its belly, steps made of rope, and the last of the purini soldiers who had stayed behind ran up to it and one by one they climbed these steps into the belly of the bird.

But by then Illani had appeared. She was running amongst them waving her arms and shouting, but many couldn't hear what she was saying because of the deafening noise the bird was making. But some did hear her. She was telling people to run. And so some started running, and then others. But many didn't move in time. They were frozen, like chinchilla under the shadow of a hawk. The bird with the rope ladder went up into sky. But instead of all the birds going away, two of them came back down fast and without warning they hurled invisible spears of thunder and fire on the gathered people.

Some people collapsed when they heard how it had ended. Others stood, speechless, as if made of stone. And yet others were breaking into sobs and wails. Cascarina's head reeled, she staggered as if under the impact of a physical blow, a vortex was rising to engulf her, but then someone spoke, she heard someone say, 'Some of us must go back. There will be wounded, children –'

'And if the purinis return. What then?' Someone else interrupted.

'So are we to do nothing?' Cascarina heard herself saying. "Are we going to let them die alone, without comfort?'

Others joined in. A few were against the idea of going to help at all. Others weren't but said that the purinis could easily come back and more lives shouldn't be risked. Finally it was decided that some should go back, but only able bodied men or those who had knowledge of medicine.

Since Cascarina wasn't a man and had no knowledge of medicine she wasn't among those elected to go. She stayed behind. But staying behind was harder than going. It was harder because in waiting there was nothing to occupy her, nothing to protect her from herself.

In the darkness of the cavern, sitting next to her sister-in-law, she heard people all around her, moaning, weeping, and some who were already succumbing to desolation and whose voices rose in keening wails. Then abruptly, not far from her, a young woman cried, 'Look! Look! Can you see them?'

'What? Where?' Someone asked.

'Can't you see them?' the woman cried. 'They're coming through the walls!' The woman could see the dead walking through the walls. Young mothers with their infants. Children. Beautiful young girls. Men in their prime, old folk… She could see their luminous, spectral bodies walking through the walls, searching for their loved ones…

But Cascarina, although she understood what the woman meant, could not see anything. And abruptly she was angry. She was furious.

'Don't be foolish!' She cried, rising to her feet. 'We don't know who's dead or alive. We've got to hope they're alive, not believe they're dead.'

'I can see them! I can see them!' the woman insisted. But others knew Cascarina was right and they also told the woman to be quiet.

Food and wood, these are the important things now, Cascarina decided. And from that moment on she began to take charge, to organise others, and in this way, by being occupied, she managed – just – to keep a hold on herself.

For three days and two nights Rumicuri and Mountain Trotter had travelled on the return journey through the forest. Now it was behind them and they had only one more hill to climb before they arrived at the gorge and the bridge that crossed it.

In anticipation, thinking of Cascarina, of the reassuring news he had for his people, Rumicuri tackled the last hill recklessly, slipping and stumbling, for once leaving Mountain Trotter behind.

Once over the hill he hurried into a flat terrain of spiky yellow-green palm bushes, of huge heart shaped leaves and trees laden with fungus and climbers, until the vegetation came to an end and he stopped, sweating and panting, on a small patch of cleared ground close to the gorge, and where ahead of him, in a shaft of sunlight, was the basket-work suspension bridge.

Home! Home at last.

Purini objects were banned from the kingdom. It was the law. But Rumicuri had made up his mind that certain things in the kingdom had to change. And among the changes would be changes in the law regarding contact with the outside world. So although the machete in his hand was a purini object, he kept hold of it as he approached the bridge.

Where were the guards?

The guard house was always manned. All able bodied men had to serve guard duty, which lasted several days and came around every three or more years. Because of its infrequency men looked forward to it as a welcome change and invariably they performed their duty without fault. Thus, when Rumicuri gazed across the bridge he had fully expected to see at least one of the two guards standing or sitting outside the hut.

Concerned, stepping onto the bridge itself, he peered more intently, but there was still no sign of the guards. Holding onto the thick suspension ropes he stepped from slat to slat, the entire bridge swaying under his movement. When he reached the other side he hastened to the guard house. He looked inside but found nothing wrong, no sign of disturbance.

Mountain Trotter wasn't far behind and it wasn't long before he, too, crossed the bridge. When he came off it he found the sovereign standing on his own, his brow creased.

'The guards aren't here,' said Rumicuri, a note of alarm in his voice. 'I haven't known this to happen before.'

Without answering Mountain Trotter went and looked inside the hut. It appeared undisturbed to him as well.

'What if one of the guards became ill, highness? The other might've had to take him back,' suggested Mountain Trotter, when he returned.

Rumicuri had thought of this possibility himself. It could be plausible if an illness or injury was severe enough.

'Let's go,' he said. 'We'll find out soon.'

'We're not in the purini world now,' said Mountain Trotter wanting to reassure him.

'No, we're not.' The trace of a smile softened Rumicuri's countenance. You've served us well, Mountain Trotter. I'm grateful.'

The old man was pleased. Few things gave him more satisfaction than being of service.

Once again Rumicuri hurried ahead. He had a better path to travel on now and so progress was quicker. He was still worried, but another part of him was increasingly expectant, happy to be home.

Although he hadn't been away for long it felt like half a lifetime. The dangers and strangeness of the outside world had made his kingdom seem distressingly distant, unreachable.

There was much he had discovered in the purini world. Time would have to pass before he could assimilate it all but he knew now that his uncle was largely right. If the Arayana were to survive he would have to prepare them for the outside world. His own son was an infant still, it was too soon to know what the future had in store for him, but when he was older, after the rites of puberty, or perhaps even before, he would send him to learn the guile of the purinis. And that no matter what Illani had to say.

Thinking of Illani, Rumicuri felt unsettled. It was two years since they'd separated but he wasn't free of her. Would he ever be? His heart told him it was Cascarina he loved but the bewitchment Illani had cast on him was potent. With her he'd always felt himself in danger. He didn't know of what exactly, unless it was of being swamped, dominated to the extent that her needs took priority over his duty to the people. And he couldn't let that happen. He had no intention of ending up like his father.

Not, it wasn't that Illani was selfish, he thought. During their bitter rows he had often accused her of being selfish. But since they'd separated he'd come to think of her differently. More than selfish, she was a woman of strong appetites. Good food, love-making, fine clothes, all these things aroused her. He hadn't known another woman so immersed in her own sensuality. Even now it made him heady when he recalled their love-making. No, it wasn't that she didn't give. It was that he couldn't give her what she demanded in return. And yet he hadn't stopped desiring her. Sometimes his longing was like a pain. It would not take much, he knew, for temptation to get the better of him. And this was why he avoided her, feared her...

With Cascarina it was different. She was another strong woman, but her strength was not complicated like Illani's. When he was with Cascarina he didn't feel the need to be on guard. It was less exciting, perhaps, but he was content with her, and if there was anything to regret it was only that she hadn't got pregnant. It was a mystery why she hadn't. They had been trying for a long time, long before Illani, and there were no remedies, no sorcery they hadn't attempted.

But such was life. There was no such thing as complete happiness, no matter what the elders claimed. Look at Illapacta, he was an elder and how happy was he? No, the important thing was that his people were safe. Most likely the absence of the guards would be easily explained. Tonight he would celebrate, he thought, with some good food, some mishqui, a little coca to ease his fatigue, and then he would lose himself in the sweet delight of Cascarina's arms...

Reaching a familiar bend in the hill, he paused to recover his breath and peer through the undergrowth to where he could make out the first terraced fields. In this particular field a yucca crop was growing. The long leaves looked green and healthy. A good crop, ready for harvesting, but there was no one in sight.

As he circumvented the field, following the path towards five huts that were as yet out of view and which constituted the lowest of the villages, he wondered with sudden anxiety why there wasn't a single person in the field.

Beyond the field the path led once more into the forest. In a short while he came to another clearing where amid various trees and bushes stood a cluster of huts. In his anxiousness he almost ran up to them but even before he arrived he knew, somehow, that they were empty.

There was nobody in the first hut. Yet again, staring in, he could find no indication of disturbance. And when he went to the other huts it was the same.

Standing outside the last hut he breathed deeply to calm his pounding heart and tried to think what possibly could have happened to make everyone, including the guards, leave their dwellings.

The birth of the world! As soon as the notion struck him he felt relief.

There were only two occasions when the entire population was required to be present and therefore the guard houses could be temporarily abandoned. One was the ascension of a new sovereign. The other was the appearance of a new elder. And before he'd left there had been speculation that a new elder was imminent. All that appeared to be holding the elders back was a propitious sign. So had they received it? Rumicuri thought that they must have. If they had received a strong sign they might not wait until he returned. He hadn't indicated when he would return and the birth of the world wasn't his domain. The elders made all the decisions in these matters. It was the birth of the world. He became convinced. He could picture it happening at this very moment. The entire community would be gathered on the hill outside the main village. The new elder – because it was late afternoon – would already be among them. He would be like a madman, delirious with strange ecstasy, and the people would all be welcoming him, full of holy gladness.

When Mountain Trotter arrived, breathing hard and looking perturbed, Rumicuri was quick to reassure him. 'I know what it is now,' he said. 'It's the birth of the world and everyone must be present when that happens, even the guards. We'd better hurry if we don't want to miss it.'

Mountain Trotter was relieved. He'd heard about the ceremony. For the people of the high kingdom it was said to be an event of profound significance. He would be pleased to witness it for himself, and so, old man that he was, this time he made a strenuous effort to keep up with the sovereign's fast, impatient pace.

When in due course they came to more huts and fields they saw at a glance that they were deserted, but now had no need to stop and inspect them and so they didn't. Had they done so, however, they would have received a shock, because, unlike the previous dwellings, some of these had not been abandoned before the soldiers arrived and their interiors had been ransacked.

Further up they passed more dwellings and fields. These higher fields had been somewhat affected by the drought but now Rumicuri noticed a fresh, young greenness and he wondered if it had rained. Perhaps it had even snowed on the high mountain? That would certainly explain why the elders had decided to go ahead with birth of the world.

As they came closer to the main village they passed yet more dwellings, fields, plantations all of which were deserted. But here there was something odd, for not only were the doors of some huts wide open, on the ground outside, here and there were bits of clothing lying as if they'd been flung there or dropped in a rush. Then, moments later, Rumicuri noticed the vultures. Emerging from a patch of forest he spotted four, five vultures circling low in the sky. His immediate thought was that some animal had died. But why were they circling above the main village? (He couldn't yet see the main village since it was obscured by the slope of a hill.) And if everybody was there, celebrating, wouldn't the vultures be scared away?

Mountain Trotter also noticed the vultures. He was puzzled. Disquiet stirred in him.

Stopping, the men exchanged looks. Rumicuri's face hardened. He was overcome by a sudden foreboding and abruptly he took off, almost running up the path between the terraced fields. Yet even then a voice was telling him that he was being a fool, that he was scaring himself over nothing, that when he reached the village he would find it all as he anticipated.

There was a screen of trees at the top of the terraced fields. Reaching them he paused, not to brace himself, but becoming conscious of his dignity, thinking it would not do for him to be seen running into the village like one demented. So for the last short distance he walked slowly and deliberately. Just before he stepped out of the trees it struck him that he could not hear any human sounds, that it was unnaturally quiet.

Then he saw the devastation.

A chaos of rubble was everywhere. Some dwellings were standing but most had been reduced to broken wood, bits of wall, piles of earth, scattered stones... His eyes expanded like rings of water. *An earthquake. There's been an earthquake*, he thought. Dazed, mind reeling, he hurried forwards, scrambling over rubble, looking everywhere for signs of life but seeing no one. He couldn't understand why there were no people. Had they all fled? Why? Even if there had been an earthquake, why would they flee? And what of the lower villages, the guard house?

He saw a dwelling that was still standing, unscathed, and he went over to it. He looked inside but it was empty. Then he heard a noise, someone calling his name. It was coming from behind the dwelling. Rumicuri hurried around the corner and there, in the near distance he saw Chotavalo scrambling towards him across the rubble of what had been the gathering house.

Rumicuri did not move. He could not move. Such was his fear, the sense of calamitous anticipation, that it took all of his strength to steady himself.

Chotavalo's purple robe was torn and soiled.

'It was the purinis,' he gasped.

Rumicuri's legs gave way. He staggered. Chotavalo reached out and grabbed him. With Chotavalo holding him, he sank to his knees like an animal dying.

'Some are alive,' Chotavalo said, squatting next to him. 'Many are dead, but others live.'

Rumicuri heard Chotavalo faintly. Everything went out of focus. He couldn't breathe. Blackness surrounded him. He was drowning, drowning...

'There are wounded; some badly. I don't think anything can save them, but with others the wounds aren't so bad. They'll live, I think.'

'How many live in all?' Rumicuri heard himself saying. 'How many all counted?'

'No one knows yet. More than half. Yes, more than half...'

Rumicuri put his hand on the ground to stop himself from collapsing. His mind was reeling still.

'Where are they?'

Chotavalo said the wounded were in Illani's dwelling and other dwellings that were undamaged. Many had fled to the river cave, but now they were drifting back and building makeshift shelters in the forest and doing what they could to gather food.

'Is Cascarina dead?' Rumicuri asked.

'I heard she's alive. In the river cave.'

'My son?'

'He's dead... Illani is badly wounded... It was the purini birds. They came four days ago. They spat fire after the purini soldiers gathered all the people together...' Chotavalo's voice faltered, unable to continue. Grief and guilt choked his soul. It gagged him.

Chotavalo and the other elders hadn't heard the missiles explode or the helicopters arrive. The sacred cave was some distance removed from the main village and no exterior sound reached the inner chambers. While the catastrophe was occurring the elders had been occupied preparing for the birth of the new elder, Cuspi.

What they had been doing had seemed so important at the time. As an elder Chotavalo had been taught not to trust the nature of reality. In a world that was forever being born he'd been taught to recognize change and impermanence as the essential reality. Among all the Arayana there was no one better prepared for an encounter with the unexpected than an elder. And this is what they'd been doing when the purinis arrived. They'd been preparing for Cuspi to meet the unexpected, preparing for him to emerge from the sacred cave and witness the world being born in all its pristine beauty. And while they were preparing for this moment when not only the elders but the whole Arayana community celebrated no less than their rightful place in the grand scheme of creation, at that very moment the purinis were spitting fired and death upon the people. At the moment when the elders were full of holy joy, at that moment the Arayana were being slaughtered.

Chotavalo had been schooled in the unexpected. But there was nothing in all his years of sequestration, in all his years as an elder, in all his experience or depth of knowledge that had prepared him for the morning when in the course of his duties he'd set off for the village and, like Rumicuri, had spotted the devastation and had feared an earthquake, but when he arrived running he realized it was no earthquake, for what he discovered among the ruins was dead and dismembered bodies everywhere, and all over these bloated corpses, these stinking, unrecognisable pieces of bone and flesh were dense clouds of humming flies and a great number of vultures so gorged they couldn't fly, so gorged all they could do was stare at him, squawking, flapping their wings, beaks bloody with human remains...

Mountain Trotter arrived. Chotavalo spoke to him. The old man's face caved in, his mouth opened but no words came out.

'Where are the other elders?' Rumicuri asked.

'Punimillo is with Cuspi, in the sacred cave. I don't know where Macaruca is.'

After Chotavalo had returned to the sacred cave and told his brother elders the unimaginable thing he'd seen, they had both hurried down with him to the village. Shock had unhinged the mind of both elders. Punimillo had returned to the sacred cave. Macaruca had started laughing and crying without being able to stop, and later froth had dribbled out of his mouth and he'd began babbling like a child even though he was over seventy years old. Finally he'd wandered off. Chotavalo didn't know where; he hadn't seen him again.

Rumicuri pushed himself up from the ground. His legs held – just.

'I'm going to the wounded. Can you spread the word? Tell the people I'm here.'

He started walking up the hill, across the rubble. He no longer hurried. He walked slumped, with laden slowness, forcing himself to take each step. Mountain Trotter followed him.

One of those attending the wounded – a woman – was returning with a gourd of water when she saw the sovereign. She stopped, nearly dropping the gourd, and then hurried forward. Rumicuri did not recognise her at first, then remembered she was from the lower villages. When the woman reached him she at once fell to her knees and laying the gourd aside she touched the ground at his feet with her forehead. Rumicuri said nothing. It seemed to him now that this ancient gesture of fealty was totally empty and meaningless. He was the sovereign of nothing and nobody. Everything was in ruins. When the woman stood up her eyes were full of tears. Rumicuri turned his head away. Either that or disintegration. And then what would happen? Everything was in ruins, but if not he, who would hold them together? Or was he to destroy even the little that was left?

There were some twenty wounded inside Illani's hut. They lay on the rough stone floor, squashed together on rescued fleeces or blankets. A small fire was burning and the smoke masked some of the worst smells but there was nothing that could conceal the sight or sound of their suffering. Many of the wounded were too ill to be aware of Rumicuri's presence. Others, more conscious, raised their heads. Behind him, two men appeared in the doorway. They had finished burying three people, and were on their way to Illapacta's hut, were there were more wounded, when they saw Mountain Trotter outside Illani's, speaking to the woman with the gourd of water. They approached the hut and paused to watch the sovereign a moment, as if to make sure it was him. Then they hurried off to inform others. Looking about him, Rumicuri spotted Illani. She was lying curled under thick blankets. Her eyes were closed. Her face was swollen, one side of it smeared with a thick paste of some kind.

But Rumicuri did not go to her at once. They were all his people, they were all known to him, and so with tremendous effort he made a semblance of playing the role he was born to and in the confined space he stepped between one person and another, gazing at the barely conscious – some of them friends or relations – and greeting in silence those who were able to recognize him.

One of these was Alayana, his father's youngest wife. Since he'd become sovereign this woman had been a constant headache because of her endless amorous entanglements in which he had to mediate. But she was kind hearted and he was fond of her and now she lay staring at him, her hand clawing at his clothes, saying, 'My children, highness, where are my children? Have you seen my children?'

Alayana had five children. Thee of them from different fathers. One of her children, the eldest, was Rumicuri's half-brother.

'Not yet, mother,' he replied. 'When I find them, I'll send them to you.'

He moved to Illani. She was barely conscious. Her breath was spasmodic. Her eyelids flickered but didn't open. Now and then her lips moved and she would utter a moan or a few garbled words before lapsing into silence again. Rumicuri squatted beside her. A thick blanket was wrapped around her body. It seemed to be stuck to her with semi-congealed blood. He feared to think what injuries lay under the blanket. Emotion welled in him. The past, the acrimony, the many things he'd held against her were forgotten in the sorrow he felt for this woman who was still his wife, the mother of his dead son.

Rumicuri placed his hand on her brow – it was hot – but Illani became restless, shaking her head, so he removed his hand. After some time, when her condition didn't alter, he stood up and turned to leave.

Illani never regained consciousness.

She died without being able to tell Rumicuri what had passed. She was never able to tell him how the purinis had kept her son and told her they would kill him if she didn't do what they wanted. But when Calchas was speaking to her, passing on the commands that the monkey-faced purini soldier was giving, Calchas added words of his own which the purinis could not understand.

Calchas told Illani the purinis weren't to be trusted. Not with the monkey-face in charge. He knew it now. They'd take the gold and stones but that wouldn't stop the killing, he told her. If she got a chance she should warn the people. Tell them to run, Calchas warned her, because they're all going to get killed.

She left her son crying. She could hear her son crying when the purinis made her leave her house and go with them. And her son's crying was a crying that hadn't stopped. He cried inside her all the time she was leading the monkey-faced purini and another one – not the one who had tried to violate her but another one, to the houses, the ones that weren't in ruins, and showing them where to look for the things from the ancestors.

And it put them in a frenzy. Even the monkey-faced one laughed strangely and she saw madness in his eyes when he seized the artefacts and adornments of gold and stones and put them in a big pouch made of fabric.

Many places she couldn't show them because it was reduced to smoking rubble. Rumicuri's own dwelling was partly ruined because the roof beams had caved in. The purinis had to scramble, move things out of their way, dig with their hands, but when they came across the stone encrusted sandals, the gold necklace and other ornaments, and the pots containing un-worked gold and silver and stones they became so crazed they started ignoring her, forgetting to guard her.

So she escaped. Little by little she backed towards the doorway. Then at a moment when they were distracted, their backs turned, she fled. Rumicuri's was a good place from which to make an escape because it was surrounded by vegetation and the forest was near. The monkey-faced purini chased her; he went right past her because he didn't notice her squeezed into the hollow trunk of an old tree. She fled again, deeper into the forest, and then she started making her way back to the main village, but always under cover, concealed.

Reaching the village itself she was forced to leave the forest. She darted from one place to another, keeping low, hiding behind walls or among rubble. But when she came closer to where the people were being held she saw purini soldiers. There seemed to be a lot of them. They were gathered in pairs or small groups, resting, not doing anything, but she was afraid they would spot her if she tried to go past them.

For some time she waited, undecided what to do. Calchas had told her to warn the people, but now she was free she was also desperate to rescue her son. Suddenly she made up her mind. She would return to her dwelling. If it looked possible she would first try to rescue her son. If it did not look possible she would come straight back to warn the people. In order to avoid crossing the main village she had to take a circuitous route to her dwelling. When she arrived there she hid in a bush and watched to make sure there were no purinis close by. Not seeing any, and with her body trembling, she left the bush and darted, crouched over, up to the door of the hut. The door was ajar. She peered in. Once quickly. Then longer. She could see a shape on the bed; it looked to be Calchas, but no sign of any purinis. She ventured in but even before she reached the bed a scream was rising inside her because she could see her son on the bed, limp, and blood everywhere: Blood on her son, on the bed, and on Calchas who was also dead.

Illani paused only to lift her son. She rushed out with him in her arms. When she was concealed again in the undergrowth she collapsed on the ground, rocking her son in her arms, sobbing silently. Presently she struggled to her feet and circumventing a field, still carrying her son, she went into the forest. There she collapsed on the ground once more, and now with the corpse beside her, she rocked backwards and forwards, her body convulsing with loud and violent sobs. But then, as if her whole personality had undergone an instantaneous change, she stopped abruptly, placed her hand briefly on the corpse's little chest, and then stood up and without looking back she started making her way towards the main village again.

When she got close to the field where the people were being held, she hid behind a half demolished wall close by. A moment later, she slipped past three unobservant purinis and was mingling among her people. Her only thought now was to warn them, to warn them that the purinis were going to kill them all and they must run, run into the forest at the first chance they got. Many were persuaded by Illani, but many others were not. Even after Illani had told them what the monkey-face purini had done and what Calchas had said, even then many wanted to cling to the hope that somehow they would be spared. They pointed to the purinis who were tending the wounded. Why would the purinis look after them like that if they were going to kill them? And what where they waiting for? If they were going to kill them all why hadn't they done so already? These were things Illani couldn't tell them because she didn't know the answers. And in fact, unknown to Illani, as yet no definite decision had been taken as to their fate. The soldiers guarding them were only concerned with their immediate orders which, after gathering as many people as they could find, was to stand by. With the Major dead, it was between two of the three remaining officers that the fate of the Arayana was being decided. The third officer did not count because he was a Second Lieutenant and therefore would have to obey the other two. Captain Maldonado, the officer now in charge was averse to further destruction, further killing. But he was weak, and Lieutenant Echiveira wasn't weak and so he was intent on persuading the Captain that it had to be done. And to the Captain it looked like Echiveira had evidence. No one could dispute the red book, or that the Major had been killed by one of the Indians. The Captain, unfortunately, couldn't question this Indian. If he had been able to, it might have helped him reach a different decision. But after killing the Major, the Indian himself had been killed by a soldier, apparently, according to Echiveira, in self-defence. So the Captain had nothing to go on except what he was being told by Echiveira. And Echiveira had a case. How could they just go back without justifying themselves for what had already been done? As Echiveira kept saying, insisted in fact, it wouldn't look good on the report. How could they just go back and say they'd slaughtered some innocent Indians by mistake? The scandal could be their undoing; his and Echiveira's and possibly even the Colonel's. So maybe there was no other way, after all. The army had to avenge the Major's death; it had to show it had done what it could in its fight against the criminal Radiant War and its subversive supporters and fellow travellers. Maybe, as Echiveira said, it was their duty?

Had the Captain only known what Echiveira had done, known that Echiveira was only interested in covering his tracks and escaping with the loot, possibly although by no means certainly, the fate of the Arayana might have ended differently. But the Captain knew only what he was being told, and so he finally reached the decision he did, the one Echiveira had already made for him, which was to leave behind as little evidence of a mistake as possible, regardless of whether these people were or were not the Radiant War, but calculating that at the very least they were follows travellers.

Among the Arayana, when the purinis started leaving and the metal birds rose into the sky, many had sudden hope that the worst was over, but Illani wasn't one of these. She feared it was just about to begin and so it was then that she started running and waving her arms and shouting, '*Yana! Yana!* Run! Run!' But too late. Too late...

Cascarina found Rumicuri under a tree. All night he had stayed awake. Many times he had stood up and fallen again, stumbling in the dark without being aware of what he was doing. Then, as dawn was breaking, he had fallen asleep. And this is how Cascarina found him: slumped on his side under a tree, his head resting on the trunk.

She didn't want to wake him. She sat down on the ground, nearby. His long hair, she saw, was all tangled and his clothes, the ones she had made for his journey, were grey with dirt. She couldn't see his face clearly, but she could sense, even though he was asleep, his pain and exhaustion.

Why had he returned? Why was he alive? Why was she carrying his child?

A humming bird flew past Cascarina. The feathers on its tiny body shimmered green and blue as it hovered over a flowering bush, its long, needle thin beak probing the red flowers. Beyond the bush, in the distance, she could see the mountain heaped with brilliant snow. The sky was deep blue. The rising sun, a warm golden disc...

Why? Why did the Father Sun rise in the heavens? Why did the Mother Earth give forth her bounty? Why did the birds not die and the flowers not wither? Why did life go on here, all around her, as if nothing had happened? Better if the purinis had killed them all. Better if they were all dead.

Rumicuri woke up. He lifted his head and sat up with a start. For an instant his face was blank; then he saw Cascarina and a tremor passed through his face as he stared at her with bloodshot eyes, overcome by complex emotions: fleeting gladness, anguish, guilt...

Cascarina felt similar emotions. Now that he was awake some part of her wanted to hold him, cling to him, but no sooner had this feeling manifested itself than it was crushed by contrary feelings of pain and guilt.

So neither of them made a move towards the other. They stayed as they were; each of them, after the first fleeting consolation of being with each other, isolated in their respective prisons.

Finally, after a long silence, Rumicuri spoke.

'Have you just come from the river cave?

'A little while ago, yes.'

'Where are the others?'

'Many are still there. Others are collecting food…'

After another silence, Rumicuri said, 'Who's alive… can you tell me?'

So she began telling him. She gave him the names, starting with those closest to her. He listened, now and then interrupting when he wasn't sure of whom she was speaking. It took some time for Cascarina to enumerate all the people she could recall. When she had finished, he asked about others she hadn't mentioned. Her voice choking she was able to confirm some of these as dead, others she didn't know where they were, if they were dead or alive.

Finally they ran out of names.

It appeared more had survived than Rumicuri had at first feared. But he was not comforted. There was nothing on this earth that could comfort him for the multitude that had perished.

With an effort Rumicuri got to his feet.

For a moment, as though in hope, Cascarina wondered if she should tell him she was with child. But she couldn't bring herself to. Not yet…

In times of need Rumicuri had always gone to the river. The tumbling water, falling over rocks, drifting into limpid pools – its constant movement and never-ending sound – was able to soothe him when he was troubled. Perhaps it was the river's impression of continuity. Perhaps, in some way, it represented, from its source high up in the mountains to its unknown destination deep in the jungle, the journey that all mortals must make. In any event, always when he needed solitude he'd gone to the river. And this is what he did now after leaving Cascarina. He walked through the forest to the river, to the pool, where, many years ago, he had found the stone, flecked with gold, which he had given to Cascarina.

But that had been a time of joy, when he was young, when his body quivered with vigour, when he had still believed his people had a place in the scheme of creation. And how could he not believe? As the sovereign of the Arayana he had no choice. If he didn't believe who would believe for him? A disbelieving ruler could only bring ruin upon the people. The Arayana nation would disintegrate. It would cease to be. So he had believed. Clinging like a tree at the river's edge…

But now? What was there to believe in now?

It would be a simple matter, he thought, contemplating the pool below him. A length of twine, tie his feet and hands, tighten the knot with his teeth. Jump in.

Everything would end. And why not? It was all in ruins. There was nothing left. Belief hadn't saved the Arayana. And without belief there was nothing. The Holy Source was only a word, the Mother Earth only a word. Empty words. Words without meaning, because without belief there was nothing to make them real. The purinis had destroyed them. He was the last sovereign of the Arayana. In the time of his forefathers the empire had fallen, the great stone cities had been abandoned, but the Arayana had survived. And the Arayana had survived after disease had killed great numbers of them, after conflict had divided them. The Arayana had survived. But this, the death-fire of the purinis, this the Arayana would not survive.

Chotavalo had found them dead. He'd gone to the sacred cave to tell Punimillo that the sovereign had returned. When he entered the last chamber he found them dead. Young Cuspi was lying on his bed, curled up with a blanket over his shoulders. On the floor, next to him, Punimillo was lying sprawled on his stomach, face down.

Chotavalo felt no emotion. He was hardly surprised that Punimillo had killed Cuspi. He'd used basago, the drug that was employed to put an apprentice elder to sleep when they were moving him from one chamber to another. Cuspi had been born unblemished and had died unblemished. Punimillo had killed him out of compassion, to spare him from seeing a world that, instead of being born, was dying.

Chotavalo left them as they were. He left the cave and returned to see what more he could do to help those who had survived. He had no illusions now. He had experienced the destruction he guessed Illapacta must have foreseen. He could understand now why Illapacta had turned his back on elderhood. He could understand why Illapacta had taken to coca and mishqui. But Illapacta was dead and he was alive. He could drug himself, like Illapacta, he could kill himself, like Punimillo, he could go crazy, like Macaruca, but he could also live. He could choose to live and search for the flaw, the hidden flaw that had allowed the whole edifice of elderhood to collapse. Maybe if he could do that he could bring some solace to himself, to the people who remained...

EPILOGUE

THE dead had been buried. The wounded were recovering. A first group of able bodied men had already departed with Mountain Trotter in search of a new place to colonize. It had been decided that they would establish themselves in the forest beyond the Jaguar's Ribs, close to Mountain Trotter's village, close to the outside world. They would save what they could of their traditions, but there would no longer be a kingdom and Rumicuri would no longer be their sovereign. He would learn all he could from the purinis, he would learn their cunning and guile, and if it worked out he would do all he could to make them strong so that the purinis would respect them and no more harm would come to them. But their life as it was could not be lived again. For the Arayana kingdom there would not be another dawn. They would adopt the ways of Mountain Trotter's people because this gave them a better chance of surviving, even if it meant that in time they became indistinguishable from the purinis... All this had been decided, and now all that was left to do was to make the necessary arrangements for the exodus.

So the river cave was abandoned. In the evenings some people remained in the main village to be near the wounded but the majority occupied the huts in the low villages, close to the bridge. Rumicuri passed the days going backwards and forwards, organizing the exodus. He slept wherever darkness took him, some nights in the main village, some nights in the low, and now and then without shelter, in the open forest. He didn't care. He did what he had to do for the people but for himself he was indifferent. He had no desire to live. At night, when he lay down to sleep, his one wish was that he wouldn't wake up again.

Cascarina had scarcely seen him. One evening, when by chance he stumbled into the hut she was sharing with others, she was disturbed by his appearance. He was a man who had always walked proudly, who washed himself every day, who took care of every aspect of his appearance. But the man who appeared before her now was unwashed and his clothes were filthy and his hair grimy. He had the tense, downcast manner of someone fraught to breaking point. When he spoke his voice was hollow and his black eyes stared emptily, without seeing.

Cascarina prepared some food for him, which he ate indifferently, without addressing her. By the time he finished it was dark. The other people in the hut lay down to sleep amid their belongings. Cascarina arranged her own blankets and fleeces to make a space for him. She lay down, waiting in silence, until at last he left the fire and stretched himself on his back by her side. After some moments she pressed closer to him, tentatively, aching to give him warmth, to soothe him, to bring a ray of light into the dark emptiness of his being.

'Amataba's magic worked,' she murmured. 'I'm with child.'

Rumicuri didn't stir. He didn't speak. But he had heard what she said.

Anger and bitterness spread through his veins. He was possessed with a blinding rage. Not against Cascarina, not even against the purinis, his rage was against the imponderable forces of creation, by whatever name it might be called, Life or the Holy Source or Destiny... whatever it was that ruled creation choked him with bitter blinding rage.

You destroy my kingdom, you kill my people, you drown my soul, and after you've done these things you tell me my woman is with child? And I'm to be happy? What cruelty is this? What world is this my child will live in? What will be his future?

He was so enraged he was afraid to move. He feared that if he moved even a muscle there would be no stopping his rage. So he lay there. He lay for a long time before his rage began to ease.

Neither he nor Cascarina spoke. But they both remained awake, until finally, a thought came to him. It came to him the way it had come to Illapacta, like a flicker from a dark horizon. Quietly, with something that if not yet peace was a flickering of it, he understood that in spite of everything that had occurred he had to believe.

And the people had to believe.

Not in what they had been. All that was gone. It was dead. But they had to believe, even as purinis living in a purini world they had to believe that all was not lost, that they would bring children into the world, that they would survive, that even as purinis in a purini world they, those who remained, would go on living. And because they lived they must believe. Every man, every woman had this struggle: to endure…

No matter what… No matter what…

In silence he lifted his arm and slipped it under Cascarina's neck. And thus they lay, feeling the warmth of their bodies, in the endless silence, in the endless night.